Tides of Impossibility

A Fantasy Anthology
from the Houston Writers Guild

Edited by
K. J. Russell and C. Stuart Hardwick

SkipJack Publishing books may be purchased for educational, business, or sales promotional use. For information, please write: Sales, SkipJack Publishing, P.O.B. 31160 Houston, TX 77231.

First U.S. Edition
Houston Writers Guild

Tides of Impossibility/Houston Writers Guild
ISBN- 978-1-939889-27-0 (SkipJack Publishing)

Forward

I had the pleasure, last year, of meeting Tim Powers, author of *On Stranger Tides*, the novel that inspired the fourth movie in the *Pirates of the Caribbean* franchise. Tim was one of our instructors at the week-long Writers of the Future workshop, my rather generous reward for one little scifi story and several years of toil. Tim is a kind and giving soul and kept us up late into the evenings, sharing his experiences in the publishing business and adventures with Phillip K Dick. The last piece of advice he gave our class of budding writers was, "marry into wealth." The first was, "Look around you. The faces you see are not your competition, they're family."

During my week in Hollywood, I saw this attitude reflected in kindness and generosity from countless luminaries of scifi and fantasy, from Orson Scott Card to Larry Niven, Nancy Kress to Stephan Hickman. It was as if we had come upon the Wizard of Oz and instead of shouting "ignore the man behind the curtain," he pulled back the shades and offered a guiding hand.

Back home, I found another branch of the family in the Houston Writer's Guild. My mailbox was soon filled with invitations and welcome, and I was joining other local authors at local venues to sign copies of the *Tides of Possibility* Scifi anthology--and making new friends along the way. So when Kyle asked me to help edit *Tides of Impossibility*, there was nothing to think over, I was in.

Putting together a volume like this is a labor of love for the craft. It takes time, planning, diplomacy, restraint, judgment, and negotiation. It means late nights and bleary eyes, deadlines, and unwelcome surprises. But I think, as you turn these pages, you'll agree it was worth the effort. We have gathered here sixteen of the most talented voices of the Southwest, some fairly well known, some not so well known -- yet. We have stories for every taste, from werewolves to Robin Hood, duty to hauteur, rejuvenating fire to ancient magic, the dark and tragic to the light and lyrical.

This is a thrilling, unsettling time for writers, a time of unsurpassed opportunity and unremitting competition for attention and shelf space. Every good word, every tweet, every handshake or signature, makes a very real contribution along the way. Enjoy, and as you uncover or rediscover your favorites, be sure to spread the word. You're part of the family too.

C. Stuart Hardwick

TABLE OF CONTENTS

Elfanticide

by Lisa Godfrees and T.J. Akers

The darkening skies couldn't dampen Hambohn's mood. The day he had worked toward all his life was here at last. His pinnacle achievement. Tonight, he would ascend to First Satrap of Serpia, a position second only to the Emperor in power and prestige. Thunder, lightning, flood, typhoon--let them all come. Nothing could spoil this day.

He strode toward the throne room's antechamber, his gate measured and head erect. His eyes darted about, drinking in the attention provided by a grand audience. Every entrance was important, if only to send the correct message to his enemies at court.

His favorite robes flapped around his legs with each stride. Made from the silk of a rare and venomous spider, the garment changed colors to reflect his mood and mesmerized those foolish enough to stare too long at its intricate shading. It had been expensive, but his tailor assured him the extravagant number of harvesters crippled in its collection was proof of the silk's potency.

He spied a mirrored fountain and moved to admire himself one last time. His robes, currently bright orange, flowed behind him like the ripples of a majestic swan. An imposing figure, if he did say so himself.

The doors to the throne room opened and a herald announced him.

Emperor Nightenshade inclined his head as Hambohn prostrated himself with a grand flourish of his arms in a most courtly bow. "Hambohn din Hammedatha, Agate of the Imperial Crown, and newly appointed First Satrap of Serpia. Come and be welcome."

A wave of genuflection moved through the courtiers as the new First Satrap marched into the Emperor's presence. Everyone, including the nobles and his former peers, bowed down, save for one: a tall elf standing sentry in the back of the room. Hambohn glared at the green-haired lout but the fool remained immovable, a tree in the maelstrom of Hambohn's displeasure. If the Emperor noticed the elf's lack of deference, he did nothing to correct the insult; so neither could Hambohn.

Fury split his insides, darkening his robes beyond scarlet fire to pitch black. *I don't know who you are, you stubborn, moss-headed elf, but I will find out. And when I do, you will grovel before me to your dying breath.*

And just like that, Hambohn's night of triumph was ruined.

* * *

Manula whispered into the First Satrap's long pointed ear. "All is ready to proceed at your command, M'Lord."

Hambohn metered his rising delight but allowed himself a faint smile. Public outbursts of emotion never served him well, especially as he was prone to slitting the throats of those nearest him when rage was upon him. He lost a great many slaves that way, not to mention a few political rivals during parliamentarian debate.

"I have a good premonition of this afternoon, Manula." The First Satrap stopped at a passing fountain. He pulled at the lines of his garment to make his person appear taller and more opposing. "The Purim Priestess personally assured me this night was a crucial conjuncture for my future."

His new spider silk-woven robes were more exquisite than the last. Finer than milkweed silk and as light as a second skin, the weave was strong enough to resist steel blades, a quality rivaled only by the best light armor. And these robes never took on a color that clashed with his Serpian gray complexion. In fact, with each color change, the garment's properties enhanced the wearer's appearance. That stubborn elf who had refused to bow would be no match for these robes. He'd kneel now from Hambohn's sheer majesty. And if he didn't, Hambohn had a plan for that too.

"Take us the long way, Manula, through the center of the Green Quarter." Hambohn chuckled as he stepped into his palanquin.

His retinue wound through the city streets and passed through the wrought iron gates of the Assimilation District. They held themselves close, each careful not to touch the nasty metal that burned most elf-kind on contact. The idea for containment had been his and had come to him by way of a visiting dwarf delegation. Protection with a sting.

Once inside, progress slowed markedly as they wove through haphazard groves of Minoan trees. This Assimilation Quarter, dubbed the Green Quarter after the Verdant Elves who inhabited it, had once been a respectable treeless area. The brainless elves tainted it by planting Minoan saplings, a species native to their own lands. The trees sprouted everywhere, maturing at an alarming rate. It was an ecological disaster. Cutting, burning, and poisoning the saplings proved useless. The plants resurrected themselves by the next day. These green-headed monsters and their pestilent trees were a rash beneath Hambohn's underclothes.

But not for much longer, if his audience with the Emperor went according to plan.

His heralds bellowed, "Make way for the First Satrap of his Imperial Highness." Their flags curled in the light breeze. "Make way."

The elves intoned the appropriate response. "Hail Gracious One, Satrap to the House of Nightenshade."

"Greetings," replied Hambohn, pleased that his deep voice resonated above the crowd like thunder from an incoming storm.

The crowds pressed in as he tossed handfuls of silver coins from his palanquin. Grubby children snatched at the money, prodding his bodyguards to form a barrier lest the dirty urchins venture too close.

Some of the adult elves offered grand displays of sycophancy, allowing his palanquin bearers to walk across their backs as they lay before the Satrap. Each earned a gold coin from his servants' gloved hands. Wrapped in a fine handkerchief woven from poisonous silk, the tokens created illness in the recipients. Despite his seething resentment of the elves, the smile upon his face was genuine.

Then the breeze shifted and became a tailwind, flapping the curtains on the palanquin closed and effectively scooting them down the path. Hambohn gritted his teeth. It wouldn't do for him to fight the curtains open as if he were interested in the proceedings outside. Frustration welled inside him. They'd only handed out a small portion of the poison-laced gifts and now the crowds were scattering as the inhabitants sought shelter from the incoming storm.

"Get us out of this wretched wind, Manula," Hambohn grumped.

At the palace, Hambohn's heralds blared their arrival over the noise of the palace attendants. "Hambohn din Hammedatha, Agate of the Imperial Crown, First Satrap of Serpia, loyal to the Imperial House of Nightenshade. May the Emperor's rule advance unhindered as the Eternal Light into the darkness."

The Emperor, unfazed by the cacophony, continued reading his parchment, ignoring Hambohn's entrance and forcing an imperial wait--a condition tolerated by the First Satrap only because the Emperor outranked him. *Next time I must double the number of heralds. See if Nightenshade can read through fifty of them.*

The Emperor rolled the parchment and passed it to his scriblerian. "I'm busy Hambone. There is little time for your usual posturing. State your request."

"It's Hambohn, Your Eminence," Hambohn bowed.

"That's what I said. You may rise and proceed. What is it you wish today, Hambone? To put the viceroy in chains? Or perhaps to lock the Purim Priestess in the dungeon?"

Hambohn bristled at Nightenshade's comments. It wasn't his fault the viceroy was caught messing around with one of the Emperor's lesser concubines. And he had nothing but respect for the current Purim Priestess; it was her predecessor who crossed him.

Hambohn cleared his throat. "The Verdant Elves are a blight on your Empire, oh Magnificent Star of the Northern Sky. Not only are their trees a contagion, their customs are spreading outside their district like a virus."

Situated in the middle of the city, the Green Quarter was the best place for more stubborn captives to be integrated into Serpian Society. Conquered species had no choice but to take on their captors' culture and appearance. It was Serpian law. The Purim Priestess's magic encouraged the conversion process, a failsafe if the transformation went too slowly. But the dratted elves had proven resistant to her spell. In fact, elfish customs and speech were becoming popular among Serpian youth.

"Hmmm." The Emperor's right eyebrow arched as he pursed his lips. "What would you suggest I do for this...blight?"

"If it pleases you, Great Mountain of Wisdom, issue a decree for their extermination. I will provide 10,000 sacks of silver to the royal treasury to defray the cost of termination."

The Emperor unrolled another parchment and scanned it.

Hambohn was familiar with this ploy; he used it himself when he wanted to consider a request and make the petitioner sweat. His Majesty was anything but obtuse. Extermination was cheap and they both knew it. Imperial enforcers would receive the elves' possessions in payment for their services.

"Very well." The Emperor handed his signet ring to the scriblerian without looking up from his scroll. "If it means that much to you, do with the elves as you see fit. It makes little difference to me."

Hambohn plucked the ring from the scriblerian's outstretched palm and retreated backwards, bowing at the waist, until clear of his sovereign's presence.

As he headed back to his palanquin in the palace courtyard, Hambohn passed a familiar figure at the gate. The elf was easy to spot because, once again, he was the only person not bowing.

Hambohn stopped in front of him. "What is your name, elf?"

"Cimadore, Exalted One." The elf stared him in the eye, not even bothering to avert his gaze.

"Why do you not bow to me, Cimadore?" Hambohn's robes flashed scarlet. The same robes that were supposed to beguile the elf and send him reeling to his knees.

"My job is to guard the palace gate. I can hardly do that if my eyes are on the ground, Exalted One." The elf's gaze passed from Hambohn and stared placidly forward.

Hambohn raised his fist and swung at the elf's face.

Cimadore caught Hambohn's fist in his hand and the crowd gasped.

Lightning struck the palace gate in a white explosion. Hambohn tumbled to the ground, momentarily blinded. Grumbles and groans surrounded him.

Manula helped him to his feet and he brushed himself off. The crowd dispersed like a flock of chickens caged with a hungry fox. All except for Cimadore, who remained at the gate unaffected as if near-death by lightning was a common occurrence.

Hambohn jumped into his palanquin and gave the order to flee the storm. The lightning goddess had spoken and he would not argue. Not when he'd already achieved victory. Cimadore might not have bowed to him today, but soon he would have no option.

* * *

Verdant Elf Elimination Day Proclamation
WHEREAS, Verdant Elves influence Serpian youth to speak and dress in a morally reprehensible and culturally inferior manner; and
WHEREAS, Verdant Elves have poisoned Serpian ecology by planting and propagating Minoan trees; and
WHEREAS, Verdant Elves have failed to integrate into Serpian society to the point at which figures in authority are not given their due deference; and
WHEREAS, Verdant Elves have proved resistant to all attempts at assimilation per Serpian law.
NOW, THEREFORE, I, Martindale Horatio Nightenshade, serving as Imperial Emperor of all Serpia, do hereby proclaim Luvainer 15th, 332, as Verdant Elf Elimination Day.
Serpian citizens are urged to remove the pestilence of Verdant Elves from our society by any means necessary.

~Signed this 2 day of Moravier, 332 with the Imperial Signet~

* * *

Moravier 6, 332

Hambohn knocked upon the First Consort's apartment door. He dressed in his official robe as required by this evening's invitation, but there was no reason it had to be the rag he received at his appointment ceremony. The black market scarlet linen and contraband dwarf-spun gold thread that his tailor had acquired made him look more presentable for the sake of the empire--a worthy cause. As long as Hambohn looked good, the First Satrap didn't care where his tailor procured his materials.

A servant answered the door; her long green hair brushed the floor as she bowed.

Hambohn stopped in the doorframe. What was a Verdant Elf doing in the First Consort's chambers?

"Lord Hambohn, is there a problem?" The First Consort stepped from the shadows, her lissome figure complemented by a simple white gown which clung to her curves like moonlight on the water.

"Your Grace." Hambohn bowed his head. "I--uh--I'm allergic to the hair of the Verdant Elves. Perhaps if your servant were to shave her head…"

The First Consort's brows twitched and then her lovely face relaxed. "Fanti, be on your way. I have no more need of you tonight. The eunuchs will suffice for the rest of the evening."

To Hambohn's delight, the elf trembled as she scurried away.

"Follow me, please." The First Consort glided towards double doors that swung open without a touch. The Emperor reclined at the head of a long table in resplendent robes of midnight blue. As she neared him, the Consort's dress darkened to the exact shade of the Emperor's. Constellations materialized and twinkled across the couple's garments, matching the layout of the eastern sky.

Hambohn was almost embarrassed of his fine robes in the presence of these masterpieces. Almost.

"Please sit down, Hambone din Hammedatha." The Emperor studied the goblet of wine in his hand. "We are pleased you could join us."

"The honor is mine." *And it's Hambohn, you imperial oaf.* Hambohn executed his most courtly bow before reclining at the table. "To be invited by the First Consort, a woman of surpassing beauty, the star of the Emperor's eye, is more than I deserve."

The First Consort's expression remained undecipherable. She was pleasant to gaze upon, as lovely as everyone said even if her complexion was a bit olive, but her mouth did not smile and her eyes did not sparkle when she glanced at him. Her every movement reflected the finer noble families of their land, although she was new to the capital. The Emperor had chosen her to replace his last consort near the time Hambohn had risen to Second in command of all Serpia. Rumors contended that she became First

Consort when the Emperor selected her from the fairest of hundreds of exquisite women.

"Where did you come from before you married our Emperor, Blessed Lady?" Hambohn, who prided himself a gourmand, slipped a morsel of roast python between his lips while waiting for her answer.

"I'm from here in the city, Satrap." The First Consort dipped a piece of cheese into a bowl of licorice sauce. "But, please, call me Threse. Titles are a mouthful; let's save our mouths for the wonderful dishes my kitchen has prepared, if the Emperor agrees."

Emperor Nightenshade smiled at his young wife and stroked her cheek with the back of his fingers. "If that is what you wish for tonight, my darling, then you shall have it."

Each dish Hambohn sampled proved more succulent than the last until his stomach protested against the tightness of his robes and his thoughts muddied from the free-flowing wine. He regaled his monarchs with story after story -- political intrigues, gossip, even a few ribald tales, although nothing too risqué in the First Consort's-- Threse's --presence.

"Alright, my dove, why did you invite us to this fine banquet? What can we do for you?" Emperor Nightenshade's expression was tender. "I will give it to you, even if it is half my empire."

Hambohn choked on a swallow of wine. Half the kingdom?

The First Consort's laugh trilled through the room like wind against hanging chimes. "Can't the First Consort invite the Emperor and his First Satrap to a nice dinner without being accused of wanting something?" She smiled mysteriously as the candlelight shimmered off her ebony tresses, creating a faint greenish aura around her. "How about this? My deepest wish is for you and our esteemed guest to come to another banquet I will prepare tomorrow evening."

The Emperor chuckled in response. His gaze never left his wife's face as he said, "Good night, Hambone. We will see you tomorrow evening."

Hambohn struggled to his feet. He tried to bow, but the room kept tilting around him. Not that the royal couple noticed.

He didn't remember walking through the palace. Big, fat raindrops fell on his uncovered head in the courtyard, bringing him back to his senses.

Cimadore, the dreadful elf, stood sentry at the palace gate. By now, the olive-faced beggar would have heard about the proclamation. Hambohn smiled in anticipation. The mold-headed nuisance was sure to not only bow at his approach, but tremble as well. The perfect ending to a superb evening.

But Cimadore did not bow. His stoic countenance showed minimal regard, as always. The elf looked unconcerned as Hambohn passed, even... disinterested.

Hambohn stumbled, but side-stepped before he fell. Cimadore was at his mercy and still did not show a modicum of deference. Was the elf was too stupid to recognize the power that Hambohn held? He reached for his short sword, but it was not on his sash where it belonged. Drat. He'd left it at Threse's apartment. And the Emperor looked as if he didn't want to be disturbed. He would have to wait until tomorrow night to retrieve it.

Perhaps it was just as well. He could strike the elf down and no one would care, but no one would see either. Cimadore had defied him in public, so Hambohn needed a public way to punish this gangrenous elf. Something long and drawn out that he could enjoy as much as he'd enjoyed tonight's banquet.

He hurried to his palanquin as the rain began in earnest.

* * *

Moravier 7, 332

"To the Agate of the Royal Crown, Overseer of Serpia, personal dinner guest of First Consort and Emperor Nightenshade the Conqueror." Hambohn raised his ornate crystal wineglass toward the ceiling. "In other words, to me!"

His wife and friends laughed and raised their glasses in return. "To Hambohn the Exalted."

Hambohn surveyed the guests gathered in his formal entertaining room. Their eyes followed his every move. Their ears couldn't drink enough of his words. Who was he to deny them? "Threse, the First Consort, enjoyed my company so much that she has invited me to another private banquet with the Emperor tonight."

Cheering and clapping greeted his announcement. He had so many friends these days. It had been no trouble for Sherez, his plump cherub of a wife, to gather them together for this impromptu mid-day feast. He smiled fondly. She'd proven a good choice in companions--luscious and adoring with just enough ambition to push him to greatness--a useful wife.

"So your life is complete then, eh, Hambohn?" A voice from the throng rang out.

"It will be once the elf Cimadore no longer has a head." He grumbled. "Oh no! Did I say that out loud?"

More laughter.

"Beheading's too good for that one. You should let him hang and leave him out a good long time so everyone can see what happens when people disrespect you." A man in bright blue robes nudged Hambohn. What was his name--Morass? Morwin?

"No one's afraid of hanging these days," said a man in red and gold that

Hambohn didn't recognize. "You should burn him alive. Let him serenade you with the music of his torment."

"But no one would recognize him afterward," said another fellow wearing dark green. "Why not impale him on the biggest spike you can find? No, the biggest spike in history. He'd die slowly and still be recognizable."

Hambohn motioned for a servant to refill the wineglass of his friend in dark green. He liked that idea. A lot.

Sherez's warm hand brushed his forearm. "I hate to see you upset, husband. You have found favor with the Emperor. Why not go now and ask permission to impale Cimadore instead of waiting for the edict to take effect? Surely he will grant your request."

Hambohn nodded. "A good idea, my pet. Make arrangements for me to be conducted to the palace." He raised his cup for more wine to drink while he waited. *Better and better.*

* * *

"Hambone, it is fortunate you are here." Emperor Nightenshade rose and stretched when The First Satrap was announced. "You're just the man to help me with something I want to do."

Excellent. "How can I be of service, Your Majesty?"

"What should I do to honor someone who truly pleases me? Someone who has gone out of his way to show service to this office?" The Emperor crossed his arms and waited.

This could only mean one thing. The emperor realized his worth, his ambition, his single-mindedness and wished to honor him at last. With glee, Hambohn considered his options for rewards. "If it were me, Majesty, I would be most honored if you would allow me to dress in some of your own royal robes, and then have one of your most noble officials lead me through the city on your finest mount shouting, 'This is what Emperor Nightenshade does for someone he wishes to honor.'"

"A most excellent suggestion." Nightenshade nodded, smiling broadly. He returned to his desk and sat down. "Please make the arrangements to honor Cimadore the elf. You can find him at the gate of the palace. Leave nothing out."

"Cimadore?" Hambohn swallowed and focused on keeping his mid-day feast in his stomach where it belonged. "If I might be so bold as to inquire, what wonderful thing has he done to receive such honor?"

"He discovered and prevented an assassination attempt upon my life." The king's visage darkened like thunderheads brewing on the horizon. "A worthy deed, don't you think?"

"Yes, of course, Your Excellency." Hambohn bowed low before Nightenshade. "Your loss sire would be the parent of all tragedy. I will see to it at once."

"Make sure you see to every detail personally." The Emperor resumed his work taking no notice as Hambohn bowed his way out of the room.

The skies opened and rain poured down on Hambohn as he led Cimadore through the city. The friends that had attended his gathering just hours before jeered from under protective awnings as he led the cursed elf around the square on the emperor's best stallion, royal crest and all. The emperor's armor bearers held a rain tarp above the elf to keep him from getting wet but Hambohn, at the front of the retinue, was drenched by the time he returned to the palace. Were he able to make use of it, the fire in his soul could have dried his robes in seconds.

* * *

Hambohn slumped into his villa in dripping robes, his throat sore from yelling. Sherez did not stand or bow as usual when he entered the sitting room. Reclined on pillows, she watched as the work crew shaved an enormous tree into the largest impaling spike in the Serpian Chronicles. The sun shone down on the workers' glistening backs. It had stopped raining once Cimadore's parade had finished and they were back in the castle. Too late to do Hambohn any good.

"I heard you spent the day parading some elf around on the Emperor's stallion." His wife's voice slippery sweet even as her words dripped condescension.

"Not just any elf. Cimadore." Hambohn threw himself upon his couch with a groan.

"I don't understand. You went to the palace so you could kill him. Did the Emperor not take kindly to your request?"

"I never got a chance to make the request." He explained the events leading to his humiliation. He expected sympathy--wasn't that the role of a wife? But Sherez turned her attention to the windows. "You've embarrassed me in front of all our friends with your witless suggestion."

"My suggestion?" Hambohn's words were loud in his own ears. "It was you who prodded me to go to the emperor and ask for Cimadore's head. If it weren't for you, I wouldn't have even been in the palace."

Banging erupted from the villa door. A servant led an Imperial eunuch flanked by five guards into the room. "You're late for the First Consort's banquet. The Emperor has sent us to bring you immediately."

Hambohn jumped to his feet. "Let me change into something appropriate--"

The eunuch shook his bald head. "There's no time. The First Consort and Emperor are waiting on you."

"It will give even greater offense to them if I show up in this attire." Hambohn gestured to his damp, mud-fringed robes.

The eunuch pursed his lips. After a moment, he addressed one of the guards. "Hurry to the palace and arrange for a spare set of ceremonial robes to be delivered to Fanti." Turning his attention back to Hambohn, he frowned. "You can change at the palace."

Hambohn walked behind the eunuch as the guards trailed behind them on the long march to the palace. He could only hope that the First Consort and Emperor were not overly upset at his delay. Surely Nightenshade remembered that his day had been spent following his orders regarding the elf. How quickly events had changed for him. Last night, everything had been perfect, at least until he'd seen Cimadore at the gate.

Hambohn squared his shoulders. If things could deteriorate within a day, they could turn around in a day. He'd simply have to be more charming, more helpful, more…Hambohn.

At least it wasn't raining. And there was no Cimadore at the palace gates. Things were already looking better.

* * *

The banquet was as fine as the previous evening, possibly finer, but Hambohn could not enjoy it. Events of the day distracted him like the stench of spoiled eggs in a poorly ventilated room. He could never be rid of Cimadore now, not after today's demonstration.

The Emperor and First Consort didn't mention his lateness. If anything, the Emperor seemed surprised at his entrance, as if forgetting that Hambohn was expected. Hambohn briefly praised the goddess for the charms of the lovely Threse.

Bellies full, they lounged at the table after the last dish had been removed. Like the previous evening, the Emperor asked, "What do you desire, my darling? Up to half my empire, all you have to do is ask." He flicked a strand of the First Consort's hair off her shoulders in a playful fashion. "Unless you care to invite us to another banquet tomorrow night?"

Threse met the Emperor's eyes, her expression solemn. "If I have found favor with the Emperor, and if it pleases him to grant my request," she said, kneeling formally in front of him, "I ask for my life and the lives of my people to be spared. We have been given to those who would slaughter and annihilate us. If we had merely been sold into slavery I would remain quiet, for that would be too trivial of a matter to disturb you."

Righteous indignation filled Hambohn. Here was his chance to make amends for his lateness. To tip the scales of fortune back into his favor.

Hambohn sat up straight. "Who would do such a thing? I will make sure they die a most horrible death."

"Yes, who would do such a thing?" The Emperor frowned. "Who would be so presumptuous as to touch you?"

Threse speared Hambohn with her eyes. "This wicked man is our adversary and enemy."

"What? No, I'm not! I would never do anything to harm you." What could she mean? Someone was filling her head with lies about him. Maybe even that horrible Cimadore.

The First Consort leaned into the light of the waning moon. Her hair's faint green tinge blossomed into verdant tresses in the moonlight. "Do you deny that it was you who wrote the edict to exterminate my people?"

Comprehension struck Hambohn like a blow to the face. Too late, he realized his blunder. The First Consort was a verdant elf. The Emperor must not have known or he would never have agreed to the edict. "I did, but--"

"Guards!" Nightenshade yelled.

Hambohn's face dug into the thick pile carpet as strong hands propelled him forward. His own hands were lashed behind his back. He struggled but could not rise with the weight--one of the guard's feet?--in the middle of his back.

Nightenshade paced the floor, his jeweled sandals passing in and out of Hambohn's field of vision. The pacing stopped, followed by a large sigh. "I cannot revoke the edict to kill the Verdant Elves. It has been made into law which is immutable, even for me."

"There is one thing that could mitigate it, if it pleases you to do so." Threse's words were tentative.

"Tell me," Nightenshade commanded, all softness gone from his tone.

"If I have found favor with you, let there be a new decree that allows the elves to defend themselves and entitles them to the property of their enemies if attacked."

"Summon Cimadore," the Emperor commanded. "He'll be at the palace gate. He has served the Serpian Empire well. Have him take Hambohn's position in my empire and do as the First Consort has requested."

"Yes, Excellency." A set of footsteps receded from the chamber.

Hambohn's thoughts spun. This was a dream. A dreadful, awful, ridiculous dream. He would wake up and none of this would be real.

The guard holding Hambohn cleared his throat. "Your Majesty, Hambohn has set up a sharpened pole in his own courtyard that stands taller than the palace. Rumor has it that he intended to use it to impale Cimadore the elf."

Someone gasped. Hambohn wasn't sure, but he suspected that it was Threse.

"I see." Nightenshade's voice dropped to a low rumble, reminding Hambohn of the calm in the eye of a hurricane. "Impale Hambone on it instead, and give all his possessions to Cimadore."

The guard jerked Hambohn to his feet.

"Please, First Consort, I didn't know you were a Verdant Elf. I would never have made the proclamation if I'd known. Please have pity on me."

Her gaze became dispassionate, the same stoic indifference he'd seen on Cimadore's face every time the elf refused to bow. How had the similarity escaped him?

Revealing every ounce of her regal bearing and unbendable will, she locked eyes on Hambohn. "Cimadore is my uncle."

* * *

Verdant Elf Defense Day Proclamation
WHEREAS, Verdant Elves play a vital role in Serpian society, influencing the culture and ecology in a positive and productive manner; and
WHEREAS, Verdant Elves have been instrumental in safeguarding the empire from treasonous attacks; and
WHEREAS, Verdant Elves are indispensable to the Imperial Crown.
NOW, THEREFORE, I, Martindale Horatio Nightenshade, serving as Imperial Emperor of all Serpia, do hereby proclaim Luvainer 15th, 332, as Verdant Elf Defense Day.
Serpian citizens are urged to protect Verdant Elves from anyone who wishes them harm. The possessions and material wealth of anyone who attacks a Verdant Elf will be forfeit and given as recompense to said elf.

~Signed this 8 day of Moravier, 332 with the Imperial Signet~

The Thirteenth Summer

by Artemis Greenleaf

"I told your father you were too young for this," Kel said as he unbuttoned his leather doublet.

Fria held her tongue. She huddled in her bridal gown, shivering in the shadows of Kel's large canopied bed.

"Come here," he said.

Swallowing hard, Fria complied. She did not see a well-developed, potent man shedding his clothes, but a towering male who outweighed her by at least two fold and was orders of magnitude stronger than her. A threat.

"You're hardly more than a child." He lifted her chin and studied her face, his meaty hand warm against her throat. "Sit over there," he told her, gesturing to an overstuffed chair by a fireplace large enough for four tall men to easily stand abreast.

Again, she did as she was bidden. Vicious beatings at her father's hand had trained her to be compliant.

Kel peeled back the brocaded silk bedspread and pulled the top sheet off the bed. Then he rolled up his sleeve, drew a dagger from his boot, and slid the blade across the back of his wrist. He blotted the blood with the sheet, and held it against the wound until the bleeding stopped. After he rolled his sleeve back down, he took a large red apple from the bowl of fruit on a table by the door. The apple crunched as he bit into it, and he artistically mussed his hair in the mirror as he chewed.

"Hadlea will be up later with some food for you, and she'll show you to your apartments. Pray, do not think ill of me for rejoining the wedding banquet. It is my duty as its host." His hazel brown eyes were warm, and the left corner of his mouth lifted into a half-smile.

Fria nodded.

Kel tossed the apple core into the chamber pot and scooped up the bloodied sheet.

"In the morning then," he bowed slightly to her as he left.

The echo of boots on stone faded. A cheer went up from the wedding guests, and Fria shuddered. She could only guess that he had held up the bloody sheet, and they'd applauded what they thought was her blood. She was glad that her mother and her younger sister, Marian, had left immediately after the ceremony.

Fria sat back in the chair and scowled at the fire. "Well, this complicates things," she said, running her index finger around the edges of the emerald and sapphire ring that glinted in the firelight.

Fria's father and Kel juggled an uneasy truce between their neighboring fiefdoms, which were separated by a stretch of old forest peasants called the Witches' Wood. Elder daughter Fria had been promised to Kel at birth. Twelve summers had come and gone, and the raw spring was tearing its way out of the belly of the cruel winter. She'd hidden the evidence that she had crossed from childhood to womanhood as long as she could, but the chambermaid had found her bloodstained petticoat and betrayed her to her mother. Her father sent a herald to Kel, and the wedding was announced.

She had been taught her entire life that Kel was a brutal tyrant, and yet her father eagerly served her up as a blood sacrifice for the sake of a political union. She had been disappointed, but not surprised, when she was summoned to her father's chambers in the dead of night. He and his spymaster waited for her there.

"Open it," her father had said, handing her an intricately carved wood box that covered the palm of her hand.

The spymaster shared a look with her father, "It is said to be of dwarvish make."

Fria had lifted the lid and discovered the sparkling green and blue ring that now graced her right hand. The spymaster had shown her the trick to opening the concealed compartment underneath the emerald. It contained a noxious potion that, once the marriage had been consummated and Fria was with child, she was to pour into her sleeping husband's ear. She was practically a crusader, on a mission to rid the world of a wicked and violent man. The thought of being a crusader had appealed to her, as her cousin had just returned, full of tales of valor and exotic places, from battling the infidels in the Holy Lands.

However, Kel had not brutalized her, as her mother warned he would. Not only did he not demand her wifely duty in his bed, he was sending her to her own apartments. Could it be that he was not the ogre she had always been told he was, or did he suspect treachery from his young bride? Either way, she would have to be constantly on her guard. If she found herself liking her new husband and not following through with his murder, her father would likely have her assassinated. If Kel was merely suspicious, rather than kind, any whiff of treason would almost certainly mean her death.

The bedroom door opened, and a dour matron in a grey frock stepped in. "Come with me, Miss," she said.

"Who are you?" Fria asked, her heart fluttering under her ribs like a terrified bird. The woman couldn't possibly have heard her thoughts, yet Fria felt she'd been caught in the act of murder.

The woman's stony face was unreadable. "I'm Hadlea, Miss. Here to show you to your apartments."

"I see," Fria replied. She glanced around the bedchamber, forgetting for a moment she had no belongings there, and followed Hadlea down the corridor.

A young man, scarcely older than Fria, passed them. She recognized John from the wedding. His mother had died in childbirth, and her new stepson was clearly a stripling version of his father.

"It is late for you to be about, sir," Hadlea said.

"Rolf sent for me. Shadow is foaling!" He glanced at Fria. "Would you like to come see?"

Tsch. "You know that would be unseemly," Hadlea scolded. "Do not shame your father with such rash behavior."

John forced a smile at Fria. "Goodnight, then." He hurried down the hall.

Fria would have loved to have seen the birth of the foal, but she knew that going to the stables with her husband's virile son would require more than one chaperone. Besides, she was meant to be recovering in her apartments from her deflowering. How would it look if she were traipsing about the estate as if nothing had happened?

* * *

The days passed, not unpleasantly. The daylight lengthened and the darkness shrank. Fria only saw Kel at supper, and not always then. John kept busy with his studies, both of literature and weaponry, but especially with the staff. When she saw him, he was friendly, but their paths rarely crossed, save for meal times. Even as the household teemed with servants, bustling with the estate's upkeep, she was alone in the rambling manor, with only a small dog of uncertain parentage for company. She had a lady-in-waiting named Blodwyn who was always at her side, but she never spoke unless spoken to, and then only answered with a "Yes, milady" or a "No, milady."

At least Kel had an extensive library and a stable full of excellent horses.

On Midsummer's Day, Kel came to her bedchamber early in the morning, before her servants had arrived to dress her. Pip, her little dog, made a terrible racket when Kel had knocked on the door, and she was hard-pressed to quiet him.

"Come riding with me, milady. You have not surveyed your domain."

"So early? It is still dark," Fria replied, trying to put him off.

"Rolf has already saddled the horses. It is a long ride around my lands."

She had no recourse but to do as she was asked. "Yes, milord. Shall I meet you downstairs when I am dressed?"

"I'll wait for you up here," he said.

Fria's jaw opened and closed. It was his right, as her husband, to see her undressed.

"…in the corridor," he finished, and closed the door softly behind him.

She chose a linen gown that was closest to what the common folk wore, although it wasn't especially close. She pulled on her travel-stained cloak, the one she had arrived from her father's house wearing, and fastened it. Night's chill would still be lingering at this early hour.

"Come, Pip," she said to the dog, and the two of them joined Kel in the hallway.

At the stables, Rolf waited in the yard with two horses – Kel's black stallion, and a dapple grey mare for Fria. She wished that she was riding astride, instead of to the left. She was an excellent rider, when she was allowed to ride properly. But today, Kel would be leading her horse around, as if she were nothing but luggage. Pip danced around the horses and yapped. Fria's grey stamped her feet.

"That one'll never keep up, milady," Rolf said, nodding toward the dog.

"Would you hand him up to me?"

Rolf glanced at Kel, who nodded. The stableman picked Pip up gingerly and handed him to Fria. The mare flicked her ears backward, but made no effort to dislodge the dog.

Fria nearly came to disaster when she caught one of her long bell sleeves between her knee and the lumpy pack saddle she was riding sideways on. As they rode, Kel pointed out various landmarks and points of interest, but he said little else. The sun was nearly overhead when they came the stretch of ancient forest that separated Kel's lands and Fria's father's. She had seen it many times before, and she didn't like it. The trees were huge and dark, and seemed to be outside of time itself, older than the very bones of the earth. Kel turned his horse to a path through the forest.

"The Witches' Wood! Why are we going in there?" Fria asked.

"Part of the tour, milady," Kel answered.

He slipped off of his horse, tied him to a tree, then tied up Fria's mare before rummaging in his pack. When he turned around, he had a length of rope in his hands.

"What is that for, milord?"

"A unicorn trap."

Kel helped her slide off the big grey horse. "And pray tell, why do you require a unicorn of all things?" she asked, fearing she would not like the answer.

"I have it on good authority that someone is planning to poison me."

"Milord!" Fria exclaimed, glad she'd left her ring at the manor. "Have you any idea who or why?"

"Perhaps," he said.

Reluctantly, Fria followed Kel into the forest. Even the squirrels were dark and mysterious here. A few dozen yards in, Kel stopped.

"This tree will suffice," he said.

"For what purpose?" Fria asked.

"My unicorn trap," he replied. "How could I possibly catch one without a virgin?"

Realization broke over Fria like a sudden downpour. She wouldn't be able to run down the path, leap on the mare and gallop away, dressed as she was. And even if she could, where would she go? She had no money, nothing of any value, and she would be unwelcome, at best, in her father's house, having failed to either become pregnant or murder her husband.

Fria backed away from Kel until her way was blocked by one of the ancient trees.

"You might want to sit down," he said, uncoiling the rope.

Pip barked fiercely, but Kel lunged at him, and he fled into the bushes, yelping. Fria hit Kel, beating his broad chest as hard as she could, but he only smiled at her. She slid down the tree trunk, and Kel tied her to it, not so tightly as to be painful, but not loosely enough for her to escape without help.

"The alchemists say," he told her, "that unicorn's horn is proof against any poison."

"But, milord, unicorns do not exist."

Kel frowned with mock sympathy. "Then you may be here a while." He started down the path. "I'll send my gamekeeper around later to see if you've caught my unicorn," he said over his shoulder.

Fria watched Kel mount his own horse and trot away, taking the grey mare with him. Tears rolled down her cheeks, and wracking sobs scuffed her tender throat against the rough hemp rope. She couldn't believe he would just leave her to die in the forest. Pip whimpered and skulked out of the shrubbery, shivering and licking her hands.

The shadows lengthened, and Fria stopped her crying. Her hands were raw and bloody from struggling against the obstinate ropes. Pip sat with his head in her lap. She had had neither food nor drink all day, and was feeling faint. She closed her eyes, just to rest them for a bit – after all, they were sore and swollen from crying, and her head throbbed. The next thing she knew, something was crawling on her face. Her eyes flew open, and she found herself looking into the sapphire eyes of a unicorn, his whiskers gently grazing her cheek.

It startled when she moved, but didn't go far. This one looked to be a baby. It was perhaps as tall as a yard, with an impeccable white coat that practically glowed in the dense twilight, and it danced around her on cloven hooves. Its wispy mane stood on end, and the creature's spiral horn was only a hand's breadth long.

Fria wondered if hunger had caused her to have peculiar visions. But the colt left tracks in the soft dirt of the path as it galloped off in answer to a vaguely horse-like call some distance behind Fria. She closed her eyes and took in a deep breath. Rain was in the air. At least she might get a drink soon. When she opened her eyes again, the tracks were still there in the dirt. Surely they were the tracks of a deer, or perhaps a wild boar, and her famished brain had concocted a unicorn, based on her conversation with Kel.

A familiar sound caught her attention. Hoofbeats. A horse was galloping in her direction. Fria shrank against the tree, not knowing if the oncoming rider was a friend or foe. Night was falling fast, and she would be at the mercy of the wolves soon. Still, they might treat her more kindly than the wrong sort of traveler. She tried to silence her breathing by taking shallow breaths, grateful that Kel had left her far enough off the path as not to be easily seen in the gloom.

The sound of hoofbeats changed as the approaching horse broke into a trot and turned down the forest path, muted by fallen leaves. If the rider stayed on the path he would pass her by, unless he looked very carefully into the darkening forest.

"Fria?" the rider called. "Fria!"

"John?" she answered, perplexed. Pip barked a friendly hello, his tail thumping against Fria's leg.

The rider leapt off his horse as soon as he reached her and drew his sword. With one stroke, he severed the ropes that bound her to the trunk. He helped her to stand up, but her legs were wobbly – they'd fallen half asleep from being pressed against the hard roots of the tree.

"How did –" Fria started.

"There's no time." John pressed a fabric packet into her left hand. "The gamekeeper's boy is coming for you. With some of his drunken friends. It will go badly for you if they find you." He drew a silver and black dagger from his belt and gave it to her. "Go. I'll try to throw them off the scent."

In two strides, he had pulled himself onto his horse. Fria stood in the middle of the path, dumbfounded by this turn of events.

"Go!" he shouted at her before he wheeled his horse around and galloped off.

Fria and Pip fled into the trees. She stumbled over tree roots in the dark, feet numb and clumsy, hampered by the unpleasant pins-and-needles sensation in her legs as the blood flow returned. Her long dress caught on every bush and thorn. It was slow going, but at last she heard the sound of flowing water. She knew a creek ran through the middle of the forest.

Water! She ran down into the ravine, set down the packet and the dagger, and flung herself into the stream, guzzling like an animal. Pip was more restrained, crouching on the bank and lapping noisily.

When her thirst was finally sated, she waded out of the creek, her dress heavy and water-logged. She groped around the area where she'd left John's gifts until she found them. The fabric packet smelled of Hadlea's glorious bread. She shared the bounty with Pip, but they were both still hungry when it was gone.

"I suppose we'd best tighten our belts and carry on," she told the little dog. "At least we're not in my father's oubliette."

Fria tore off the ragged remains of her impractical sleeves and used the dagger to split her long skirt so she could move more easily. Just as she was about to leave, the glare of a lantern caught her eye.

"Wot makes you think she came this way?" grumbled a male voice.

"It's a little scrap of linen caught in the bush here, innit? Linen don't grow on trees."

Leaves crunched under their feet as they got closer. Fria crouched under the edge of the ravine. Pip started to growl, but she circled her fingers around his muzzle and blew in his ear.

"Wot's that, then?" asked the second voice.

"It's a fox, I reckon," answered the first. "Look over there. That's a lantern for sure. Bet it's her."

The footsteps receded into the distance.

"Are you hurt?"

Fria whipped her head around. A shadowy figure stood before her in the gloom. The voice, however, sounded female.

"Not too badly, ma'am," she replied.

"You can call me Ash, not ma'am. Not to worry – they'll be following that Will-o-the-Wisp for miles."

"Good riddance to them," Fria replied.

"What brings you to the forest this time of night?" Ash asked.

"I've been here since midday. Tied to a tree. My…husband said he was trying to catch a unicorn, but I'm sure he meant to leave me for the wolves. Although I hadn't thought it would be the two-legged kind."

"None worse. I can show you to the edge of the forest, if you'd like."

"Your offer is very kind, but I've nowhere to go. I think I might be better off staying here."

"Do you know how to hunt?"

"No."

"Fish?"

Fria shook her head. "But what else am I going to do?" Pent-up tears burst their dams and streamed down her face. A sob escaped her throat. "I have nowhere to turn."

"Are you asking for my help, then?"

"I would beg of you any help that you could provide."

"Come with me, then," Ash said putting her hand on Fria's shoulder. "I don't live far from here."

The walk through the impenetrable dark of the forest seemed longer than it was, and eventually, they arrived at a small cabin in the woods. Thick vines embraced the walls and roof, and Fria could have believed the house had sprouted from a seed at the dawn of the forest. The cottage wasn't large, but light spilled cheerily out of the windows. Ash opened the front door and they went inside. Some trick of light made it seem much bigger inside than out.

"Ashleigh Rowan! When will you stop trying to rescue every livin' thing you find in the woods. I've told you those don't make good pets," exclaimed a woman in an apron, who waved a wooden spoon.

"She's not a pet, Mother. She asked for my help."

"Did she now?" Her eyes rolled skyward.

"I suppose you'll be wanting some dinner, then? What's your name, child?"

"Fria," she replied.

"Fria," repeated the woman. "You can call me Mrs. Rowan. And wash up in the basin over there."

Pip barked.

"And who is this wee thing?" Mrs. Rowan asked.

"That's Pip. He's been my only friend and companion since the wedding."

"A wedding, you say! Bit young for a bride, aren't you?"

"Yes," Fria said, staring down at the worn oak floor.

"Go on with ya, clean yourself up."

The meal – crusty bread, vegetable stew, roasted potatoes, and berries - wasn't the rich fare that Fria was used to, but it was the most satisfying one she ever remembered having. While they ate, she told them of her wedding and how she came to be in the forest. She left out the part of the story that contained the poison ring, as she feared they would think badly of her and cast her back out into the forest.

"Can you not simply return to your father's house?" Ash asked.

"The wedding was nothing but an alliance strategy. Kel has rejected me, and thus the alliance. My father is certain to blame me. And the worst of it is that the marriage was never consummated, even though false evidence was presented that it was. That makes me useless to him. I would be afraid for my life, should I return to his house."

Mrs. Rowan frowned. "Ash, you're leaving in three days' time. Why don't you take this one, and her pup, with ya?"

"They'd not accept a human for training, would they?"

"They might do. She'd be no worse off there than here."

* * *

It had been seven years and a day since Ash and Fria had left together, bound for the strange land of Faery, not found on any map. They'd spent their time learning woodcraft, weapons, and demon lore. Fria had grown from a near-helpless girl to a strong and fierce woman who was deadly with a sword, but even deadlier with a bow. So deadly, in fact, that she was the leader of a team whose sole purpose was to hunt and capture demons. They sat at the wooden table in Ashleigh Rowan's mother's house, drinking cold well water and eating bread and butter. Two others shared their meal, Tuck - the Abbey Lubber, and Alan - the gancanagh. Ash herself was a descendant of the Tuatha de Danann, the folk who had lived in Ireland for centuries before humans had arrived there.

Demons had recently established a trade route through what Fria had once known as the Witches' Wood. Her team was here to stop them.

"Does your mum not have any ale, then Scarlet?" Tuck asked. He had nicknamed Ash 'Scarlet' because she had recently taken to wearing a red cloak.

"Not a drop. Now stop asking about it," she replied. "You know," she looked at Fria, "should anyone ask who you are, you can't tell them your given name. Too many people know of you here. It wouldn't be good to set tongues wagging."

"What do you suggest, then?" Fria asked. She adjusted a strap on her leather armor.

"Good Lady Fria
Out to hunt the goblin
Locals can't know
Who's doing the robbin'," sang Alan.

"That does not even rhyme," Ash said.

Fria shrugged. "Robbin' the goblin? Still," she tilted her head to one side. "Robin's a common enough name."

"You're forgetting one thing," Tuck said. "We're short a team member. Don't know why Bran left us in the lurch."

"I think he didn't want to be parted from his sweetheart. We may be only four, but we can at least get the lay of the land until we get a replacement." Fria pulled on her green cloak.

"You mean now, I suppose," Tuck said, almost sullen.

The team followed the banks of the creek through the wood. After a while, Ash's sharp ears detected the noise of an approaching group. The voices were gruff, possibly demon. Fria and company hid themselves, and became invisible to mortal eyes. The company of men passed single-file over the narrow bridge just in front of Fria, and while they may have been outlaws, they were not demons. After they had passed, Fria rose and dusted herself off. Her hood, which had helped to conceal her in the tall grass, was still pulled up, obscuring her face in shadow.

"I think we should cross here," she said, and stepped onto the makeshift bridge, facing her team and taking a few steps backward.

"In a moment, perhaps," said Alan. He looked past her to the opposite bank.

Fria glanced over her shoulder. A large man, carrying a heavy staff, had started across the bridge from the other side. An imposing figure, he had matured a great deal in the last seven years, but Fria knew him in an instant. *John.*

It was too late to hide, and she feared he might recognize her. She nocked an arrow and drew her bowstring. Lowering her voice as deeply as she could, she called out, "Sir, I was on this bridge first. Kindly remove yourself so that I may pass."

"I am already halfway over. You move. And do put down your bow. I mean you no harm." John continued across the bridge.

Fria found herself in an untenable position. She could not shoot John in cold blood, but he was so much bigger than her that she wasn't sure she was strong enough to win in a fair fight. Why hadn't she just said nothing and let him pass, hiding her identity under the hood of her green cloak? She did not want to appear weak in front of her team, either. If she backed down to a mere man, how could she stand up to demons?

Alan was nearest to her. She seized his magic-infused staff and strode out onto the bridge. Each step caused it to creak and shudder. When she reached John, she stopped, planting the staff in front of her.

"Go back, or I shall knock you off this bridge," Fria said in her deepest, gruffest voice.

"Go back yourself," he replied, flipping the bottom of his staff up into his other hand so that it was parallel to the ground.

"A challenge, then. The winner crosses the bridge, and the loser takes a bath."

"As you wish," he said, and pushed forward with the staff.

Fria stopped his advance with her staff held at his chest. John dropped his staff's tip to push her block to the side.

Back and forth they went, feinting, parrying and swinging. Fria did not wish to injure him, just knock him into the creek. She saw her opportunity, and attacked, but his staff whizzed past her face and caught the edge of her hood, pushing it back from her face. For a full second, John gazed at her, dumbstruck.

Snap! One of the boards gave way, and she toppled into the water.

"Fria!" John bellowed, and jumped in after her.

The water was not deep, but the current was strong, and the rocks were slippery. It was perhaps a hundred yards before they could extract themselves from the stream.

"I feared you were dead," John said, helping Fria to her feet.

"Some forest folk took me in. You mustn't tell your father that I'm alive, I beg of you."

John closed his eyes. "My father is dead."

Fria squeezed his hand. "That is ill news."

"He would not have left you to perish. Father told the gamekeeper to fetch you, but he was not well, so he told his boy to go. Unfortunately, he and his companions had been at the ale house, and their thoughts were befuddled by drink. It was pure chance I heard them as I was returning to the stables. My father just wanted you to know that he knew about the poisoner's ring, and warn you against using it."

"My father's spymaster gave it to me the night before the wedding. I was told to pour the contents in Kel's ear while he slept, once I was with child."

"Would you have murdered my father?"

"No. Your father was kind to me, and he never touched me. Even had he been otherwise, I could not have completed my task, although I expect my own father would have killed me for sparing him. I never wished to be his wife, much less his executioner." Fria paused. "I have often wondered why you didn't just take me with you instead of setting me loose in the forest."

"I have wondered that myself. I had been strictly forbidden from being with you without a chaperone. I believed that you would simply follow the path through the wood and return to your father. I did not know you feared him so. When you did not arrive safely at his home, I searched for you for weeks."

"Robin! Are you hurt?" shouted Ash, from the far side of the creek.

"Robin?" asked John.

"My nom de geurre, as it were," Fria replied. "Yes, I am unharmed," she called out to Ash, Alan, and Tuck. "Just renewing my acquaintance with an old friend."

"There is a sturdier bridge further downstream," Ash yelled. "Let us make our way there."

"Agreed," Fria shouted back.

The fae folk moved quickly and soundlessly through the trees, and were soon out of sight. John moved quietly, for such a large man, but to Fria's well-trained ears, he was as loud as a herd of cattle.

"I suppose you will be headed back to your estate. Pray keep my secret – it is best that none know I am here," Fria said.

"As my stepmother, you are part of my household."

"As I told you, the marriage was never consummated."

"It is just as well, then. When my father was falsely imprisoned and then executed, I lost all claim to his holdings. I have been living here in the forest for the past three years. Strange I have not seen you in the wood."

"I have been away, with the kin of my companions. Pray, tell me how you came to such misfortune." She squeezed his hand again, but this time he held onto hers. Fria did not resist.

"The peace between our fathers' houses was ever unsettled, and became much worse after your disappearance. The old Sheriff passed away, and the king appointed your father in his place. My father and I attended the banquet held in the new sheriff's honor. My father suddenly fell faint – I suspect his wine was drugged – and he was carried to a bedchamber. The next morning when he awoke, the chambermaid lay dead on the floor, and blood was smeared on his sword and hands. No one doubted that the scene was fabricated, but as your father was the sheriff, there was nothing that could be done to save him."

"I deeply regret that this has happened. My father has much to answer for." Fria had no doubt that a man who could send his thirteen year old daughter as a bride-assassin was capable of executing his rival under fictitious charges, not to mention taking the life of the unfortunate chambermaid. "Do you know," she asked, "what has become of my sister, Marian?"

"She is betrothed to the pernicious Guy of Gisbourne, who has usurped my father's estate."

"Do you know when the wedding will take place?"

"A fortnight, if the proclamations in the village are to be believed."

"Not if I can help it." An idea both absurd and genius popped into Fria's head. "If there was a way to avenge your father's wrongful death and possibly regain your holdings, would you pursue it?"

"Wholeheartedly."

The three fae approached them. They had already crossed the bridge and come around the opposite path.

"We thought you'd never arrive," grumbled Tuck.

"I think," said Fria, reaching up to grip John's shoulder, "that we have found our fifth member."

* * *

It had taken some convincing on Fria's part, but John (Tuck had ironically nicknamed him "Little John," because of his size), had proven himself invaluable. Because he'd been living in the forest for the past three years, he knew all about the routines of those who travelled the wood regularly. Fria had decided that the best way to bring the demons out was to start intercepting their merchant caravans through the forest. To add insult to injury, they would freely distribute among the local villagers any of the demons' gold that they should acquire.

Now Tuck had an inordinate fondness for good ale, and insisted on acquiring some, and by some, he meant an entire wagonload of casks. Fria had decided to put this acquisition to good use. Ash had discovered that one of the merchant demons was a silk trader. John knew that a silk trader passed through the forest just after midday every Tuesday. Most likely, they were one and the same – silk was uncommon in this part of the world.

They parked the wagonload of ale across the path where it narrowed, so there was no way around, and removed one wheel. Tuck, wearing the brown robe of a monk, sat in the driver's seat. The other four waited in ambush. Before long, the purveyor of silks and his company of two walked down the path, with a donkey pulling a covered wain. The largest of the three was dressed as a fighter, with leather armor, a sword on his left thigh, and a dagger on his right. The other two were cloaked and hooded, one in grey, the other in tan. Demons could disguise themselves as men, and easily fool actual humans, but their artifices were no match for the fae's keen discernment. Ash whistled once like a kestrel, and twice in the voice of a common redstart. Fria knew that one of the party was a demon and two were human.

"A pox on that crooked sheriff and his bloody taxes," grumbled the man in grey.

"The price of business," shrugged the tan-clad one.

"Hey! Get out of our way, you!" growled the fighter.

"I should very much like to," responded Tuck with a smile, "but as you can see, my wagon is broken. I've sent my squire off to the village for a wheelwright, but he has yet to return."

"MacDonald! Help the friar move his cart," said the figure cloaked in brown.

Fria caught a yellow flash of eye in the dark under his hood, and knew he was the demon. Once the grumbling fighter had his shoulder under the wagon, Fria rose, bowstring drawn, and let fly an arrow that pinned the grey-clad human to a tree. It passed through his shirt and cloak, but not his flesh, and drove deep into the trunk. Little John stepped out of the shrubbery, sword drawn, and held the fighter at bay.

Alan had the most unusual weapon. In his hands, he held a clear crystal pyramid. The top third of it twisted to one side, revealing a vacant chamber. Alan crept up behind the demon and touched him with the device. Instantly, he was converted to a fluid and pulled into the pyramid, as his compatriots watched with morbid fascination. With a flick of his wrist, Alan snapped it closed and the essence of the demon swirled red and orange inside his prison. John also stood flabbergasted, for he had never seen such a thing.

That gave MacDonald the advantage he needed to slip out from under the beer wagon and draw his sword. Fria quickly hobbled him with an arrow to the calf, and Ash relieved the grey-clad man of his gold-filled purse.

Fria, whose face was hidden by her green hood, took the pyramid from Alan and lowered her voice, saying, "The wicked are not welcome here. Robin of the Wood and company will see to it that they are brought to justice."

"Robin of the Hood, more like," snarled the man in grey. "Show your face, coward."

Fria nocked an arrow and sent it flying. It struck the tree, between the edge of the man's hood and his ear. "It is only by my good graces that you yet live. Pray, mind your tongue, lest it be silenced."

Ash used her dagger to cut a strip from the demon's cast off cloak. Little John snapped the fletching end off the arrow's shaft, pulled it out of the fighter's leg, and Ash wrapped the wound in the strip of cloak to stop the bleeding.

"We have no quarrel with you, only your masters," she said.

John used one of the casks as a fulcrum and a heavy staff as a lever so he and Alan could lift the edge of the wagon while Tuck put the wheel back on. When it was done, Alan climbed up on the seat next to Tuck, Ash perched on the casks behind them, and Fria and John sat on the back end of the wagon. Tuck clucked to the horses, and the wagon rolled toward the village, leaving the fighter and the man in grey to make their own way back to town.

"You have learned a lot in seven years' time. The king's own archers could not best you," John said. He shook his head. "And all this time, I thought alchemists and priests were the only ones who had dealings with demons, nor did I know they could pass as men. They have a much different visage than I suspected."

"Their true faces are like those of serpents; yet, they are good at fooling the eye. It is similar to what the fae call 'glamour.' And I would say that you have improved yourself as well, since last we met."

His lips hinted at a smile. "We have caught the silk trader. What next?" he asked.

"Rare it is to find a solitary demon, for they often travel in packs. Still, time grows short to save my sister from an ignoble fate. Perhaps we can restore your lands in the same adventure."

"I have lately grown fond of living in the forest," he replied.

* * *

In one week, Fria and her team had captured five more demons and liberated a small fortune in gold and silver. They kept little for themselves, just enough to cover their needs when they went amongst the townsfolk. The poorest villagers benefited the most from the demons' misfortune and news of Robin of the Wood's largesse spread on nimble feet throughout the village and local farms.

The sheriff, however, disliked this tax revenue reduction, and vowed to capture Robin. He decreed that, in honor of his daughter's coming nuptials, he would sponsor an archery contest. The prize would be a golden arrow.

"A most blatant trap," Ash said when Fria handed her one of the proclamations.

"Of course it is. But I have a stratagem."

John scowled. "Just because you know it's a trap does not mean you cannot get caught in it."

"I have heard more and more about Guy of Gisbourne, and I like him less and less. He wears malice as a doublet and cruelty as a cloak. I will not have my sister fall into his clutches."

"You haven't spoken to her in more than seven years. You cannot know her mind. She may fear her father's wrath more than she values her salvation, and thus betray you," John said.

"That may be so, but we have a secret weapon." Fria smiled at Alan.

John crossed his arms. "He is certain fair, but likely not enough of a temptation to lure your sister from her groom."

"I beg to differ with you," said Ash. "Our fair Alan is a gancanagh, a love-talker. No female can resist him, if he desires her. That is his magic, and it is perilous strong."

John shifted his weight and his eyes darted between Fria and Alan.

The day of the tournament, one day before Marian's wedding to Guy of Gisbourne, arrived. Fria slung her bow over her green cloak. Tuck, in his usual brown frock, Ash in her red cloak, and Alan dressed in blue, accompanied her. She had asked John to wear a helm, and over it a cloak, so that he was not recognized. The contest was being held at the estate that had been stolen from John, and, although he was still opposed to Fria's plan, he agreed to participate. The team staggered their entrance, and merged into the throng one at a time. They kept an eye on the sheriff, even as he and his spies sifted through the crowd. Fria handily won each competition, and soon the archer in the green cloak was marked as Robin of the Wood. The final contest was between the top archer and Guy of Gisbourne. A prudent combatant would have made sure to miss the mark, but Fria was not so politically minded.

Gisbourne shot first, and the arrow struck dead center of the target.

"Do you concede?" he asked. "You cannot hope to have a better shot."

Fria said nothing, but smiled as, over Gisbourne's shoulder, Alan took Marian's hand and led her from the spectator's box and toward the edge of the wood. The whistle of a kestrel caused Fria to look up, but she saw no birds in the sky.

She stepped forward and pulled an arrow from her quiver. She nocked it, and the crowd fell silent.

She felt her own heartbeat as she pulled back the bowstring.

She breathed deeply, willing her heartbeat to slow. Then she found its rhythm.

In between pulses, she let the arrow fly.

Fletching scattered and wood splintered as her pale arrow drove straight down the black shaft of Gisbourne's.

Another heartbeat, then the crowd roared.

Fria reckoned that while her father, the sheriff, was evil through and through, he was not stupid. He would not risk the wrath of the crowd by making a spectacle of seizing Robin of the Wood. It would be subtle and unobtrusive, a knife in the ribs, or poisoned drink. She was prepared.

The sheriff raised Fria's right hand in victory. She did not pull back her hood, and her father failed to recognize his own daughter. "We have a champion!"

Fria inclined her head.

The sheriff presented the golden arrow, but whispered next to Fria's cloaked ear. "Robin of the Wood, you are a marked man. I will see you in shackles before nightfall."

Fria put the golden arrow into her quiver, as she would any common arrow, bowed again, and turned to leave. She passed behind John, and a green-cloaked figure emerged from his shadow, but it wasn't Fria. Fae folk are most excellent shape shifters, and Tuck imitated her perfectly. The sheriff's spies would follow him for a while, until Ash, John and Fria were safely free of the compound, then he would shift into his usual appearance. In the meantime, Fria, hidden between John's massive form and a small alcove, slipped the golden arrow into his belt, and turned her cloak inside out so that now it showed blue. She let it cover the bow and quiver altogether.

John left the compound first. Then Ash, followed by Fria. When she arrived at the rendezvous point, she looked at her sister. She had grown into a pretty young woman with porcelain skin and haunted eyes.

"I hope you do not pine overmuch for your groom," she said to Marian.

Marian looked longingly at Alan. He smiled back. "This misadventure may yet save me from the poisoned chalice I had prepared myself."

Fria threw back her hood, "Marian, my sister! Never, ever entertain such ideas again. You are safe now."

"Fria!"

The two sisters embraced each other, and tears glistened on both their cheeks.

"Where is John?" Tuck asked as he lumbered up to the group.

"John?" Fria released her sister and looked around. How had she failed to notice he was not there? "We must find him! Alan, stay here with Marian and keep her safe."

Fria ran back down the path towards the archery competition. A noise to her left caused her to change her course and follow a barely discernible trail. She proceeded through the thicket, following the sound she had heard earlier, for perhaps a furlong, before she came to a clearing.

John was on his knees, face swollen and bloodied. Guy of Gisbourne stood behind him, the edge a sword pressed under John's jaw. Blood trickled down his throat.

"Did you really think I wouldn't recognize this spawn of dogs?" Gisbourne said. He let his human disguise drop, and his long forked tongue flicked over his hard, scaly lips. The pupils of his tawny eyes contracted to vertical slits in the afternoon sun.

Fria took a step forward. "Release him. It is me you want," she said, realizing too late that the kestrel's whistle she'd heard earlier had been Ash's warning that there was a demon about.

"Very noble. But I intend to kill both of you. Or perhaps all four of you." His mouth gaped in a gruesome parody of a smile.

Tuck and Ash had caught up with Fria, and stood behind her. There was a nearly imperceptible click from her right. She watched out of her peripheral vision as John's hand inched toward Gisbourne's boot. Guessing that he was trying to give her a chance to escape by yanking his captor off his feet, and almost certainly cutting his own throat in the process, she whirled to her right and took the open demon trap from Ash's hand.

She hurled it as hard as she could, aiming for the bridge of Gisbourne's nose. He dodged out of the way.

But not quite enough.

The tip of the open pyramid brushed against his cheek. His sword clattered to the ground as he was sucked into the crystal. Ash reached John first, and clicked the top of the pyramid into place. Fria fell to her knees in front of him and held his bloody face in both her hands.

"Such a touching reunion," the sheriff's voice sounded behind her, freezing her heart.

Steel sang across leather – a sword being drawn from its scabbard. Fria's lips brushed John's as she pulled the golden arrow out of his belt. Then she threw off her cloak and turned to face her father, bow in hand.

He stopped in his tracks. "Fria?" Then he laughed. "Luck is with me today. I have regained my claim to Kel's holdings and unmasked Robin of the Wood."

Fria nocked the golden arrow and drew her bow.

The sheriff snorted. "You will not shoot me in cold blood. You are much too fond of goodness and–"

The golden arrow pierced his heart, and he fell back into the forest litter with a thud.

John recovered from his wounds and reclaimed his family holdings. He and Fria were soon wed. And though she bore him four robust children, the pair of them often disguised themselves and made their way to the forest, along with Ash, Tuck, Alan, and Marian to keep the demons from establishing a foothold there. Alan took Marian to wife, and he lived with her on her ancestral estate. Many generations of their children claimed their fae ancestry with pride.

Age did not trouble Ash, Tuck, nor Alan, but Fria and John were mortal. After a time, they both found their heroic exploits in the forest too taxing. It was time to lay the legendary Robin of the Wood, also known as Robin Hood, to rest. The local prioress, whose convent had benefited greatly from the outlaws' spoils, agreed to assist in the ruse. Fria and Little John donned their outlaw garb and made it known that Robin of the Wood was ill and was going to the abbey to be bled. They had cached clothes there, for even after all these years, no one suspected that Robin Hood was a woman. Once they entered the abbey, the prioress caused a grave to be dug, and ruefully reported that Robin had been more ill than she suspected, and she accidentally over-bled him.

Thus ended the life of Robin Hood, but so thoroughly had Fria's team routed the demons that none ever set foot in that wood again. Their eldest daughter saw to that.

The Queen of the Elves

by Steven D. Malone

Alfnoth the deacon, servant to the children of God at Lydbury, to Henry, by the grace of God king of the English and duke of the Normans, sends greeting and eternal blessedness in Christ.

I cannot render adequate thanks, as you have deserved, for the friendship of your brotherly love, which you often for the sake of God showed to me in my necessities. I pray Almighty God that he may recompense you in the high summit of the heavens with the reward of his favor eternally in the joy of the angels.

It pleases me to reply to your request for my witness to the visit paid your blessed and loving father William, late king of the English and Duke of the Normans, by the rebel Edric of Shropeshire and his wife Godda, known as the queen of the Elves. However, I fear the wrath of God for keeping memory of such vanities and the displeasure of you, my king, for the false and deceived railings of this woman, a true daughter of Eve.

I served faithfully as a soldier by your father's side in all the years since, until full of the infirmities of age, I entered in service to Almighty God some six years ago.

In this duty, I was present on the day traitorous Edric gave up his rebellion and swore fealty to William. To the lesser thegns like myself, the rebel was known as Wild Edric. The peasants on the fens taught us that name. He earned it in our eyes for he fought well and we lost many in the three years we faced him. We all marveled, your father not the least, at Wild Edric when he bowed down for his oath. He showed all the weight of his defeat in a haggard brow and tattered raiment but he stood proud and with arrogant eyes. It was I that whispered into the king's ear the rumor that set us on the road of our separate dooms. Wild Edric is married to the queen of the Elves, I whispered.

William marveled anew at Edric, immediately falling into conversation with the rebel. Wild Edric boasted of the truth of my assertion. Before all of the host, your good father required Wild Edric to wait upon the King's court accompanied by his elfish wife at her earliest opportunity, for this was a wonder of the English their conqueror dearly wanted to see for himself. The tattered rebel bowed his assent.

The herald of Wild Edric appeared at the burnt doors of York some weeks later, as your father drank in celebration of the ravaging of the northern shires. This unholy thegn dressed in Edric's green raiment and decorated himself in the talismans and jewelry of the old gods' Yule trappings. The fierce man's horn sounded like Gabriel's doom and his voice came like thunder. All of us cowered before him and your father also, God forgive me, such was his visage. The herald announced, without so much as a by-your-leave, that it pleased Godda, queen of the Elves, to appear before William on the day we call St. Cuthbert's Day near Eastertide. The man's great horse reared and neighed mightily and was gone leaving us staring of into a foggy twilight.

There was talk of little else among William's host amid the desolate North Country or along the road to Winchester castle where your father held Eastertide. Everyone from thrall to earl, in anticipation, doubled and redoubled their efforts in preparation for the event. All of the Norman and English churchmen, and as many London burghers as could get invited came for the night of marvels. Your father demanded the best food and drink brought in from all the surrounding lands. His craftsmen busied themselves preparing the gifts he required. Though all was prepared, few slept on St. Cuthbert's Eve.

After noon it was when we heard music and song coming from the west road. Wild Edric and his company arrived. Edric led wearing armor of leather and bronze and clothes of green wool. His levy of warriors followed behind with musicians and singers and thrallmen. Behind those came several heavily laden carts. The whole company glittered in the sunlight from jewels and bronze armor and merrily colored clothes. But there was no queen of the Elves with them.

King William and Wild Edric approached each other with greetings. The King's was cold for there was no wife with Edric. Edric's was proud and haughty and not that of a defeated enemy. He did, finally, kneel before the King.

However he spoke his wife's apology while on his knees saying, "The queen, my wife, believes the King will understand that there are duties and constraints that come with her office and begs me to give you the time of her coming as required by her station. She will be before you when it is neither day nor night, she will come neither walking nor riding, she will see you neither under the sky nor under a roof, she will be seen by you when it is neither dry nor rain."

"God's very beard!" came your father's oath. "Will she come as I command or not?"

"She will come when all these things come to pass, my King," Edric said. "Queen Godda knows that her primary mission here today is to prove she is who she is. She will come!"

The King's doubt remained but he led us into the great hall where a great feast sat spread across the tables. Edric and his company, comely and happy, were good guests. They enjoyed the King's table with great delight. Their conversation was refined and charming though each declined to talk about the lady Godda. Finally sated, Edric rose and addressed King William saying his company came with entertainments and diversions for the host if it pleased the King. William answered that he would be pleased.

Edric stepped to the center of the hall and shooed away the thralls that continually kept our drinking horns filled. He then began a story of long ago when Godda's elves roamed the English isles freely and without fear of man. It was a wondrous story filled with passion and war and revenge and tragedy. It was the tale of how Godda and Edric met and loved. Such was the tale that all the host cried and clutched at their hearts sharing the grief of the two lovers. But, then Edric's tale turned. His story filled with ribaldry and errors and farce. The hosts' tears were now of laughter and their sides hurt from an excess of mirth. Finally, your father called a halt to the story unable to withstand Edric's verbal onslaught. All of us were grateful for the relief.

"Now, my Lord and all here, some of my friends and I offer you magic and music and magic again," Edric proclaimed.

To the hearth came a peculiar man of heavy brow and sparse beard, dressed in a thick hide robe glittering with golden thread and sparkling stones. This one carried a harp of wood, inlaid with more gold and carved in elaborate monstrous shapes. To his haunting music and rocking dance, Edric sang a song in a strange language. The beat of the music raced faster and grew in volume. The strange man began to twirl. Faster and ever faster he twirled. A wondrous green smoke rose up from his great robe until he fairly disappeared in the cloud. There sounded a great crash from I know not where. The one man, tall and commanding, became two, short and dwarflike, before my very eyes. Men rose up in alarm. Women screamed.

Wild Edric, joined by the two dwarves, sang a new song of such sweet melody that all the host stilled without words from the singers or from your father. With the new silence Edric's song ended.

One of the small men stepped forward as Wild Edric returned to sit by the King. He announced that he and his little friend were knowers of all secrets and the two proceeded to prove it to all the host. His little friend began to leap and bound and contort himself about the hall stopping first near this person and then another. With each stop he would hug or stroke the hair or clasp the hand of a man or a maid. The first of the little men then would tell that one's name and then another's secret such as the name of the hall where they lived or maybe what was in his pocket or some such thing. They were a marvel to all and a great diversion for the passing of time.

Without our knowing it, the afternoon waned and evening approached. Such was our wonder that none noticed Queen Godda arrive.

I was first to feel the breath of cold wind and to see the Lady Godda. However, as one all the host by an unheard signal turned to see her. The great doors, barred though they were, guarded though they were, stood open. Godda, Queen of the Elves, sat astride a small paint pony with feet touching the floor. Neither standing nor walking. The pony's front legs were in the hall the back legs stood in the grass. Neither inside nor outside. Behind Godda lay a thick misty fog dark in the twilight. Neither rain nor dry – neither day nor night.

Lady Godda wore flowing, and most immodest, gauze that first seemed a silvery white but on closer scrutiny seemed to be a shimmering flow of rainbow that covered her head to ankle in a luminous veil. Godda was neither clothed nor naked, in my eyes, for as the thin, shining veil covered her it exposed her. My Lord, words fail me. I cannot describe her beauty.

The pony stepped from beneath the elfish woman and she entered a silent hall and bowed to the king.

"Greetings in Christ to you, Lady Godda," William said amused and maybe a touch red-faced.

"Ave, conqueror of England," Godda said. "You demanded the presence of a queen of the Elves."

"I required the presence of the wife of Edric of Shropeshire to see if she was Queen of the Elves."

"See her then," said the lady from beneath clothes of rainbow.

"What proofs, wife. What proofs do you have for the king?" said Wild Edric.

"Do you require proofs, duc de Normandy?" Godda said.

"Forgive my caution, Lady, my priests," your father gestured to his prelates at table. "My priests teach me to doubt such things."

"The court of the Queen of the Elves is a proof." She gestured to her company. "My entrance here is a proof."

The King sat silent. Wild Edric stood and brought forward two of the Shropshire men to give witness. The first told a tale of money. The Lady Godda came to him asking for implements made of iron for elves defer from working iron. The man left iron tools on his stoop evenings, mornings saw a silver penny in their place. The second man chanced upon Lady Godda and her sisters in his forest at a twilight. They danced and frolicked in the mist as he watched. Their singing, he claimed, set a spell on him so that he slept. When he awoke, seemingly unharmed, he returned to his home to find he had been gone a year and a day.

"I've seen no elven pennies," said the King. Many of the host grumbled agreement.

"Have you, any of you, looked in your purses of late?" said Lady Godda.

The King and everyone fished their secret places and out came silver – a silver penny from the days of Penda of Mercia. I confess I was not alone in being delighted. Everyone seemed delighted save the King.

"I've not seen Lady Godda as clearly as did the good man who saw the dance."

The two dwarf-like men began to play. Lady Godda began to sway. Came the thunderous crash of the King's hand slapping the board before him.

"I do not expect to sleep a year and a day, my Lady!" he cried.

Perhaps I saw the smallest of smiles on her lips, the smallest of nods, as she continued to sway. Perhaps I saw nothing.

The music played faster. She began to dance. To frolic. The drape of silvery cloth twirled and glittered and shone in the lamp light. As it twirled to the alien music, Lady Godda stepped out of it by some elfin magic and danced before the dumbfounded king as naked as a minnow. Long golden hair flowing loose down her back. Skin the color of moonlight… (Illegible, possibly erased – ed.) …(s)aw nothing of her that proved her more than a mortal woman. The wondrous dance enthralled all present with no blush on cheek or shame in heart.

The music ceased leaving the hall in silence, Godda kneeling bent over her knees supplicant and modest despite her nakedness. All the host sat bewitched at our cups. The King, your blessed father, broke the spell.

In a flash of blood-red light and a resounding thump, he freed his sword from its sheath turned it and drove its point into the table. He rose to stand before the host a fierce scowl on his face.

"Enough! Enough tricks and songs and dances. No proof lies here. No truth. Fear me, the King of England, if this be a lie," William shouted.

"I do fear the wrath of the Conqueror. All of the twilight realm fear you,

William of Normandy," Lady Godda said though I saw no fear in her. "Feel the fear of the Ealderfolk!"

The distant thunder sounded and grew louder coming ever closer. The floor beneath my feet trembled. The walls shook. Serving dishes and ale cups danced and clattered. Wine spilled. The host screamed and signed to ward off evil. Lord, I have never known such fear as that in my belly and throat as I did that night. At the Elf Queen's command, the Wild Hunt roared above us.

I saw Lady Godda stand and command her robes with a gesture. Of its own the cloth of rainbow flew from the ground to wrap around her shoulders.

"Silence!" she commanded. The shaking stilled. The Wild Hunt receded into the distance.

This daughter of Eve looked again into the eyes of the King.

"What proof do you require, my Lord? For once and for all, know that I am Queen of the Elves."

King William, dazed, stared out at the woman. Slowly, he returned his sword to its scabbard and sat again.

"It is said," he said with a strained voice. "That the Ealderfolk are far-seeing and can tell past and future. See for me the future."

"Lord, I do not see the future."

"Lady, see the future or earn my wrath," William said though I felt hesitation in his voice.

"I say again, Lord, the time not yet come is not given me to see."

"I ask one last time."

"My Lord, allow me to dream for you. Only my dreams have weight in future times. Even then, things are not always clear but muddled," she said and awaited his pleasure.

The King nodded his head and the Lady gestured to Edric. The thegn rose from his bench and approached his wife. Lady Godda pulled from her shining robe a strangely wrought spear point.

"Sire, the Spear of Saint Brigit, matron of poets and healing and the metal forge," Godda bent a knee and sat the spear on its point. A flick of the wrist started the copper colored thing spinning slowly. By itself, the spear point stayed upright as it turned round and round.

Lady Godda, her husband beside her, sang a haunting song in her silvery Elfish language. She swayed slowly back and forth with eyes closed as her dwarves played on lyre and pipe. After a time, her singing ceased, though not the music. She stiffened as if asleep.

Wild Edric touched her forehead. Lady Godda fell backwards caught by her husband. He placed an arm under her and lifted her above the revolving spear point. Edric stepped back and the Lady floated in midair!

Before the alarm of the host could sound, Edric turned to hush us with a gesture. "Allow the Queen of the Elves her sleep and her dreams," he said.

We watched the floating apparition as a wind of unknown origin stirred the draping robes as if pushed by the dwarves' music. Lady Godda spread forth her arms, twirled upright in the air, and flew to hover above your startled father. A voice came from the air, deep and throaty, that might have been Lady Godda's though I did not see her lips move.

"Ave, William, conqueror of the English. Hear the dream of the Queen of the Elves. Born from the breast of a Griffin with a holy scepter are three birds. The first, a noble hawk, wars against the Griffin and lives by rapine and unfulfilled avarice. He will die chained in a cage. The second, a cruel and fearful eagle, rules the Griffin's prize by unholy violence dying apostate. The third, a cough, the thief of birds, steals his legacy but holds it forever sitting on a hoard of gold…"

My lord William jumped from the table throwing his ale horn to table with a great crash.

"Cease these lies, Hell thrall!" he cried. Torn from her dreaming, Lady Godda fell to the floor and the spear point ceased its spinning. "How dare you slander your king?"

Helped upright by her husband, Godda slurred. "Lord, I dream only of birds."

"Silence!" The King strode forth to stand over the couple. He considered them with a fierce scowl while the host trembled and waited.

I waited for the order to kill the Lady and her husband. We all knew she spoke evil lies.

My Lord Henry, forgive me for writing to you of what follows. I fear your wrath but I write at your command a true witness of this unholy night.

Your father turned from Lady Godda to look upon his children at their benches. One at a time, he looked first upon you at suckle on the paps of your wet nurse, then at your brother Rufus, called so even then for his devilish red hair, as he sat grinning at the deeds of this woman, and finally at the darting dark eyes of cursed Robert, the first born. Your father turned back to the wife of Wild Edric.

"I see those birds, Lady. It does no good to a king to renounce what is there to see in his eyes and in his heart." King William softened his glare. He turned to his butler, known as Hugh of Ivry. "Bring forth gifts for the Queen of the Elves. Make music. There is time enough to worry over my little birds. My doom is not yet come."

The next morning, Wild Edric and Lady Godda dispatched to Shropshire gift laden. William returned to London happy in the knowledge that he entertained the Queen of the Elves. That said, I never knew your father to look upon his sons the same way again.

This is my witness truly told of the night Wild Edric and Lady Godda came to the court of your father. This is the birth of the legend of the Children of the Conquering Griffin. I know not of the truth of any queen of elves, though I believed it that night. To this day, it is said that William Rex thought of Lady Godda when he divided his domain between you and your brothers, giving Normandy to Robert where he might live by his sword, and England to William Rufus so that he might be saved from apostasy, and giving you only money so that there would be no stealing. In all my time of service to your father, I heard no such consideration. I did not fight your father's wars with Robert. I did not attend your brother Rufus when he fell to the ash wood arrow in the new forest. I saw no theft when you entered the treasure room to become the last heir of conquering William.

The Lord almighty bless you and direct your whole life.

* * *

Editor's Note:

Eadric Silvaticus (the Wild), a Saxon nobleman in the West Midlands, resisted Norman rule after 1066. Mention of him is made in the Anglo/Saxon Chronicle in 1067 and possibly again in 1075. His marriage to an elf comes from Walter Map in his De Nugis Curialium.

William bequeathed Normandy to his eldest son Robert despite their bitter differences (Robert had sided with his father's enemies in Normandy, and even wounded and defeated his father in a battle there in 1079). His son, William Rufus succeeded William as King of England, and the third remaining son, Henry, was left 5,000 pounds in silver.

Robert Curt Hose, inherited Normandy but was not allowed any revenue with which to pay his followers and was expected to be content with an empty title and bide his time until William Rufus died. Often helped by the King of France, he continued to wreak havoc against William and later against younger brother Henry. Henry captured Robert in 1106 and imprisoned him. Robert lived in captivity another 28 years and died in his early 80s.

William Rufus (the Red), is described as a devil-may-care soldier, without social graces, with little show of conventional religious piety or morality and, according to his critics, addicted to every vice. It is also said he was a wise ruler and victorious general. He taxed the nobility and looted the Church to pay for his wars. Rufus finally died while hunting. Speculation has it that his death could have been an accident, an assassination, and even that Rufus may have been the last Western king to be sacrificed in a pagan ritual.

Henry was present when Rufus died and hurried to secure (steal) the royal treasury. His succession was quickly confirmed while his brother Robert was away on the First Crusade. Henry's 28 year long reign, a period of peace and prosperity in England and Normandy, was filled with judicial and financial reforms.

Wind and Ash

by Corinn Heathers

A pale, slender hand slipped from beneath the dark cloak, clad in a jeweled half-gauntlet that left the fingers bare. That hand traced a complex series of strokes in the air, leaving behind a wispy trail of blue-white light. The traveler's fingers repeated the strokes, scribing a short series of eldritch runes with practiced ease.

The traveler's form faded into the appearance of just another shadow cast by the torchlight. The cloaking charm was temporary, but it would not take long to evade the patrols that made their way around the keep.

The living shadow slipped through an alleyway and pressed herself against the walls of the keep while a patrol of six passed. Young and strong, the half-dozen men of the guard wore light armor suitable for long hours on garrison duty. Lightweight sabers were strapped to their hips and they each carried a pistol. The acrid scent of smoke powder informed the traveler the weapons were ready to fire should trouble present itself.

The scent became stronger as the guardsmen approached. The traveler was less than a meter from the nearest guard, but his bored expression did not change. Against the dark stone of the keep, an unmoving shadow was invisible.

The city of Ashenvale slept, but the night watch and city guard would be out in force, checking the papers of anyone not wearing the lord's emblem. The traveler wore no emblems and held no papers, and thus wished to avoid any potential confrontation.

It took a few moments before the patrol disappeared into the city streets proper. For the next quarter hour, this alleyway would be unobserved. The traveler darted deeper into the alley, following the keep's walls as they became a narrow corridor. A short distance away, the traveler could see a heavy wooden door set into the keep's exterior wall.

The door opened and a man clad in polished steel stepped out into the alley. His sword was drawn and held ready, the naked steel reflecting lurid torchlight. "You are expected."

The traveler smiled — the guard could not see her face yet — and canceled the illusion as she drew the hood of her cloak back. She shook out wavy hair of an ethereal silvery-white. The traveler's features appeared human, resembling that of an attractive young woman in her late teens, but were... *different*. Her face, the color of her hair, the gem-like shade of her amber eyes and her too-fluid movements, all held a tangible sense of *otherness*.

"Lord Ashenellar is waiting for you in the study." The guard's tone was nervous. "I will take your cloak and have one of the servants care for it."

"Thank you." The traveler's voice was clear but spoke the common tongue with an unusual precision, lacking the smooth drawl of those native to the Vales. She shrugged off her cloak, unclasping the garment and letting it fall into the guard's outstretched hand. The traveler was not surprised to recognize the captain's insignia engraved into his armor; Lord Ashenellar would not wish to reveal her presence to anyone who he could not trust absolutely.

"The halls have been cleared for the night. Head down this corridor, take a right and enter through the first staircase. It will take you to the second floor study."

The traveler nodded her thanks and headed down the hallway as she had been instructed. It only took moments to reach the study. Lamplight flickered on the walls, covered in heavy oaken shelves lined with books and scroll cases. The traveler walked through the open doorway and stopped in front of the lord's desk, a slab of polished wood carved from the trunk of a great oak.

Behind the desk sat her client, Lord Vincent Ashenellar. A powerfully-built man in his middle years, his great mane of brown hair showed only faint traces of gray. Ashenellar's well-muscled arms were hidden beneath the sleeves of a fine silk tunic dyed a deep crimson. Judging by the sheer brawn the lord displayed, it was obvious that Ashenellar was no stranger to hard physical labor.

The traveler's gaze scanned the study. On a nearby divan lay her mission. Her eyes widened in surprise as she caught the faint tingling sensation of awakening magic emanating from the inert form of a young girl.

"Thank you for coming on such short notice," the lord rumbled, a bass voice that seemed to rise up from beneath the ground. "I am Vincent

Ashenellar, Lord of Ashendale."

The traveler inclined her head in the ghost of a bow. "My name is Lynna."

"Please forgive the poor reception, Lady Lynna. Had the situation not been so dire, I would have had the kitchen prepare a late supper, but I am afraid all I can offer you is wine."

The fey woman ignored the offer of refreshments. Instead, her gaze was focused on the girl locked in deep, unnatural slumber. "How long has she been like this?"

"Two days." The lord uncorked a bottle of red wine and poured himself a glass, filling it nearly to the rim.

Lynna could keenly feel the man's distress, but she hoped that he wouldn't get too drunk when there was important work to be done. "What is her name?"

"Eleanor. She prefers to be called Ellie."

Lynna transfixed the lord with a piercing amber stare. "Tell me everything. Omit nothing, no matter how inconsequential or trivial. The life of your daughter may hang in the balance."

"Eleanor is the fifth child of House Ashenellar and my only daughter. She was born nine years ago. The delivery was difficult; my wife passed shortly after Ellie's birth. The midwives swore to the Dawn that Ellie would likely die of the wasting before she saw her first year, but they could not have been more wrong."

"The child was healthy." A frown drew across the woman's face. "*Too* healthy."

Lord Ashenellar's expression darkened. "Yes. The signs were all there, but I could not bear to entertain the thought. Ellie grew strong and fast. She proved to be sharp of wit, learning to speak simple phrases much more quickly than her brothers had. It was harder to deny when her need for sleep began to decrease, but still I did not want to believe such a thing."

The big man sighed and gulped at his wine. "At first I rationalized to myself that my daughter was simply more gifted than her brothers. Thus I was able to blind myself to the truth for years. Two months ago, I could no longer remain blind. My daughter's servant came to me, terribly distraught, clutching Ellie's favorite hairbrush. When I managed to calm the woman, she would offer no explanation except the brush itself."

Lynna's eyes narrowed in suspicion. "You found gem-colored hairs caught between the bristles."

"Yes... strands the color of fine rose quartz."

The fey woman turned toward the slumbering girl again. Ellie's long hair only showed the faintest traces of the pale honey-blonde common to children of the region. The rest of it had already been stained the same iridescent pink the lord described.

"Continue," Lynna prodded, refusing to allow the man to shut down while she still needed information.

"The change in my daughter had become too obvious. I decided to restrict her to the children's quarters in the keep. The servants had their discretion insured through various means, but Ellie did not react well to being limited in her movements. It was difficult enough to keep her from wandering outside of the keep when she only spends half the night asleep. She would slip past the servants and avoid the sentries with remarkable ease.

"This more or less continued until a few nights ago," Ashenellar continued. "There was a terrible explosion of wind and lightning from the children's quarters. Two of the servants were injured and my daughter — " The man choked on his words, nearly dashing for the wine bottle on his desk.

"Don't get drunk," Lynna snapped. "Losing your wits at a time like this will serve no one, your daughter least of all."

The big man scowled. "I'm no fool, Lady. I know what this means."

"Do you?" Lynna arched a silvery eyebrow. "She has been spellshocked by the release of her own magic. I can repair the damage, but I cannot turn back time. Your daughter is feytouched."

Lord Ashenellar turned his anguished gaze upon the fey woman. She could have shoved her sword through his gut and it would not have caused as much pain and fear as her plainly spoken words.

"You can halt the transformation, can't you? You must!"

Lynna gave the noble a cold stare. "It cannot be stopped, and I will not suppress her. It is far too late for that now."

"Please, Lady, have mercy upon my family!" Ashenellar's deep voice held a shrill edge of desperation. "Ellie is my little light, the last gift that Sophia left me."

Lynna only gazed intently at the small body on the couch.

"I will — I will hire you to train her." Ashenellar's voice grew in strength as his plan took shape. "Heal my daughter and teach her to control her power. You will be handsomely rewarded — in gold, in title and anything you could desire!"

Lynna's eyes widened in mild surprise. She hadn't expected this at all — at best, she'd expected Ashenellar to abandon the child to the care of another feytouched. At worst, well... the Seekers of the Dawn had a much darker solution to the problem.

The fey woman turned toward Ashenellar, the man's eyes shining with tears that streaked down his face and into his meticulously-trimmed beard.

Lynna approached the divan where Ellie lay comatose and placed her gloved left hand upon the girl's forehead. "Do you understand the implications of your offer, Lord Ashenellar?"

"I do." The steel in Ashenellar's voice was unexpected. "The political ramifications do not concern me, Lady Lynna. My daughter's life does."

Lynna kept her attention focused on the girl. "Your rule and authority will be harshly questioned if it becomes known that you fathered a feytouched child and allowed her to live. The fear of the citizenry will aid your rivals more than you know."

"Should it come to that, I will bear that stigma for the sake of my daughter."

Lynna nodded and woke the power within her. The lines of force inlaid into her glove began to seethe with brilliant blue-white fire. She closed her eyes and sank deep within the magic.

The soul-aching chill of the otherworldly energies enveloped her body from within and began to seep out into the room. Lynna's mind made connections, rerouting and diverting the astral energies, bending the chaotic spiral to her will.

With absolute focus, the fey woman began to examine the girl's astral pattern. To her mystic sight, the lines of force were twisted, warped and damaged from the sudden release of far too much unfocused magical energy. The resulting overload was not potent enough to cause permanent damage, but Ellie *would* die without proper treatment.

"This will take some time."

Slowly, re-aligning one line of force at a time, Lynna began to repair the girl's damaged pattern.

* * *

Lynna sat at a small table in one of the keep's bedchambers, watching the edge of the sun peek over the horizon as dawn broke across the Vales. With such a spectacular view, clearly the room had been intended for visiting dignitaries. Lord Ashenellar decided the room's out-of-the-way location would be an ideal place for the feytouched woman and her newly-acquired apprentice.

The fey woman sipped at a mug filled with strong coffee, diluted with cream from the keep's own dairy cows. The beverage filled her belly with a pleasant warmth that did well to combat the chill from such a draining procedure, but Lynna would not allow herself to rest just yet.

Ashenellar's daughter still slept, peacefully at last, only occasionally shifting as she slumbered. It had taken two hours, but Lynna had managed to smooth out the girl's damaged connection to the Astral.

Rose-colored locks shifted. Lynna sat her mug down and watched intently as the girl drew herself up from her slumber. She sat upright, her pink hair tangled and disheveled, a bewildered expression on her face.

"Good morning," Lynna offered, her tone as soothing as she could make it. The girl blinked ruby-colored eyes and stared intently at the arcanist. "W-where am I? What happened?"

"Many things, but the most important is that you are alive. How do you feel, Ellie?"

The girl gawked at the fey woman. "Who are you? How do you know my name? Why do you look so odd?"

"My name is Lynna, and I know your name because your father gave it to me." The arcanist laughed. "Why do I look odd? Well, I don't consider my appearance to be strange, but I am feytouched — as are you."

Ellie's shocked expression was predictable. "W-what? I'm... feytouched?"

Lynna lifted her mug to her lips and sipped slowly. "It is not easy to explain to one as young as you, but it means that you are different than other people. The blood of the Starfarers flows through your veins."

"I'm a... monster?" Ellie cried, her eyes round and wide with fear.

"Of course not! Do I look like a monster to you?"

Ellie shook her head. "N-no, not like a monster at all! But the priests talk about feytouched — "

Lynna raised a hand to stop her. "The priests are wrong. The people of this land do not remember the Starfarers fondly. You have learned the history of your homeland?"

"Y-yes. There was a big war, hundreds of years ago, and we lost. The Starfarers conquered human lands and made men into slaves. They stole women and took them into their sky-ships. Our ancestors fought them, but they were too strong, and a lot of people died."

"Do you know what happened after that?"

The girl shook her head, her ruby eyes wide.

"The Starfarers were engaged in a great, terrible war with a faction of their own people, one that had gone on for thousands of years. They found our world by accident, you see. One of their astral vessels, badly damaged, took refuge here."

"What did they want with us? Why did they take people?"

Lynna drained the last swallow of coffee from her mug and grimaced. "Warriors. The Starfarers are a very long-lived people and take many decades to reach maturity. They were losing warriors faster than they could raise and train them, and humans mature quickly by comparison. The 'big war' you speak of is called the Harvesting."

Ellie shivered, the abhorrent thought clearly understood in its entirety by the girl despite her young age.

"The Starfarers remained here for a time, attempting to take as many people as they could in order to develop a method to quickly produce soldiers for their war."

Ellie wrapped her arms around her legs, her knees tucked under her chin. "Did they figure it out?"

"We assume they did. The Starfarers disappeared only twenty years after the war, but they left behind a legacy — what humans call 'feytouched.' Buried within our blood is the remnants of Starfarer experimentation. Sometimes these traits will emerge within a human child."

Lynna stood up and walked across the small but luxuriously-appointed room, sitting down on the bed next to the child. She took Ellie's small hands into her own and gazed into the girl's ruby eyes. "Feytouched are the likely result of the Starfarer's magical transmutation of our bodies. They wanted slave warriors they could control easily, who would rapidly mature to breeding age and quickly yield multiple offspring within their first fifteen years of life before being sent to die in battle — "

The blank look spreading across Ellie's face prompted Lynna to stop mid-sentence, realizing that her words were lost on the nine-year-old girl. The arcanist smiled. "My apologies. I didn't mean to confuse you. It's best we focus on the here and now, in any case."

"It's okay," Ellie said. "So lots of people hate feytouched because it reminds them of the war?"

"That's a bit oversimplified, but yes." Lynna released Ellie's hands and tucked an errant lock of silvery-white behind her ears. "They also fear us because they feel threatened by us. We live longer, we need less sleep, we are healthier, more resistant to disease and infirmity. And we have a strong connection to the Astral."

Ellie stared at Lynna with a mixture of fear and curiosity. "Seeker Ethan says feytouched are evil witches and sorceresses that can control the minds of men and make them do terrible things."

Lynna sighed and turned away. "The Seekers of the Dawn use the fear of feytouched for their own political ends. Fearful people are easier to control and manipulate. You probably don't understand now, but you will when you're older."

"Whenever Seeker Ethan gave sermons about the feytouched, the people put more money on the offering plates."

"Ah, so you do understand, at least to some degree." Lynna smiled at the girl, who returned the smile tentatively. "That's not important now; we have more pressing matters to attend to. Your father hired me to train you."

Ellie's smile drooped into a frown. "Train me?"

"How to use your abilities without hurting yourself or anyone else," Lynna replied. "That is why we are here, in this part of the keep. We will live here and I will train you to properly control your connection to the Astral."

"But what if someone sees us here? Won't that be a problem for Father?"

The girl's insight was certainly impressive. Lynna shook her head. "He has declared this section of the keep off-limits to all but his most trusted subordinates. Your servants and your father's personal guard will ensure that we have everything that we could need."

The girl's lips twisted in disappointment as she realized what that meant. "That means I can't go outside anymore?"

"I'm sorry, but you can't." Lynna stood and motioned toward the door leading to the keep's eastern corridors. "The east banquet hall has been converted into a training room. We will spend much of our time there. In fact, I would suggest you get dressed. We begin immediately."

Ellie glanced at the neatly-folded pile of clothing next to her bed: a simple dress of woven white cotton and a pair of brown leather boots. Compared to the richly-decorated silk nightgown the girl wore, the new clothing looked plain indeed. Ellie shrugged and slipped off the bed, pulling her nightgown over her head and tossing it onto the wrinkled bedsheets. The girl picked up the dress and pulled it on. "Can you tie the back?"

"Of course." Lynna's slender fingers fastened the laces, careful not to tie them too tightly. "There is fruit and bread on the table. Eat and meet me in the hall."

Ellie nodded, her small face devoid of confusion or fear. "Okay."

* * *

Ashenellar's servants spent the night stripping away the banquet hall's banners and finery, leaving bare stone behind. Small areas of the stone floors were cushioned by training mats borrowed from the guard barracks. A wooden table was set up at the west end of the room, accompanied by two battered chairs. The hearth at the room's northern end burned brightly, a large stack of green firewood sitting beside it. A chamber pot sat in another corner, partially shielded by a folding screen.

"How unfortunately backwards." Lynna stood beside the table and filled a dented cup with water, eyeing the chamber pot with a considerable amount of enmity.

The table itself was heaped with preserved food — hard biscuits, great hunks of salt beef and jars of pickled summer vegetables. Channeling astral energy was hard on the body and Lynna made certain that Ellie would have ample provisions available.

The feytouched woman took several swallows of water and awaited the arrival of her young charge. She could sense Ellie's presence; newly awakened, the emanations of the Astral burned brightly from her being. This, among other things, Ellie would learn to control.

The door opened. Lynna glanced toward the sound and watched as Ellie made her way through the room to her new teacher. The girl's behavior would have been considered strange by an outside observer but in truth Lynna expected this. The awakening dampened emotion as well as granted access to considerable power. It was for this reason that Lynna took it upon herself to nurture feytouched children.

"Hello, Lady Lynna." Ellie bowed deeply. She punctuated the gesture with an abbreviated curtsy.

Lynna chuckled under her breath. "There's no need to be so formal. Call me Lyn."

Ellie nodded. "Okay, Lyn. What are we doing?"

"First I would like to take your measure. From there, I can decide how to proceed." Lynna flexed her gloved left hand and focused on a formless emptiness in her mind — the mental manifestation of her physical connection to the Astral. The jeweled glove responded to her silent commands and brought forth an awakening of senses, enabling her to detect and analyze the properties of nearby magic.

Ellie gave the arcanist a blank look. "So... what do I do?"

"I want to see you really cut loose. Go all out, with all of your might!" Lynna's lips spread in a feral grin. "Let it *all* out. Push the power through you, out of you and into the world."

Ellie looked dubious. "You won't get hurt?"

"I am well-protected," Lynna assured her, waving away the girl's concerns. "I need to see what you can do in order to proceed with your training."

"O-okay." Ellie still didn't look completely convinced, but the girl did as she was instructed. Her red eyes closed, her small face twisted in an expression of deep concentration. Lynna watched as the girl shivered from the sensation of intense cold that accompanied an evocation.

Ellie's eyes flew open. Her head tilted back and she shouted out a wordless cry as the connection was completed. A faint glow of building astral energies rapidly increased in intensity until it became a radiance almost too painful for Lynna to look upon.

The brilliant aura pulsed rapidly before it collapsed back upon Ellie's body and blasted outward in a tremendous explosion of magical force. Arcs of crawling lightning played across her body, striking the floor, the table, her teacher — but Lynna remained unharmed despite the thunderclap detonations all around her. The static discharge, brought about by the shock waves compressing and distorting the air around them, dissipated harmlessly into Lynna's barrier.

The storm of wind and lightning faded away, leaving Ellie on her hands and knees, gasping for breath. Sweat beaded on the girl's forehead, the muscles in her arms and legs trembling from the sudden emptiness that resulted from such a release of magic.

Lynna bent down and helped Ellie stand, handing her a cup filled with water and several strips of salt beef. The girl took the vessel and drank greedily, draining the cup before gasping for breath.

"Steady," Lynna murmured. "Can you stand?"

Ellie nodded weakly. "Y-yeah. I think so." She bit off a piece of salt beef and chewed, swallowing quickly. Lynna knew she would need to eat and rest after such a release of power.

"You did very well, Ellie. Honestly, I'm impressed that you managed to channel so well after only just recovering from spellshock."

Ellie swallowed a mouthful of salt beef. "I knew that if I let any more out I would have hurt myself. I feel it, boiling under the surface, trying to escape. It doesn't want to stop, but if I let too much through, I'll die, and people around me will get hurt."

Lynna brushed a sweaty lock of iridescent pink from the girl's forehead. "That feeling is normal. With training, you will learn mastery over the powers you possess."

"I want to learn. I don't want anyone to get hurt because of me." Ellie's gaze dropped away and she turned toward the door.

So she is aware of what she inadvertently did, Lynna mused. She gazed upon her young charge and placed a reassuring hand on Ellie's shoulder. "I will teach you how to control it."

* * *

A swarm of sparkling motes exploded outward from a central point. Lynna's eyes hardened as she focused her defenses, strengthening them at a single point as the potent little projectiles converged and bore down unerringly on her midsection.

Such was her surprise when the eight energy stars seemed to notice, breaking off as if they were a group of birds in flight. Lynna found herself unable to react in time. A smile spread across her face as the motes slammed into her at four separate target areas – all locations where her barrier was weakest. Bracing herself for the inevitable concussive blasts, Lynna's smile didn't falter as her student's force missiles detonated and nearly knocked her from her feet.

"Good! Very good!" Lynna waved a hand and called an end to the exercise. "That's enough for today; I'm not sure I could keep this up myself!"

Ellie's grin dominated her face. "You shouldn't harden your barrier in a single location when defending against such a spell. Didn't you tell me that yourself?"

Lynna sat down heavily at the table and gulped water from her dented cup. "Of course; that was the point of this exercise, after all." Her sharp eyes caught the sway in her young charge's stance. Concern suffused her face.

Ellie seemed to barely maintain her feet. Exhausted far beyond the niceties of noble manners, she yawned without covering her mouth. "I'm feeling a little unsteady."

"I'd say that's an understatement. We'll skip paper lessons for today. Lay down and rest yourself before supper."

"What if Father comes — "

Lynna raised a hand to stop her student. "He will have to come back later. I doubt you would make good company while dozing off, in any case. Go, Ellie; you've drained your astral capacity and need to rest, else you'll risk damage to your pattern. I trust I don't need to explain what that means?"

Ellie's eyes grew wide and she shook her head.

"Good. Now get yourself to bed. I will wake you when the servants bring the evening meal."

Lynna accompanied Ellie to her room as the girl did as she was told. Ellie was so exhausted from her perhaps over-enthusiastic display of magical prowess that she didn't even bother to undress, but simply fell facedown into the bed.

The arcanist felt the hinting of a smile tug at her lips as she peeled back the blankets and tucked the girl into bed as best she could. The sun still shone brightly through the window, but Ellie's slumber was only partially natural. She would be unable to awaken for at least an hour.

Lynna turned to head back to the training hall but was interrupted by the less-familiar sight of Lord Ashenellar. To keep Ellie focused on her studies, Lynna insisted that he keep his visits scheduled to avoid interfering. This was the first time he'd come to the restricted area unannounced.

"Lord Ashenellar." Lynna's tone was neutral, but her expression was guarded.

"I did not expect her to be asleep," the man whispered, keeping his voice low.

Lynna gave a dismissive wave of her hand at the lord's consideration. "She has exhausted her astral capacity. Her slumber is deeper than natural sleep; do not fear to wake her."

Ashenellar's eyes narrowed. "When will she awaken, Lady Lynna?"

"Not for at least an hour." Lynna turned toward the shuttered window and opened it more widely, allowing in a gentle breeze. She noticed that Ashenellar seemed agitated. Perhaps it was merely that he wished to visit with his daughter... or perhaps it was that his daughter was steadily becoming less human.

"She has already grown taller," Ashenellar observed in a flat tone. Lynna said nothing as the big man gazed at his sleeping child. The arcanist could have sworn she saw the faintest hint of fear in his eyes, but the split-second of vulnerability was quick to pass.

"She will continue grow at an accelerated rate." Lynna sat down at the small table near the bed and motioned for Ashenellar to do the same.

"What do you mean?"

"The feytouched were created as weapons, Lord," Lynna muttered, trying to keep her own expression calm. It was not something she relished explaining to humans. "We were molded to suit the needs of the Starfarers long ago. Those who continue to appear as a result of the mixing of feytouched bloodlines will exhibit the same traits as the original — "

Ashenellar scowled. "That much is known to me. Explain why my child appears to have aged a winter in less than a fortnight!"

"I was attempting to," Lynna snapped. Her expression softened but only slightly. "The Starfarers needed powerful warriors that could be quickly replenished in the event of staggering losses. The feytouched were intended to reach full maturity twelve years after birth, so that the Starfarers might seed the next generation of warriors to fight and die in their — "

Ashenellar was aghast at the obvious implication. "My daughter... my Ellie..." The lord gathered himself with tremendous effort and looked Lynna squarely in the eye. "You are sure of this? Completely sure?"

The arcanist did not waver. "Of course. I experienced it myself, many years ago."

"Is there nothing you can do to help her? Nothing at all to stop her from... from changing?"

Lynna shook her head. "I can only train her so that she will not be a danger to herself and those around her. Lord Ashenellar, your daughter is not *becoming* a feytouched. She *is* one, and *we* are no longer human."

"I hired you to help her!" Ashenellar snapped.

"You hired me to heal her spellshock and to train her." Lynna sighed and fixed the man with a harsh glare. "I am not doing less than I was asked. If witnessing the changes causes you distress, then perhaps you should refrain from visiting — "

Ashenellar's face went red and he jumped to his feet, nearly upending the table they sat at. "Eleanor is my daughter! She's just a child, just a little girl!"

Lynna shook her head, her eyes shining with an ancient and eldritch sadness. "No, Lord, she isn't. Not entirely, not any longer."

The big man was silent. The blood seemed to drain away from his face, tempering the heat of his anger and leaving him appearing ashen and drawn.

"If you wish to visit with Ellie, she will awaken for the evening meal. I must record the results of today's training. Please, excuse me."

Lynna stood up and walked across the bedchamber and through the door leading back to the training hall, leaving Ashenellar alone with his daughter and his thoughts.

* * *

Lynna and Ellie settled into a familiar routine over the next few months. The two would spend much of the day within the training hall engaged in magical sparring. Ellie found her teacher to be a stern taskmaster, pushing the girl to exhaustion, but with every passing day, Ellie learned both to control her power and to make practical use of it.

Lord Ashenellar would occasionally visit his daughter, but since that conversation in Ellie's bedchamber, the visits had become less frequent and more strained. It had been over a month since his last visit, and the big man only stayed for barely half an hour. Lynna understood why — the man's eyes held both the pain of the present and the pain to come in the future. His daughter's love for him would fade away, a slowly withering flower plucked from the soil.

Lynna knew that eventually his daughter would become more distant from him than a stranger on the street. The Starfarers believed the breaking of familial bonds was necessary to maintain a level of mental stability. After the breeding years passed, the living weapons would be sent off to fight and to die, leaving their offspring behind forever.

The fading of emotions was not only from Ellie's perspective, either. Her rate of growth was speeding up; after only four months, Ellie had grown several centimeters in height. While her body grew rapidly, her visible signs of aging would slow, all but halting after her sixteenth year.

Ellie's mental maturity had accelerated even more rapidly than the physical. Her mind was sharp and agile; Lynna had begun to instruct her in language, mathematics and the sciences along with the physical and magical training. The young feytouched girl absorbed knowledge with incredible, single-minded focus. This attitude toward mastering new skills was yet another legacy of their origin.

Ellie glanced up from a paper scribbled with arcane formulae, a pencil clutched in her left hand. "What's wrong, Lyn? You've got an odd look."

The fey woman blinked. "An odd look?"

"Faraway and introspective all at once."

Lynna offered the girl a reassuring grin. "I was thinking of how proud I am of you. Only a season's passed and you've come this far and learned so much."

Ellie shrugged and scrawled a new formula onto the paper, working through the equation. "Wasn't it much the same for you?"

"It was, but that was quite a long time ago." Lynna sipped coffee with cream from her dented mug, savoring the bitter flavor. "It's been many, many years. I do remember the events clearly, but the emotions are... elusive."

Ellie didn't respond, instead focusing on her work. Lynna waited patiently until her apprentice handed over the paper for inspection. Lynna studied the equations and their solutions with a critical eye. She made a few marks next to several of the mystic functions.

"The field strength equations can't be rounded off. When calculating barrier capacity, an error of a single decimal place can mean the difference between deflecting a bullet or arrow and watching your shield shatter before your eyes."

"Ah! I'm sorry," Ellie blurted, leaning over to peer at the marks left by her mentor. "I don't know what I was thinking."

Lynna sipped at her coffee. "You're distracted; that much I can see."

"Yeah." Ellie rubbed her dry eyes. "I just... I mean, the maidservant told me that my father will be coming by to visit this evening." There was hesitation and uncertainty in her voice. Lynna placed her hand atop Ellie's and squeezed it lightly.

"You're nervous about the visit?"

"The last time he visited, he was so tense," Ellie murmured. "I asked the maid a little about what has been happening in the keep. It seems Seeker Ethan has been a regular visitor. The maidservant told me all about it."

Lynna caught the note of concern in her pupil's voice. "I doubt the Seekers actually know what's going on."

"How can you be so sure?"

"We're still alive."

"But why would he come to the keep, then?"

"Perhaps your father is in mourning," Lynna offered, though in truth she felt more than a little uneasy. "He knew that you would soon be lost to him.

Like many who have lost or will lose, he seeks comfort that the Seekers can offer through faith."

Ellie blinked. "But I'm not dead."

"It doesn't matter. Death is not the only way a person can lose a loved one. You may have learned how to control your magic and keep the power from spilling forth without cause, but you can't hide what you are. You will always be in danger here."

"So we're to leave, then." The girl didn't seem to know whether she should be upset or relieved.

Lynna nodded and set her mug down. "Yes. The feytouched who remain within human lands rarely live long, happy lives. You cannot be locked up within the keep for centuries, even if your father wishes it to be so. He will not be the lord of Ashendale forever, after all."

"Where will we go?"

"My home." The fey woman looked almost wistful. "It will not be an easy or short journey, but you will be safe there."

Ellie set the pencil down and looked at Lynna with interest. "What's your home like? Can you tell me about it?"

"I've been on assignment within the Vale lands for the past seven years, but I would never forget my home, even if I was away for seven centuries. It is a place like no other on this world; you will see wondrous sights. Tall spires of shimmering metal and glass, beautiful gardens filled with flowers — my home is a lovely place."

Before Ellie could respond, the door to the training hall opened and Lord Ashenellar strode into the room. Ellie immediately got up from her chair and bowed respectfully to her father. Lynna noted his expression: nervousness kept hidden behind a stoic front. This wasn't altogether unusual, but a century of experience told the arcanist she should be wary.

"Ellie, my child." Ashenellar strode forward, his arms parted for a warm embrace, but his eyes widened, his step hitching just slightly. The big man struggled to appear as if nothing was amiss, enfolding strong arms around the girl.

"Hello, Father." Ellie stiffened in his grasp, clearly uncomfortable, and returned the gesture. The girl's voice was nearly devoid of familiarity or affection.

Lynna stood up herself and approached the lord and his daughter, intending to deflect attention away from Ellie to defuse the tension of the reunion. Unlike Ellie, Lynna did not bow. "Lord Ashenellar."

The lord inclined his head. "Lady Lynna. You are looking well today."

"Let us skip the pleasantries. Ellie's initial training in the astral arts is complete. She no longer poses a danger to herself or others around her."

"Thank the Dawn." Lord Ashenellar strode across the converted banquet hall and paced in front of the blazing fire. He knew there was more to be told and Lynna could tell that he already expected it.

Lynna leaned against the wooden table, her fingertips running across the hilt of her sword. "Ellie and those around her are safe from the power of her own magic, but she remains in danger so long as she lives within Ashendale. Her presence here places your entire family and household at risk."

The lord of Ashendale turned to the hearth, away from his daughter and her teacher, and stared into the flames. For a long moment he simply watched the flames flicker and dance as they consumed the split logs Lynna had stacked earlier that day. "So it is true. You will take her away." It was not a question.

"Ellie cannot stay locked within these halls forever. I have taught her to control her magic, but I have only scratched the surface of her training. According to the laws of our people, Ellie must train for many more years to be considered a proper mage."

"Impossible. I hired you to teach her to control her magic so that she might keep it hidden," Ashenellar snapped. "I did not hire you to steal my daughter away."

"You hired me to save her life."

"I hired you to heal her!" Ashenellar thundered, his huge hands clenching into fists at his hips. "I did not hire you to fill her mind with fool notions, to poison her against me, to warp her body into this *mockery* of my daughter!"

Lynna's eyes narrowed. "I explained this to you months ago. I understand the pain of separation and make allowances for that, but do not speak to me in such a manner."

Ellie, still standing between her father and her teacher, looked to be on the verge of tears. "Father, this is not — "

"Enough!" Ashenellar snapped, cutting his daughter's objection off. His glare, however, was focused squarely on Lynna. The fey woman appeared to be unperturbed despite the furious outburst of emotion.

"Father, please!" Ellie took her father's hand and pulled at it. "Lyn has done nothing wrong; she only did what you hired her to do!"

"She has twisted your heart and your body! I can scarcely see my child within that form! Eleanor — what has happened to you? What foul sorcery has been wrought upon you?!"

"No such thing has happened, Father!" Ellie glared up at her father, her ruby eyes gleaming in the firelight. "Lyn didn't do anything — "

Ashenellar's scowl was so deep his eyes nearly disappeared beneath his bushy eyebrows. "What monstrous designs have you for my child, witch? Have you betrayed me this entire time? Did you always intend to force womanhood upon her, to steal her from me and use her as a breeding mare to bring forth more of your foul kind?!"

"Father, that's insane! Lyn would never do something like that!" Ellie's horrified shriek was amplified by the tears that streamed down her cheeks. "The Seekers have filled your head with falsehoods and your heart with fear! Please, I'm still Ellie! I may be feytouched, but I'm still your daughter, Father! Lyn didn't do this to me, I swear it to you!"

"It's okay, Ellie." Lynna placed a hand on her apprentice's shoulder. The familiar warm touch seemed to pull the distress from Ellie's heart, softening the girl's expression. She glanced at her teacher and smiled bravely. Lynna knew that despite her assurances, this was unlikely to end well.

"Take your hands off my daughter, witch! Guards! Attend to me!"

The door leading to the hall burst open and three members of Ashenellar's personal guard marched into the vast chamber, weapons drawn and ready. The three men were outfitted in fanciful dyed leather armor adorned with the Ashenellar crest. Each was armed with a cocked pistol, all three aimed for a shot that would pierce Lynna's heart. The prominent basket hilts of their sabers told Lynna that even if she somehow managed to avoid the initial volley, the bite of cold, sharp steel would immediately follow.

"Father, don't do this!" Ellie cried. "You're wrong! This is all wrong!"

The lord of Ashendale ignored his daughter's protests. "I will not tolerate this insolence from a witch."

Lynna was at a disadvantage. Her own smallsword was on the table, well out of reach. It would also be impossible to strike with magic before the three honor guards shot her dead. Without preparation, her passive barrier would not be able to withstand more than a single projectile strike.

The fey woman glared at the enraged Lord Ashenellar. "I have dealt honestly with you, Lord Ashenellar. I was forthright with you. I still act in the best interests of you and your family."

"Liar!" Ashenellar strode before the woman, staring down at her from his great height, and jabbed a meaty finger in her direction. He turned to his guardsmen. "If the witch moves, shoot her."

Ellie took hold of her father's hand and clutched it tightly. "Father, please! Stop this madness!"

"Stay out of this, Eleanor," Ashenellar snarled, wrenching his hand away from the girl's grasp. Ellie's expression became increasingly distressed as her father fixated once again on the feytouched arcanist.

"Seeker Ethan told me you would lie and deceive to hide your true goal." The rising note of fear in the big man's voice was disconcerting. "I have committed a terrible sin, but the Dawn has graciously forgiven me and bestowed upon the Ashenellar family a blessed and holy duty."

"You *told* the Dawn Temple that you had dealings with me? And that your daughter is feytouched?" Lynna's voice was incredulous. "Are you *insane*? The Seekers of the Dawn will kill you — "

Ashenellar shook his head curtly. "I have been given a chance to seek redemption. If I slay you, then the Dawn Temple will not trouble House Ashenellar further. They will look the other way, and Eleanor — my daughter will... stay. Stay with me. Seeker Ethan promised that the Dawn Temple would forgive my sins for performing this sacred duty."

Lynna silently cursed her carelessness. She should have taken precautions for such an eventuality, should have realized the depths of desperation a terrified parent would reach. Lynna was far too experienced to have let her guard down like this, and yet she relaxed, failed to arrange contingencies. Her mind raced as she proposed and rejected scenarios of attack, defense and retreat, ultimately discarding them all. The situation was nearly as hopeless as it could possibly be.

"*No!* I won't let you do it!" Ellie cried, shattering Lynna's thoughts of desperate tactical planning. The feytouched arcanist opened her mouth to object, but it was too late.

Ellie brought her hands together violently. An argent sphere of sparkling astral energy materialized in the empty air, positioned directly beside the pistol-wielding guards. Howling winds and lightning-laced shock waves slammed into Ashenellar with the force of a charging warhorse. The guards, astonished by the sudden working of magic, stumbled as they were buffeted by fierce gusts of wind.

The sphere pulsated rapidly and collapsed inward upon itself as it detonated. Lynna lifted a hand to shield her face from the piercing flash of light, feeling herself sway on her feet as the power blasted against her defensive barrier. Her shield held and she managed to keep her balance.

Closest to the explosion were the honor guards. The attack happened so quickly and come from such an unexpected source that they didn't even have time to get a shot off. The force of the blast tore the pistols from their grasp and flung them through the air.

No longer held fast by the barrels of three musket-pistols, Lynna retrieved her sword from the table and drew the slender blade from its scabbard, keeping the weapon held in a guard position as she surveyed the scene.

Lord Ashenellar groaned and stumbled as he tried to stand. He blinked, half-blinded from the silvery flash. His honor guard was sprawled across the stone floor. It was impossible to tell if they were dead or simply unconscious.

"Father..." Ellie walked past her teacher and stood before her father. Lynna watched Lord Ashenellar warily, refusing to lower her guard or her blade after she had already made such a nearly-lethal mistake.

"Father, I'm leaving with Lyn," Ellie continued, her voice growing stronger. "I am your daughter, but I am not your property. I am a person, my own person. You are also your own person, and Father, you are better than this. You fought valiantly for Ashendale in your youth, defended the people of this land with all of your heart."

Ashenellar said nothing, unwilling to look his child in the eye.

"You were a knight of honor long before you were lord of the keep, Father." Ellie's proclamation struck the lord of Ashendale with more force than the magic she released only moments before. Shame and despair burned across the big man's face. He turned away from his daughter and limped toward the door leading from the hall.

Ashenellar hesitated at the open doorway. "I will order the guards to allow you passage through the siege tunnels. They run beneath the city and out into the hills." The big man didn't bother waiting for a response as he passed through the threshold and disappeared down the darkened corridor.

Lynna sighed and lowered her blade, retrieving the scabbard and sheathing the weapon with a single fluid motion. The fey woman attached the scabbard to her sword belt and turned to her pupil. "Ellie, it's time."

The feytouched girl nodded at her teacher and smiled without a hint of pain. "I'm ready."

Lynna returned her smile with one of her own. "Let's go home."

Bone Flowers

by K. J. Russell and Adrienne D'Agostino

Antimony couldn't smell the smoke, but she could feel it between her skin and her bones where the Drakscul stirred. It felt as she almost remembered an illness would feel, a heavy malaise seeping through the pits in her flesh. Antimony's thin fingers tightened around her staff, the skin on the back of her hand so pale that she could almost see the inky Drakscul pulling on her tendons just like her muscles had done when she was alive. Through her arm, shoulders, spine and chest, the dark presence roiled and tightened, drawing her upright like an inside-out puppet.

With a soft gray light glowing inside her empty eye sockets, Antimony turned a frustrated scowl into the arctic winds of fast-coming winter. She watched the horsemen burning the fields of lichen, and the Drakscul in her chest twitched unpleasantly. Her quiescent heart seemed to stiffen against her ribs.

She met the Drashar Nomads as they trekked eastward away from the burning fields, turning their backs to the hoofbeats of the torch-bearing foreigners. They drove their herds of echinodu on foot this year. The animals were massive, slow, with dozens of meters-long spines swaying above them, long tails dragging behind them, and heads almost brushing over the stony earth in search of lichen to eat. Every animal in the Drashar's herd was hungry and thin, and she counted fewer of them than she had in past years.

The Drashar Nomads looked like tiny echinodu walking on two legs, their thick furs dragging on the ground behind them, each holding a single long spine with an 'S'-shaped metal hook on the end. With roughly two dozen of the nomads flanking the herd, a party of six led at the front, pulling along a single echinodu that was heavily burdened with sacks and satchels.

Their furs shifting on them heavily, they paused as they noticed Antimony's presence on the eastward route, lifting their faces to look out from beneath the thick furred hoods they wore. Sparse snowflakes hung against their hardened brows.

Antimony waited to see how they would react to her. Some of the Drashar still looked on the undead of the Shy'Kimlea as a terrible threat. She kept her staff close to her and leaned on it, the wind rushing through her thin robe, over her skin, and didn't draw so much as a shiver from her. It was an exercise impossible in its parameters, to appear friendly and approachable after one's death. Still, Antimony tried a static smile at the edges of her lips.

The Drashar Nomads stood still as the echinodu herd began to pass around them, strangely enough providing protection from the haze of smoke that was sliding over the stones. One among them looked at the others and muttered something in the Drashar tongue, a deep and complicated language wherein Antimony couldn't distinguish the end of one word from the beginning of the next. Then they looked back at her and waited.

Right. Antimony straightened herself and pried one of her stubborn hands from the staff to lift it in greeting. "Hello." When she spoke, the Drakscul shifted inside her throat, imitating the vocal chords that had long-since withered away. It lent a steely echo to her voice. "Do any of you speak Aster?"

The Drashar spoke in hushed voices to one another, at least one of them visibly unsettled by Antimony's voice, though she couldn't take it personally. One of them stepped forward from the others, only distinguishable inside the thick furs by being slightly shorter and broader, hardened red brow and dark eyes watching her neutrally. The Drashar gestured towards the burning fields of lichen, now invisible behind the herd of echinodu moving around them. "We tried to tell them we needed the lichen."

Antimony frowned at the strange response and returned both hands to her staff. Her short, discolored hair shifted in front of her empty eye sockets. "I'm not sure I understand what's happening."

"Aster soldiers are destroying the lichen." The Drashar plucked a sack from beneath heavy furs and presented it open. Inside of it, the white stalks and petals of a soft plant had been pressed tight together, melting into one another. "Because of this."

"The bone flowers?" The Drakscul inside Antimony's fingers twitched, and she cast her gaze at a break in the echinodu. For an instant, she could see the red uniforms of the Aster soldiers on horseback, the flicker of their torches. She felt the grease of oil on the air. And then the echinodu blocked her view, and she turned back to the Drashar. "How long has this been happening?"

"Two months." The echinodu shifting around them were thin, bony shoulders and hips almost visible beneath their fur.

Just before the coming of winter, the bone flowers pushed up through the lichen fields of the Drashannar Reaches, like ribs through the skin of a sunken chest. Poisonous to the echinodu who needed the lichen to feed on and seen as a bad omen by the Drashar, the nomads had once collected and burned the plant. Until an undead nation had arisen two decades ago and been willing to trade for it.

Antimony looked away and seethed in silence at herself for arriving so late in the season. She blamed her other client, Naunet, for forcing her to stay in the distant southern cities far longer than was scheduled. How was she supposed to get her current client, a man named Viscid, enough of the bone flowers now? So late in the season, with the supply compromised?

"They intend to starve you." The Drashar's voice lifted and stole her attention back.

"Hm?" Antimony's gray-glowing sockets flickered as she looked at the eyes beneath the furs.

"What happens to the Kimleans without the flower?"

Her eyelids slid down over the empty holes on her face. Thinking past pure business, Antimony was struck with a sense of deep violation. That the Aster saw the undead, the Kimleans, as an abomination was well-known. The Kimleans required the bone flowers for the alchemy that preserved them. It was the closest thing to sustenance that they required. Were the Aster really willing to inflict famine upon the Drashar just to starve out the undead?

Of course they were. History left no doubt of that, nor did the echoes of the hoofbeats and the smoke over the fields.

Antimony's jaw screwed shut, and spoke through her teeth. "You were able to harvest some of the flower before they burnt the lichen? I need to buy all that you have."

The Drashar, having predicted her need, were already pulling a number of smaller satchels from their pack-echinodu's side. The one who stood before Antimony nodded. "You are far from the first Kimlean to do business this year. We have sold our full supply each day, it seems. And each day, the price…" Weathered hands emerged from beneath the furs and spread in a widening gesture.

Antimony blinked. "I'm sure we can negotiate…"

The Drashar's hands widened.

She bit down on her frustration, the Drakscul beneath her face tightening. Her poor punctuality was costing her, as it should. Still, Viscid had hired her to obtain as much of the bone flowers as she was able, and he had not placed a limit on the price she was to pay. "Very well."

* * *

Burdened by four satchels full of bone flowers and significantly free of the coin that Viscid had trusted her with, Antimony turned herself happily away from the hoofbeats and the burning fields to begin the trek back to the city of Shy'Kimlea. There was enough light left in the twenty-two hour late-autumn day that Antimony didn't worry about the wind blowing southward, seemingly from the gates of Shy'Kimlea itself. But as the evening temperature fell below freezing, the Drakscul in her limbs grew languid, her thin robe blown flat against her body.

She hoped to find respite at the last highway station on the long road to Shy'Kimlea, but as it came into view all thought of the soothing bonfire fled. Usually visible for kilometers, the light of the fire was absent, and the sight of the highway station was dominated by massive sails shining with a ghost-like light against the overcast sky. Beneath the sails, nine masts and three dark-bodied hulls hung in the air, two close to the ground on either side of the highway and one above them, positioned lengthwise across it. The airships seemed to have formed a makeshift gateway.

Antimony paused in the road, mouth ajar at the sight. "Oh, no. Not them as well." She tightened her grip on the straps of the satchels hanging from either shoulder and marched onward, fearing what she must be approaching.

Instead of the light of a single great bonfire, she saw only the cold metal frame of where it was meant to stand. Therefore the southward passage would not be safe; Kimlean traders would be trapped in the city if they did not wish to freeze to death on the road, one of the only ways that those animated by Drakscul could truly die. In place of yellow flame, airship repulsors lit the Highway station with a blue glow that dappled the sides and bottoms of each of the three vessels to keep them afloat.

Smaller red lights rode on the shoulders of the Bemure mystics. Moving about on the decks of the ships and on the road beneath were figures in thick, sanguine robes, hoods lined with fur so soft it might have been feathers. They wore shifting brambles like armor over their shoulders, and the brambles burned with hot fire that did not harm them, but kept the cold away.

As Antimony approached, she watched a merchant on the road in front of her, a well-preserved Kimlean who looked almost like he was alive except for the thinness of his gait and the way he did not ward against the cold. The man was burdened by thick satchels, and Antimony guessed the contents were the very same bone flowers she herself carried. Any Kimlean merchant who did not dedicate themselves fully to the bone flower market in this season simply was not interested in profit. The man was bold in his approach, and the Bemure mystics intercepted him almost immediately. With their eyes flickering red beneath their hoods, the Bemure reached for his satchels, their fingertips adorned in crystals shaped like claws.

The undead man and the Bemure exchanged harsh words out of earshot, and then the undead man produced in his hand a crystal sphere that seemed to be made of the same material as the Bemure claws. In his pale hands, the sphere roiled with magic, and Antimony understood his boldness. This undead man was not a Kimlean at all; he was not an undead Aster. He was an Axon, an undead Bemure, and a mystic himself. He spoke their language and could voice his objections, and now it seemed he would use his magic to evade the Bemure blockade and proceed to Shy'Kimlea in spite of them.

But barely had the Axon begun to summon magic inside the sphere before the crystal claws on the Bemure Mystics' fingertips flashed a dark blue color. The light inside the sphere vanished, and as one of the Bemure ripped it free of the undead fingers, the other took the man by his shoulders and pulled him backwards. Then, with a strange gentleness, the Bemure lay him on the ground, and he did not move. The Bemure took the satchels from him, looked inside, and then dropped the man's crystal sphere and a pitifully small coin purse in his inert hands.

When Antimony neared what she was fast-realizing was a small blockade, she noted the many others gathered there: Kimleans and Axons waylaid in lines against the ships to either side, the merchandise on the ground in front of them. Red-robed figures searched their bags, and she was sure they were looking for bone flowers. Far off to the side of the road, she noticed a much smaller airship alight with blue repulsors lowering itself over a migrating herd of echinodu, causing the animals to scatter in a panic and forcing the Drashar nomads who tended the herd to struggle for control over them. Antimony had heard about behavior like this in other parts of the world: a military forcing people to 'sell' certain goods to them at an incredible loss.

The Bemure who had taken the Axon's goods from him pulled the stachels to one side and tied their straps together. He then reached over his shoulder to the brambles on his back, crystal fingertips flickering, and the burning wood came to life in response. It unfurled from his back, spreading wings of fire, stretching talons of thorns, moving a wicker head with volcanic eyes. The Bemure gave the bags to the burning construct and it flapped its wings to carry them away, up onto the deck of the utmost airship, where Antimony could almost feel the fire that likely burned the flowers immediately.

She might not have the heat of a fire to thaw her, but anger warmed her limbs enough that she pushed against the rigid coolness in her Drakscul to march forward beneath the blockade. Her footsteps took her to the side of the fallen, rigid Axon, and she crouched over him. The man wasn't dead, and she hadn't expected him to be. Nor was he frozen. She could feel the enchantment holding his limbs in place like magic pins through his joints.

Casting a glare at the Bemure, seeing the red hoods turn towards her, Antimony lay her staff in front of her and reached out to the Axon's limbs. The power she summoned in her fingertips caused the Drakscul in her hand to recoil, and she flinched at the burning sensation beneath her skin. The divine power she wielded was the antithesis of the dark power that gave her life, but she used it carefully. In swift gestures she plucked the curses from the Axon's bones, and his rigid body jerked as though waking up.

The man's first action was to clutch the crystal sphere, as well as the bag of coin that did not even begin to cover his expenses. Green light flared inside the sphere like a sick sun breaking over the mountains, and though it blinded Antimony she did not wince against it, as she had no retinas to burn. When the light faded, the man was no longer present. He crouched thirty meters away, well past the blockade in the road, with lines of mist rising from his shoulders and head. He lifted his gaze to look at Antimony, green light boiling inside of his fogged eyes, and his expression was heavy with grim frustration.

Antimony thought she saw something in his eyes more disturbing than simple death.

Then the Axon rose, turned, and ran towards Shy'Kimlea, leaving Antimony and the blockade behind. Putting her staff against the ground, Antimony lifted herself by it and watched his back, wishing she had a similar trick to get herself away.

The click of crystals behind her head made her snap straight, eyes wide, turning around and taking a step back to glare at the red-hooded figure that had been reaching for her satchels. With what she thought was significant bravery, she eyed the two points of blazing red beneath the hood with ire. "Excuse me! Did you want something from me?"

Crystal claws on dark-skinned fingers pulling back beneath his sleeve, the Bemure mystic responded with a chuckle and looked over his shoulder to speak to his companion. The words flowed smooth like magma, lazy and simmering in the air. Antimony was able to follow some of them, but the language of the Bemure drifted between the two men as though without destination, loitering in the shifting of their sleeves and the clicking of the crystals they wore on their fingertips.

Letting her empty eye sockets flicker between the two men, Antimony twisted her staff in her hands and ignored the lingering burn in her fingers as the Drakscul worked its way back over her knuckles. "Gentlemen, if you want to speak about me or to me, you can do so in the language of Aster."

This drew another chuckle from beneath the hood in front of her, and when he gestured with his claws they flashed with red light. She almost expected him to cast some kind of spell, but the only heat she felt came from the exhaust of the airship repulsors blowing down on them. "Xeno languages taste like dirt. You will sell us what you are carrying."

"What I am carrying is none of your business." She pushed the satchels behind her back as if to protect them. "Bemure has no authority over what Kimleans purchase, where or at what price."

"Price doesn't matter. Surrender it. Take what we give you."

"That is not how trade works." She lifted her head proudly. "If you wish to negotiate a price, you may contact my employer through Shy'Kimlea's trade commission. You may even do so in your own language. He is an Axon named Viscid."

The Bemure mystic's shining claws dropped to his side and the hood shifted. He looked over his shoulder at his companion. "Viscid."

The other's Sanguine shoulders lifted in a shrug. The Mystic spread his arms, but that was the moment that the flaming brambles fell upon him like a bird alighting upon the summit of a tree. He barely even shifted under the weight as the flaming limbs wrapped around him, and he spoke casually in that slow language.

"Ah, yes." Antimony leaned her head forward, eyes narrow. "That is his name."

The red hood turned back to her. "All right, Xeno. Go." And both of the figures turned away from her.

Snapping her head back, blinking, Antimony lifted her hand as if to stop the men and inquire further. A question pressed at her lips, resting against the Drakscul in her cheeks, but she bit down on it to stop herself. Perhaps it was because her employer was an Axon? But judging by the man that had gone before her and, once again, history, the Bemure did not distinguish between different ethnicities of undead.

Still, Antimony swallowed her question. She cast a look at the Kimleans and Axons still corralled for searching alongside the other ships, saw their goods taken and lifted into the airships above by wings of fire, saw them offered small handfuls of coin in exchange for what was actually an entire month's worth of revenue. The red hoods and their clicking crystal fingers sorted through them as though they were filing paperwork. It left her feeling nauseous.

She turned her back on the sight, lifted her face to the cold wind blowing out of Shy'Kimlea, and began homeward again.

* * *

Antimony thawed at one of the bonfires nestled in the Kimlean marketplaces, half a kilometer beneath the Drashannar Reaches. The structure that had once been the underground fortress of High Necromancer Laesam served the Kimleans and Axons well as a city as long as the fires continued to burn. The open air of the city was a great shadow, interrupted by the vast fissure the high stony ceiling through which she could see the pyrite-and-snow peaks of the Cannibal's Crown. The wind did not blow down from mountaintops, but up from the unexplored depths of the bottomless tunnels below the city. She almost didn't even feel the cold, standing as close to the fire as she did.

Curling her fingers, watching the Drakscul loosen from its half-frozen state beneath the skin of her palm, Antimony knew she owed these constant fires to Axon mysticism. But mysticism brought to mind the unsettling green glow of the fleeing Axon's eyes and the red gleam from beneath hoods. The weight of the bone flowers on her shoulders felt like it was trying to bear her downward towards the lower levels of the city, the Axon's district of Axis, where her client, Viscid, waited for her delivery in the darkest, coldest part of the city.

Before that, though, Antimony went to the Corpus Trade Commission, a structure crafted from white slate just like the rest of the city, making it resemble bone. As Antimony squeezed between the thin buildings and various raised tiers that characterized the city's architecture, she pushed past undead men and women doing business with one another, listening to steely voices speaking in the accents of Aster, Bemure and Drashar. She passed the churches to the Aster god, Tatsianuk, and the Kimleans that congregated there, eyes glowing gray or yellow. She passed the temples of Bemure's various cults and the Axons that gathered there, their undead eyes gleaming eerie blue, red, purple, or just carrying shadows in the pits of their skulls.

As she climbed the steps of the Trade Commission, she looked inward to the center of the city, out past one of the hundred great balconies that spiraled up and down the inside of the circular, many-tiered city, looking over the depths of the pit. From the cold dark rose the Drakscul Pillar, the source of all undeath. It reached towards the light above but shied away from it, an impossible tower of black meat boiling like thick ink. Occasionally, polished bone rose to the surface, skulls and femurs and vertebrae clacking against one another and then melting back beneath the surface of the pillar.

The Drakscul that wrapped Antimony's spine drew her straight at the sight. It had long ceased to terrify her. After that had come fascination. Now it just rose inscrutable out of nothing.

A deathly calm lay over the halls of the Trade Commission. Antimony had expected it to be bustling with news of the bone flowers, everyone busy dealing with an economic crisis that could threaten the nature of their existence. But when she entered there was no one immediately present, and the only voices she heard were hushed whispers that seemed to come from the shadows in the corners. Her staff clicked with surprising volume against the floor, making her feel like she'd interrupted some solemn air.

Corpus had more than enough temples without the Trade Commission becoming one, though. She clicked her staff more firmly against the ground. "Excuse me! I need to speak with a commissioner."

The whispers in the shadows ceased, and the sound of shuffling cloth slid along the floor like tectonic grinding.

Antimony frowned, her eye sockets flickering tersely down the hall one direction, and then the other. These doorways and windows were usually populated by merchants attempting to violate levies and the agents that had noticed them. Perhaps such activities did not occur as often during the bone flower season. Or perhaps…

A pair of thin bodies emerged from one of the doors down one hallway, the commissioners of the dead garbed in silk robes as thin as her own. A slight woman stood in front of a small man. Her eyebrows were iced over, but her steely voice held not the slightest shiver, "Where is everyone?"

"I should ask the same question." Antimony narrowed her luminescent gaze, but realized that she knew the answer to the woman's question. "The Bemure have set up a checkpoint on the western highway. There might be more in other places. They are delaying travelers and taking bone flowers."

The woman blinked and stood taller at this, her reaction solemn. The man behind her, however, snapped upright, his eyes flaring brightly. He exhaled a strange sound and shuffled back into the room he'd come from A racket of moving paperwork came soon afterward.

Twisting her staff in her hands, Antimony bit the inside of her lip. "There are Aster horsemen burning the lichen fields, as well. The Drashar are starving, and the bone flowers are…"

Another strange groan came from the room down the hall, this time with a voice exclaiming, "Oh, no! That cannot be permitted!"

The female commissioner lifted her icy brow. "That… makes perfect sense."

Antimony shifted, then paced forward towards the woman. "Does it?"

When the woman cast her gaze towards the ceiling, her eyes burned a subtle green, and Antimony balked with realization. So thin that she looked like she was made of sticks, the woman's long sleeves fell to her elbows as she raised both hands to her chin in thought. "Oh, no. Perhaps not entirely."

"What-?" Antimony was interrupted when the short man burst from the adjacent room, carrying an incredible weight of paperwork and leather folders, brushing past her and blowing out of the room like a sudden chill wind. Eyelids sliding closed, concave over her empty sockets, Antimony turned back to the woman and cast her gray glow at her. "What doesn't make sense?"

"Well the Aster burning the fields makes sense. It's aggressive and stupid. They can't attack us but the Drashar won't fight back. It's boorish. Typical xeno thinking. No mystery there. But the Bemure, that's-..." The woman's icey brow fell. "My name is Cogent."

"... Antimony."

The woman snapped her head back up and took a step back, her fingertips drumming against her sharp chin. "The Bemure have neither military fear of us nor cause to obliterate us. The cult of Dathe wants to see Drakscul as a new god, a child to be guided."

"Maybe the motives are economic." Antimony began forward again, the Axon's body language at least not threatening. "I mentioned that I was acquiring bone flowers on the behalf of an Axon named Viscid and they-"

"Viscid!"

"Yes. Why do people keep doing that?"

"Hm." The woman, Cogent, dropped her hands about her waist. Then brought them back to her chin. "Viscid."

Antimony's eyes dimmed. "Yes. Viscid."

"What color were their eyes?"

"Who's eyes?"

"The Bemure at the checkpoint. Obviously."

Pursing her lips, Antimony hissed. "They were red."

"Oh, that's terrible." The woman vanished into the room she'd come from with even more speed than the small man had managed. Instead of a clatter of paperwork, there was the instant shuff of cloth and a familiar, disturbing click that made Antimony retreat several paces. When Cogent returned, she was wrapped in an additional robe the sickly green color of illness, the fingers of one hand adorned in crystal claws. These flashed only briefly before her long sleeves concealed them, but the crystal sphere in her other hand remained visible.

The Drakscul in Antimony's face pulled her jaw back uncomfortably, and she ground her teeth against the sensation. "I'm not sure I understand."

"I will explain." Cogent swept forward, a tall twig with cloth billowing away from her. "But don't you have a delivery to make in Axis? We should go talk to Viscid."

The thought of descending into the shadows, voluntarily walking into the Axon district with its many temples and mystics, seemed to summon back the ice in her Drakscul. Her movements felt sluggish, but in the next moment she was following Cogent down the steps of the Trade Commission and onto the road, the Drakscul pillar looming through the buildings to one side. Despite all this, Antimony had a job to complete.

* * *

"Viscid is known to the Axons for two things." Cogent lead Antimony down the stairways that wrapped the inner ring of Corpus. It was impossible to get closer to the Drakscul pillar than this. Antimony watched bones seethe against the surface of the dark meat, skulls emerging to peruse the city with empty gazes and then vanishing again, as Cogent spoke. "Before his death some hundred years ago, he was a director of economic policy for a union between three different Cults inside Bemure. Such a union has not existed since his death."

"So he is highly qualified." Antimony muttered, filling the silence between Cogent's statements so that she would not have to endure it. The Drakscul in her hands was fixed about her staff as though solidified. The light from the surface faded as they descended, down dozens of flights of stairs. While the steps of the undead did not tire, living visitors would have frozen to death ten tiers up.

"Oh, yes!" Cogent spun and walked backwards down the stairs, her hands behind her and eyes shining green. "The second thing he is known for is that, during the war on the living, he was one of High Necromancer Laesam's primary aides. In necromancy. He was a necromancer. A very good one. Also very terrible. So you have two of Laesam's old inner circle as clients, right? Naunet as well, right?" Her path abruptly turned from the steps and into one of the shadowed lanes four tiers deep in Axis. After only a few steps, Cogent was only a vague silhouette against the darkness, her green eyes glowing beneath her hair, green light pouring from her sleeves and the concealed crystals therein. Behind her, small lights were barely discernible, the blue, green and red colored fires outside of Axon temples. "Viscid's office is on this tier, isn't it? Have you ever been there?"

Antimony stood outside the shadows, twisting the staff in her hand. "I have never been to Axis before, no."

Cogent's tone dropped with a snap, "I will not wait for you, xeno. Walk."

Her expression souring, Antimony pushed herself forward with a click of her staff and a huff. "I did not ask you to wait."

The light of Cogent's eyes spun away, but the crystal claws behind the woman's back shone eerily. Her fingers drummed against her palm, the claws clicking. "Viscid hired thirty acquisitions agents to obtain bone flowers this season. All xenos who do not realize who he is. You were just the first to come to us and make me think to check. It's strange!"

Antimony kept her gaze forward, following the light of Cogent's claws. She couldn't even distinguish the road from the walls in this darkness. "I don't see what's strange about that. If he is a businessman then he knows their value, and if he is a… Mystic. Or an alchemist. Then he knows how to use them."

The claws stilled and the green-glowing eyes swung back to look at Antimony, though Cogent continued to walk. She began to ascend invisible steps in the dark. "Shush."

"Did you just-" Antimony tripped on the first step of the stairs, but righted herself to continue upward. When she lifted her disgruntled gaze from her own feet, Cogent had drifted ahead an unlikely amount, as though she'd teleported. Antimony bit down hard and hurried forward. If she lost Cogent in this darkness she might never be able to find her way out. How did Axons live here?

Before Antimony could catch up to the woman, Cogent took a sharp left and then vanished into shadow. Antimony rushed blindly forward to that spot, extending her staff in front of her like a blind woman. The gray glow of her eyes illuminated her sleeve and her hand, but only slightly. In moments, her staff thudded heavily against hard wood, and she pressed close to it so that her eyes illuminated the grain of the door. Feeling like an invalid, Antimony ran her hands over the door until she found the handle and pulled it open, hoping she was following Cogent and not about to walk in on some Cult's ritual.

The inside of the room seemed even colder than the outside, a breeze blowing outward as though from the pit itself. But a light illuminated the room, a colored fire burning in one corner. It shone a sickly yellow, very unlike that which glowed in the eyes of Kimleans at the churches in Corpus. Bags of linen and leather lined all four walls. The yellow light making her green robe a dark gray, Cogent turned her glowing eyes on Antimony and gestured to the bags. "And now you know where the confiscated bone flowers are going."

Antimony inhaled, a thing completely unnecessary for a dead woman. The Drakscul swelled in her chest and pits between her ribs leaked. But when she exhaled, she felt steadied against her disorientation. Grateful to finally have some kind of light, even if it came with a repugnant sensation upon her skin, Antimony turned her gaze on the rest of the room just in time to see the man in the center of it all turn.

Broad-shouldered and thin-hipped, the man's rotted arms hung at his sides, his sleeveless robe leaving them exposed and pale. His head was bald, his face flattened from rot. From one clouded eye and one empty eye socket there glowed the same sick yellow light. His voice rasped low, like his vocal chords had been replaced with coarse thread instead of Drakscul. "That's an… interesting accusation, Cogent."

"Oh!" The woman spun around, clicking the claws of her one hand against the sphere she held in the other, drawing both up to her chin. "And Antimony, this is Viscid. And Viscid, this is Antimony. Good to meet one another? Introductions are important."

Antimony gave the top-heavy man a dubious look, finding no words to say. He turned to her, looked her over, then just pointed at the satchels on her shoulders and gestured to the other bags around the room. At this, Antimony frowned. "I hope you don't expect me to just drop these off and leave. The value of this product has expanded significantly, and you owe me additional recompense for difficulties encountered."

Viscid turned to the other woman. "Why are you here?"

Cogent answered cheerfully, "Why is the Cult of Zarathustra confiscating bone flowers from other merchants and delivering them to you?"

He waved it off. "I don't know anything about what Bemure is doing." He gestured to the many satchels in the room. "This is all just careful business."

"Oh, Antimony! Do you know how bone flowers work?" She spun on Antimony, smiling. "They're an important part of necromancy. Powerful sorcerers use them to enthrall the minds of the mindless. Hey, what kind of undead were you during Laesam's war on the living? Were you one of the mindless horde?"

"That is," Antimony's mouth hung open for a silent moment. "An extremely personal question."

"I'm sorry." Cogent laid the crystal sphere against one of her sunken cheeks and tapped it idly with her claws. "If you were mindless then a necromancer was in control of you. Powerful alchemy, and the bone flowers were part of it. We use them these days to preserve not only our bodies, but our minds. So we maintain control over ourselves, see? Self-necromancing! You're like an amateur necromancer."

"I am not." Antimony knocked her staff against the ground.

Viscid wandered over to one of the piles of bags, opening it and revealing the congealed mass of white flowers inside. One of his wretched hands produced a small sheaf of paper. He pretended to count flowers. "Can't you two have this talk elsewhere? I'm very busy."

"No you are not." Cogent flashed her broken teeth at him, then looked back at Antimony. "Anyway. Hey, so what happens if we run out of bone flowers? We all go mindless. And then what if a necromancer shows up who has lots of bone flowers? Oh, he could really take over, couldn't he? That's why on policy all bone flower production and use is overseen by the Trade Commission. Profit is well and good, but we don't want another Laesam taking over."

Viscid turned, his yellow eyes flickering over his shoulder. "It is time for you to leave." One hand stretched towards Antimony, suddenly adorned with crystal claws, and she flinched away from it. "You as well. Take your flowers elsewhere. As you can see, I won't miss such a pathetic amount."

Pulling herself up, Antimony glared at him. "We signed a contract, sir!" By some primal instinct she had not imagined she possessed, she summoned a small amount of divine power into her fingers. They grew hot, just in case she needed to defend herself against the man's outstretched hand.

"Oh, Viscid." Cogent snapped her hands forward in front of her with a loud click of crystal upon crystal. "I just want to make sure everyone understands what is about to happen here. And you do know what is about to happen here."

Something moved behind Antimony, and she flinched heavily to one side, looking over her shoulder into the deep shadows there. At first she saw nothing, then light flicked off claws, and she could discern the shape of an Axon stepping into the room as though from the shadows themselves. In the next moment, the newcomer's claws began to glow green, and then others joined them in the shadows. A dozen handfuls of claws seemed to move against the dark recesses between the bags of bone flowers.

"I don't," Antimony muttered, stepping away from the wall and looking at Cogent. "I don't know what's about to happen."

"Yes you do, xeno." Cogent turned to her. "I can sense power in you. You are a priest of the Aster god, aren't you?"

"Not by profession."

"But by training, right? So you understand how gods and cults move."

Antimony snapped, "The Church is not a cult."

"Yes, it is. Shush."

Viscid sealed the bags he had opened behind him. His fingers slid into his pocket to deposit the sheaf of paper, and when he withdrew them they bore crystal claws, now on each finger of both hands. He turned to face the room with his long, decomposed arms hanging to either side. He faced not only Cogent and Antimony, but also the nearly invisible Axons lingering in the dark behind them.

Cogent watched Viscid, and her smile faded. It then renewed itself as a strangely hollow expression. A dead woman's smile. "Viscid. The Cult of Drakscul gives you one chance to surrender yourself."

Antimony flinched. "Cult?" She turned to look around her again, noting the universal green glow of eyes, claws, and crystal spheres arrayed behind her. Then she looked back ahead, to Viscid, and the unique off-yellow glow of his eyes and claws.

"Drakscul is not a god." The top-heavy man gestured with his claws, and they crackled with visible power. "Granandor destroyed the world four times. Zarathustra once. Yet the world returns. We died, and we return. Drakscul is a tool of the returners. The truest god will not be the killers or the returners, but she that masters the return. The undeath. The inventor of necromancy."

Cogent snickered. "That sounds very stupid. Don't make me call the Arch-Herald on you."

"Your Arch-Herald is a pretender. Laesam's champion is still the Arch-Herald of the dead, and she will still lead us to cure the world of the illusion of life."

"Are you counting on her to help you? No. Antimony, isn't Naunet a long, long way from here?" Cogent never actually looked at Antimony, though, keeping her eyes on Viscid. "Are you going to surrender or not?"

Viscid knit together the claws of both hands, and they resonated against one another, glowing bright with prepared power. "Laesam will-"

"Okay!" Cogent hefted the sphere in front of her and slammed the crystal claws of her other hand down upon it. The sphere shattered, and green light poured out like liquid in all directions. Cold burst from it, not as wind, but radiating out like heat from a fire. Then darkness broke from the sphere as though from a backwards sun, and a cacophonous silence rushed over Antimony's skin.

There was nothing. Antimony couldn't even see the light glowing from her own eye sockets. She shifted in confusion, but didn't feel like she was going anywhere. The heat that she'd summoned into her fingers was completely overwritten by the cold. She sensed no one around her, no walls, no ceiling. There came a subtle howl, like wind through distant limbs, and Antimony spun towards it.

Cast in grays, she saw the vaguest image of Viscid, the man almost indiscernible from the black around him. The howling came from somewhere above him, and he stood stock-straight staring up at it as though he'd been nailed to the void and could not move. The black nothing above him writhed and gained definition, glistening like ink. It bulged downward.

Polished bone began to seethe against the surface, skulls emerging and turning empty eye sockets on the man.

Then the darkness slammed down, the crash shaking Antimony's bone. The Drakscul in her chest and neck tightened as she watched the pillar crush Viscid and then swell towards her. She threw her hands up in front of her, summoning incredible heat that seared her bones and made the Drakscul in her limbs retreat towards her shoulders. The swelling pillar of black matter slammed against the holy energy she'd summoned and knocked her backward.

Her back hit the door and threw it open, and Antimony tumbled into the darkness outside. Even in the complete blackness, she could see the polished bone roiling in the building as if the walls were no longer there. The howling filled her ears, the sound now grating like a rodent's screech. Bodies moved around her, polished crystal claws crackling with green light as their bearers rushed towards the building.

Antimony rolled to her feet and ran . She turned her back on the polished bone, ducking her head and pulling in her shoulders to struggle past the bodies of the Axons moving towards Viscid's office. Her panicked mind unconsciously tried to count the bodies that she brushed against, but kept losing track. She just fled back the way she thought she'd come, with no way to be certain, stumbling down steps and swinging her staff beside her.

She emerged from the shadows and onto the steps that would take her back up to Corpus with a suddenness that nearly took her over the inner edge of the walkway. She fell to her hands and knees just a meter from the drop off, her staff flat in front of her, and found herself staring outward at the massive Drakscul pillar. It roiled with that same dark substance that Cogent had somehow summoned. She could feel the Drakscul in her shoulders tighten, the fibers pulling inside of her ribs.

* * *

Antimony still sat there, her hands tight on her staff, when Cogent emerged from the shadows of Axis. The woman wore an idle smirk, her arms swinging and her sleeves snapping, fingers empty of the crystal claws they had boasted earlier. She paused upon seeing Antimony, then brought her hands in front of her. "You did not do badly. I appreciate a xeno who knows when to let the Cults take over."

Her lips feeling frozen in a straight line, Antimony lifted her gray-glowing eye sockets to the woman. "I don't understand what happened."

"Oh, everything's been taken care of. You will be compensated." Cogent nodded, and idled, as though waiting for a response. Then she shrugged, "Goodbye, then," and turned away to start up the stairs.

Antimony stood slowly, using her staff to support herself. "But I don't understand." This protest did not seem to reach the Axon's ears. Cogent just continued up the steps without pause. Antimony thought about following, about insisting, but the Drakscul in her legs felt weak and frozen. And she didn't wish to see the green glow of the woman's eyes again.

The Way She Grows

by Erin Kennemer

Nothing could be done for a Mantica rose with a brown stem. Turn it to toothpicks or burn it for warmth, but don't bother trying to save it. Sherry sat down on the lawn chair and swore. She thought about going somewhere to cool down before talking to Melody, but their apartment was so tiny, there wasn't really anywhere to go.

That stupid rosebush meant more to her than anything else. Seeing it battered and twisted in its sad little pot was too much. As she stared at the cracked, dry soil, her temper flared.

"What the hell did your brother actually do?" Sherry shouted. One week of vacation and everything had fallen apart.

Melody stepped out on the patio and shrugged. "I told him to water it."

"Well, he didn't."

"You can just get another one, right?"

"I wouldn't even know where to begin. Just don't expect things to be too good around here anymore." Sherry pressed on her eyes with the palms of her hands.

"Sher, don't take this the wrong way, but I never really believed in that 'lucky rose' business."

Sherry let out a growl that was probably this side of childish and stood up. Why bother arguing? Mel would see. Luck without magic was a swinging pendulum, and they had a long way to fall.

* * *

"What the hell, Sher!" shouted Melody from the bathroom/laundry room. "You tied all of my bras together? I told Ted to water your stupid plant. You don't have to be so childish. And the thing with the cereal was over the line."

"What thing with the cereal?" asked Sherry, already bored.

"The fake- JESUS!" Melody started yelling unintelligibly and raced half-clothed from the bathroom.

Sherry stood up, nerves on fire. The luck was turning downward again.

Melody spun on her, eyes narrowed and poisonous. "What. The. Hell. A plastic snake in the toilet bowl? Are you mental? This is way worse than killing some plant. You're making me live with a sociopath. I'm done. I am absolutely out of here."

Sherry bit her lip and headed for the kitchen and grabbed a pair of oven mitts and tongs. Melody followed behind, continuing her stream of grievances. The midnight fire alarm, the accidental sign up for insurance quotes, the cats in heat getting stuck in the walls; it was a damning list, but hardly Sherry's fault.

"How are you blaming me for the cats? How does that make more sense than Mantica mojo?"

Melody knit her eyebrows together. "What are you doing with the tongs, Sher?"

"Just open the front door and stand in the living room, okay?"

"No, I'm coming with you. I don't want you hiding any more plastic critters- Oh my God, it's moving!"

Melody wrapped her arms around Sherry's chest and pulled her backwards.

"Let go, Mel!"

"You are not touching that thing. It is definitely poisonous, and you will die."

Sherry extracted herself and took a deep breath. "I had a pet snake as a kid. Let me handle this."

"Bet you didn't have a pet cobra," muttered Melody, but she backed into the living room. Sherry heard the front door open.

Stepping into the bathroom, Sherry took a deep breath. She hadn't had a pet snake as a kid and knowing her luck these days, it probably was a cobra.

In the bowl of the toilet was a long green snake, doing its best to swim. Green meant garden snake, which meant not poisonous. Sherry struck quickly, pulling the snake from the bowl with one quick scoop. She hadn't used the tongs because she didn't want to hurt it, but the oven mitts were making it hard to grip, and it was writhing. She held it behind the head so it couldn't bite her… unless she was unlucky enough to drop it.

"It says here that it's a green mamba-" Mel walked into the bathroom holding her laptop. "AND you're holding it." She ran out again.

Sherry dashed for the front door. She chucked the snake as soon as she reached the threshold, and it went tumbling end over end until it disappeared into the bushes.

"Mel, it's time to go plant shopping. Get your purse."

* * *

Tienda de Poder was a small shop in the seedier part of the warehouse district. It was exactly the kind of place that Sherry's granny would have forbidden her to go if she were still alive. Of course, if Granny was still around, Sherry would be going to her for help.

Melody looked around like she was expecting gunfire and had one hand firmly on her purse. Sherry tried to keep her head forward, but the truth was, she was just as nervous. This wasn't her element.

"So, your grandmother taught you about plant magic?" asked Melody.

"Phytomancy and not really. I didn't have any talent for it. My first spell ended up molding and going all mushy. Over-watered."

"Ah. Okay. So what makes you think you can do it this time?"

Sherry stopped walking.

"Oh, Sher, I'm sorry. I didn't mean it like it sounded. I'm just trying to understand."

"It's fine." It really wasn't. "I'm sure the upstanding proprietor of 'Power Store' will be able to guide me. Granny's heart wasn't ever in it."

Sherry didn't want to mention that Granny had specifically banned her from sprouting spells. She'd been trained enough to maintain a nice established incantation, like the Mantica, but sprouting was tricky. Hopefully, Tienda de Poder carried potted luck.

Melody pushed right in when they reached the dingy office-turned-store. Sherry followed after, trying to ignore the little-bitty granny voice in her head. *Get your butt home, young'n.* The air inside was heavy with soil and manure.

Behind a reclaimed wood counter that was either trendy or cheap, an older woman with bright red hair lazily flipped through a magazine. She looked up, a large smile splitting her face. "Welcome, young ones, I'm Hilde. Do you seek the power to change your destiny and claim riches and success?"

If she could grow that kind of spell, why would her shop be out here, in the middle of nowhere? Sherry tried not to laugh; words from Granny's own mouth. Buying spells was so gauche. *A spell is hard work. You get out of it what you put into it.*

"Have you heard of a Mantica rose?"

The shopkeeper cocked an eyebrow and gestured them over to a table of potted flowers. None of them looked like the Mantica. Hilde crowded in beside them and pointed at a couple of the pots.

"This one will give your enemies warts, this one makes all your casseroles turn out well, and this one will give you whiter teeth." Hilde smiled wide again, showing off her pearly whites. "Perk of working here."

"I'm looking for a general luck spell, actually."

"Aren't we all? Are you familiar with Phytomancy? It doesn't really work in general."

Melody laughed, and Hilde glared at her.

"I mean to say, you have to be specific. Each plant does a *specific* thing, no more, no less. If you try for something too ambitious, the results can be disastrous."

"Well, what about a Mantica rose? My Granny sprouted me one and it always brought us reasonable luck."

"Even reasonable luck is too broad. I have a tulip that makes you lucky at Go Fish."

Sherry let out a sigh while Melody wandered off. Granny was right about plant merchants; they were no place for a real Phytomancer.

"Look, I'll be honest. I had a general luck spell, and it died. Now we're having a hell of a time finding matching socks and car keys. I just need something to bring things back to neutral. I don't have to have luck again. I just want to stop waking up to a cockroach on my face."

Hilde frowned. "I have a cleansing plant. Very expensive, but necessary when spells grow wrong. How lucky were you? Things could get very ugly, my dear. You never had any near misses, did you?"

Sherry cocked her head to the side.

"Near misses! Almost deaths? 'Holy crap I could have died if it wasn't for' kind of thing?"

"No, no, nothing like that." Sherry waved the woman off, but it did make her think. Would she have noticed if she almost died?

"Sher, come check this out! It looks just like it." Melody was on the other end of the store, looking at the seed packets.

Sherry didn't want to have to explain in front of the old woman that she was a failure at sprouting, but Hilde was determined to stay on the only customers in her shop.

Melody looked up as Sherry approached. "It doesn't have a label on it, but it looks exactly like your rose before…"

"It was murdered? Yeah."

"Let's get this and give it a try." Melody shrugged.

Hilde eyed the seeds over their shoulders. "I don't offer any warranties or guarantees on my blank spells. The sprouter determines the quality, not the seed."

Sherry shook her head. "The lady was just telling me about a cleansing plant that could take care of our problem."

"It's a fern, dear," said Hilde.

Sherry rolled her eyes for Melody. "A cleansing fern. It's already sprouted, and it should cancel out any effect from the dead Mantica spell."

"At just 600 dollars, it's a bargain."

"Hell, no!" said Melody.

"That's a bit high." Sherry didn't know what to do. She needed Melody to pitch in. She couldn't afford 100 dollars, much less 600.

"How much are the seeds?" asked Melody.

"Ten. No refunds."

"We'll take them." Melody was already fishing around in her purse.

"Mel, I'm not that strong of a sprouter. Maybe we could just borrow the cleansing plant?"

The old woman laughed derisively.

* * *

"Okay, so I Googled it, and apparently you're supposed to chant before you plant. Let's just pull the seeds back out."

"No!" shouted Sherry, knocking Melody's hand away. "You'll piss them off. We'll just do the chant now."

"Geez, okay. You do it, though. I need a beer." Melody headed to the kitchen.

Sherry felt a little embarrassed, but she knew what the stakes were. The chant took a few minutes, but Melody never returned with the beer. After 'staring at the naked earth and wishing it good fortune,' Sherry needed her next line. Melody's computer wasn't on the table anymore. Sherry headed for the kitchen.

"That's nice and all, really, but we didn't order it." Melody stood by the front door, talking in a hushed voice. Her hand was gently on her waist and her hip was thrust out, the flirting pose.

"I might as well leave it with you. We're going to have to remake it for 'Phillip Mamoufwifartz.' We have a 30 minutes or it's free policy."

"Shouldn't it be free for him, though?" asked Melody.

"You'd think so," said the pizza boy. He was cute and happened to be giving Mel his best smile.

"Well, thank you, Brandon." Melody accepted the pizzas and closed the door on his face. When she turned and saw Sherry, she started to laugh. "You should see the look on your face. Lighten up."

"Did you crank call a pizza to our house?"

"No. Why would I do that? I'm 20, not 12."

"Crap," said Sherry. "That isn't bad luck, but I'm not sure it's good luck, either."

"Is everything about the stupid plants?"

"We'll see." Sherry grabbed her friend's computer.

* * *

The stink of pizza hung in her hair most of the day, so she wasn't surprised when even after a shower, she could still smell it. She turned over in bed, catching another whiff. It was in her pillow. She let out a disgusted sigh and tried to breathe through her mouth.

Someone had ordered pizza for the staff at her office on Monday. Tuesday, pizza boy had come by with another offering for the fair Melody. Wednesday, Melody and the girls had all insisted they go out, and the consensus was, of course, pizza. It wasn't until today that things got undeniably ridiculous. Three different deliveries from three different pizza places, all pre-paid.

Melody had tried to call it a coincidence, but Sherry saw the writing in the pot, so to speak. She was growing a pizza-every-day primrose.

Mew. Sherry let out a heavy sigh. The cats were in the walls again.

Mrrrrrrr. That sounded oddly close.

A heavy weight landed on Sherry's chest, and she screamed in surprise.

Melody came running in, eyes wide. "You okay? When did we get a cat?"

"It must have gotten in somehow."

"We'll just shoo the thing out. It'll be fine. Don't freak out again, please."

Sherry glared, not dignifying that with a response. She was the one who had grabbed the snake. Herding the cat out the door turned out to be harder than previously thought, however. After an hour, they still hadn't managed it.

At the moment it sat on the top of Melody's dresser, just far enough back that they needed a stick to reach it.

"How about we just have a cat now," Melody said, exhaustion in her voice.

"I don't care anymore."

Melody shrugged and went into her room, their new pet still hissing at her. Sherry couldn't sleep. She walked out to the living room, where the shrine to their new plant glowed.

The grow lights were blue and made everything look slightly sinister. The plant itself was coming along well, but Sherry had more doubts than ever. She hadn't trimmed it yet, just let it grow. Clearly it didn't have any effect on their Mantica curse. It just delivered pizza. She'd have to start trimming if she wanted to change the menu or their luck.

Carefully, she brought the shears up to the lowest bough and snipped. Now it only had three branches, a powerful number in Phytomancy. It should bring them health, wealth and wisdom. Sherry would have settled for a little quiet, though.

* * *

The next morning, Sherry woke up drenched in sweat, Melody knocking on her door.

"The AC is out," Mel said through the door.

"Did your brother forget to water it?"

"I called someone over, but you're going to have to split the cost with me."

"Won't the apartment pay for it?"

Melody eased the door open and stepped inside. "Yeah, I had maintenance out first thing. They said it was clogged with pet hair, and seeing as it's a pet-free apartment, they're calling this one 'our bad.'"

"That's not even possible. The stupid cat has only been here for one night." Sherry sat up, making a face as a fresh cloud of pizza odor mingled with body sweat.

"Yeah, guy said the same thing. 'This is clear evidence of permanent pet residency, and it violates your lease, little lady.'"

"Seriously?"

"I know, right? Who says 'little lady'?"

Sherry threw her pillow at the door, and Melody retreated. She might think this was all amusing, but more bad luck could mean that the primrose was doing poorly. If she killed another spell, they might catch Ebola or something.

"Want some pizza?" asked Melody from the kitchen.

Sherry didn't bother to answer and gathered her things to take a cold shower. After an hour in the bathroom, she was feeling human again.

A knock at the door drew Melody from her computer as Sherry made coffee in the kitchen. She was due in the office at noon, and nothing was worse than insurance coding without caffeine.

"Hello, I'm here to check out the AC." The man at the door was four foot nothing and balding. His gut protruded through the doorway before he even stepped inside. From the kitchen, Sherry could see the sweat-stains under his arms. She couldn't really judge right now, though. She was about to go into work looking about as sweaty.

"Just point me at her," said the man.

Melody walked Floyd, as it said on his jacket, over to the AC unit.

"See, what you've got here, I can easily fix. Not everyone can; you're lucky you called me." His watery eyes disappeared when he smiled.

"Yes, very lucky. If you would just fix it quickly, I'm in a hurry to get to work. Sherry, you can go ahead. I've already called in sick."

"Thanks, Mel. Thanks, Floyd." Sherry started towards the door, coffee in hand. Her foot came down on something squishy and sharp, causing her to stumble. The coffee flew from her hands and landed on Mel as the object under her rushed forward in a fury of claws and fur.

Poor Floyd would have been better off with the hot coffee. The cat hit him with full fury, biting and clawing his leg and climbing up his back to swipe more effectively at his neck. Sherry rushed forward for Melody, who waved her towards Floyd, but she could help neither of them.

The cat left Floyd, who was whimpering and cursing. He let out a wracked breath and backed slowly towards the door.

"Floyd, please don't go. We'll lock the cat up somewhere," said Sherry.

"I think he can open doors," muttered Melody.

"Shut up, Mel!" Turning back to Floyd, Sherry finished. "Please, we really need the AC fixed and you're the only person who will come out on a Friday without charging a weekend rate."

"You're worried about weekend rates? You're about to pay a hospital bill. That cat of yours is insane."

"You two will be calling other cities before you find someone to come out here. I'm warning all the guys away. Hope y'all roast!" With that, Floyd was out the door.

"Sher, go to work, I've got this. That litigious asshat can't possibly know all the AC guys in town."

* * *

Work took a backseat to Googling plant magic tips and tricks. There weren't many Phytomancers left, and they didn't have much of a web-presence. However, Sherry did manage to learn a thing or two about general spells.

One, they were hard to pull off, and two, they could grow extra branches without warning. Sherry thought fondly of her Mantica. It was such a steady and reliable spell. They hadn't even noticed it.

Extremely good coupons in the mail and quiet neighbors were two wonderful benefits of the late Mantica. Sherry couldn't be sure, but she suspected her skill at FreeCell might also have been plant-powered. Their bad luck just seemed so disproportional! Maybe the Mantica was haunting them from beyond the grave. How long could a plant hold a grudge?

She made a few rough sketches of cuts she could make to shape the primrose more towards fortune. Too bad killing a spell always ended in trouble, or else that pizza-primrose would be on its way to a landfill.

* * *

When Sherry got home, a surprise was waiting for her. On the couch, Melody snuggled closely with the AC repairman, her arms around his neck. No, not Floyd. Bill. Or at least that was the name on the back of his jacket.

"Hey, Bill. Enjoying my roommate?" asked Sherry, sarcastically.

"Oh Sher, you'll never guess what's happened." Melody disentangled herself, still maintaining some contact with Bill. "This is Bill, *the Bill*! From ninth grade summer camp?"

Mel pulled Bill to his feet and walked him over. Sherry hadn't even made it fully in the door and already she wanted to run out again.

"We lost contact years ago, but both of us always knew we were meant to be together. When he got the call to come fix the 'devil women's' air conditioner, he had no idea it would be mine!"

"It's all like some strange Shakespeare play, isn't it, darling?" said Bill, pulling Melody into another kiss. Sherry, in the splash zone, pushed past the two lovers.

"Not a Shakespeare play," whispered Sherry. "This sounds like 'comically misleading luck.'" She headed straight for the plant, only to find someone else had beat her there.

An orange tabby was chewing on a new growth of the primrose. Sherry shrieked and ran at it. "Didn't you get that stupid cat out of here?"

"I did!" insisted Melody, talking with her mouth full. "That's a different one."

"How are they even getting in?" Another cat crept out of the hallway, as if on cue. It was headed right for the plant. This had to be Mantica's work. The primrose was getting powerful, and her spoiled old spell was determined to stop it. Her comical-luck primrose was in trouble.

As Sherry ran to chase away the new brown calico, a British shorthair leapt onto the plant altar. It managed to remove the newest branch with one chomp. Sherry's heart sank.

A knock at the door caught all of their attention. Melody went to answer it while Sherry picked up the pot and held it to her chest. The cats would have to go through her cold dead-

"Pizza!" said a voice from the door.

"We didn't order any pizza," said Melody, about to slam the door closed.

"Oh now, Melly-welly, I'm kind of hungry. We'll take the pizza." Bill went to the door and started negotiating with the wayward pizza boy.

"We have to come up with a way to keep these cats off the plant until we can get them out the door, Mel!"

Melody's face lit up. She turned to the pizza boy and yanked the pizza out of his hand, throwing the lid open and tossing it onto the ground. The cats made beelines for it.

"Great idea, Melody!" said Sherry, relieved not to have any more cats clawing at her legs.

"I was going to eat that." Bill looked forlorn.

"Okay, Mel, slowly drag the pizza out the door and see if the cats follow you. Hopefully that will keep them off me and prim."

It worked. Melody lured the cats outside and Sherry set to work. She found the branch the cat had snipped and grabbed the laptop. Her granny used to be able to graft growths from one plant on to another. It should be no problem to replace a branch.

Sherry cleaned off as much of the cat bites as she could, whittling down the new growth to just a few leaves. It looked bedraggled, but still alive. She cleaned the wound and reattached the branch.

She didn't have any planter's tape, so she used duct tape. Whispering an apology to the poor spell, she pushed back and looked around.

Nothing seemed different, but at least there weren't any cats. Melody had shooed Bill and pizza guy out the door and was now sitting on the couch looking at the tips of her hair.

"Does it look longer to you?" asked Melody.

Sherry eyed her roommate. It did seem longer. She touched her own hair and sighed. The graft wasn't working like she had hoped, but it was doing something.

She spent the next few minutes trying to prop the fallen branch in the exact position it had been before the cat attack. It wasn't going great. She couldn't remember if it had been more to the left or forward.

She added a little glue and hoped for the best. If she could just return the plant to comical luck, they could at least go from there and hope for the best. Anything but pizza.

A knock at the door startled both her and Melody. "No more pizza! Get them out of here."

"I've got it," said Melody.

The door opened on the red-haired woman from the plant shop. She looked grimmer than usual. Sherry stepped in front of the plant and did her best not to look guilty.

"I got your address from the credit card receipt. When you didn't come back into the shop, I thought something terrible might have happened."

It was then that Sherry saw what Hilde had in her hands: a small green fern in a blue pot. "Is that it? The neutralizing fern?"

"Yes, dear. I wanted to give you one last chance to buy it for 500."

Melody just blinked from the door. "Why would you even come here?"

The old woman pushed past her. "I just thought, from what you said, that you might need it." She looked around. Sherry did as well. The apartment looked normal, except for the unctuous aroma of pizza. There was no sign of the chaos from minutes before. "I see that I was wrong. How about 400, in case you need it later?"

"No," said Melody, before Sherry could answer.

"Can't afford that, huh? I could do 100, but believe me, that is generous of me," said the old woman.

"The way I see it, you'd only be trying this hard to sell it if it didn't work." Melody had her hand firmly on her hip.

With her lip curled up in a sneer, Hilde replied. "I assure you, the fern works."

Sherry thought she might have fifty bucks in her checking account. Maybe Melody would cave for the other forty. After all they'd been through, surely she was willing to shell out the dough.

Melody just shook her head, an annoying look of confidence on her face. "Spill it, lady. What's your angle?"

Hilde looked defeated instead of offended, like Sherry had expected. "It works too well, if you must know. None of my other plants have any mojo anymore. This stupid thing nixed them all. It's so powerful, I tried keeping it at home and it still affected the shop. I'm not stupid, I know I can't kill it. I thought maybe if it changed ownership the effects would fade."

"We'll take it for free, then." Melody tossed her hair behind her shoulders.

Sherry sucked in a breath.

"Fine. Whatever. Just don't kill the thing. Who knows what might happen if a spell like this died." Sherry rushed forward for the fern, and Hilde caught sight of the primrose. "Oh Lord. Little plant, I did my best for you. Blame them if anything goes wrong."

Hilde put a hand on the doorknob and waved them close. When they were within whispering distance, she spoke. "That is the most powerful plant I've come across. It's well and truly yours now. Keep it happy."

They both nodded, confused. Did the woman think the plant would hear her if she spoke louder? After Hilde was gone, Sherry walked over to the fern to give it a closer look.

Its leaves were glossy with no sign of insect damage. From above, it looked like a fractal, its shape so perfectly crafted. Shelly lifted the pot, examining the radiant blue patina that reminded her of summers spent firing pots for her granny.

On the bottom of the container, in a faded black scrawl, was her grandmother's name. The fern was one of hers; it would work.

With a deep sigh, Sherry reveled in their victory. They were completely safe. Nothing would ever go wrong again. That is, as long as the fern didn't die.

Talisman

by Patricia C. Hughes

"'Twere the fires o' Hell burned that night--hot enough to melt armor, they were--and did. Burned until there was nothin' left except the stone walls."

"Aye." An audible consensus sounded throughout the smoky pub. The locals watched David carefully, testing for any sign of disbelief or derision from the outsider. David did not react. His reasons for being there were stranger than the villagers' tale.

The bearded mortician puffed stoically on his pipe. "The stones cracked from the heat. Some ran together. You can see them still."

"The dead have walked there since," the carpenter stated flatly.

A murmur of agreement filled the room again.

"I saw the witch me-self," hissed the mortician between puffs. "Last month at full moon--the ghost o' Brenna--hoverin' o'er the keep."

Ice fingers rippled up David's spine--something about the name, something shadowy on the edge of memory. *Brenna.* The repetitive chant from the dream murmured in his head: *Bren, hexe! Bren, hexe!* The similarity of sound, perhaps?

"Brenna?" David asked.

"Granddaughter o' the last laird o' Moryn Castle," responded the mortician. "The girl's mother eloped without the laird's consent. Disowned her, he did. Years later, she returned--a widow with a near grown daughter of her own. That girl was Brenna. Dark haired, as her name means. Beautiful, she was, but wicked. The old laird sealed his doom when he recanted and took them in."

A burly farmer set a pint upon the table and pulled up a chair. "The old fool should've listened to that young wench he'd wed. Elspeth warned him, she did."

The mortician gestured with the stem of his pipe. "Don't speak ill o' your elders."

"My elders close to perished from the spells o' that demon the old man nurtured," rejoined the farmer. "Stock died. Crops rotted in the fields. The people near starved."

"Some folk did die," said the carpenter. "Mysterious deaths."

"Then came the fires," said the mortician.

"The fires o' Hell," murmured the crowd.

There were no unbelievers among the locals. Generations had learned the lore upon their grandfathers' knees, and they took it very seriously.

David took it more seriously than he liked. The next morning he stood on the edge of a cliff staring at the forbidding view below. The skeletal remains of the old fortresses rose above thrashing waters and gaped at each other atop rocky islands. The villagers had told him that one was an island only when the tide was high and a peninsula when the tide was low.

With binoculars, David verified part of the villagers' tale. Some of the stones were cracked; some, fused.

The fires of Hell.

Gray chill emanated from the thick stone walls, from the craggy shoreline, and beyond to the horizon, where the choppy waves merged with the slate sky. At intervals along the shore and cliffs, great piles of wood stood ready for the Midsummer's Eve vigil.

David's eyes followed the coast. *Why am I here? I should be home in Southern California with Voy and the kids, spending my weekends in the sun, not shivering in a breeze that feels more like winter than June. How can I expect Voy to understand when I don't?*

Against all reason, the dream had compelled him. He closed his eyes and recalled its horrific images: the clip clop of his horse's hooves; the crackle and hiss of flames lashing at the figure bound to the stake; the acrid stench of burning flesh; the hypnotic drone of the mob, *Bren, hexe!*

Suddenly unsteady, David stepped back from the cliff's edge. Emotions surged: grief, outrage, regret--a promise broken. *What promise?*

The chant repeated through his head. *Bren, hexe!*

Burn, witch! thought David. *German. But how could a dream of medieval Germany bring me to a village in Britain? It makes no sense.*

Turning away from the desolate cliffs, David began the long hike back to the village inn. Well-manicured fields reflected centuries of cultivation. Pastures had the look of lawns. The sun peeped through the clouds, banishing the gray.

As he entered the village, he heard, "Hello, fellow outsider! Are you enjoying your holiday in Penmorven?"

"Uh... yes," David stammered.

On the other side of a stone fence, a raw boned woman leaned on a hoe. In work gloves, tweed, and sensible shoes, she hardly appeared his "fellow outsider".

"Are you a tourist, too?" he asked, disbelieving.

"Absolutely. A stranger like yourself." Her eyes smiled as warmly as her mouth. "I've only been summering here for the past seventeen years."

David grinned.

She removed a glove and extended her right hand over the low fence. "Eleanor Throckmorton. And this," she said, gesturing at the stone cottage behind her, "is Priest's House. So called because it used to be one."

They fell into conversation, and she invited him to tour the ancient dwelling.

"Actually, the villagers are quite friendly," she assured. "There's just that little something in their eyes that says you're not quite one of them. And for goodness sakes, don't dare insinuate that there might be some flaw in the local legends."

"Did you?"

"Yes!"

They both laughed.

"Superstition notwithstanding," said David, "something super hot did a number on those castles."

"Indeed!" Eleanor poured him a cup of tea.

David accepted the offering. "Why were there two castles in the same bay in the first place?"

She sipped the hot liquid with satisfaction. "The castle on the island belonged to Sir Louis d'Argent, whose family imposed its authority after the Norman Conquest. Moryn Castle, on the peninsula, was the ancestral home of a wily lineage of Celtic lords, who managed to maintain the bulk of their power despite any conquerors. The Normans found it advantageous to leave the Celt in place."

"I still don't understand the rationale behind the burnings."

"I've never heard a reason why either castle burned. That Brenna was a witch seems reason enough for the locals. I have heard there was some sort of romantic tryst between Brenna and Raoul d'Argent." Eleanor folded her hands and paused. "Let me show you my most recent find."

She led him to the fireplace and removed a loose stone. "This stone has always bothered me. The mortar was slightly lighter. I realize this place has had many repairs over centuries, but there was just something about it. My curiosity finally got the better of me, and I found this." Ancient pages, simply bound, were nestled in a metal box. "We must not handle it. The pages are fragile. It's the journal of a priest, dating from the time of the legendary fires. When I realized how old it was, I could not believe it had not turned to dust in my hands. It's written on parchment, not paper, but its survival is still remarkable. I called my cousin who deals in antiquities in London. He should be here tomorrow."

Eleanor replaced everything without opening the book. "It was fascinating to read about the people of the legends in the present tense." She blushed. "I could not resist reading some of it, although that ancient script was quite a challenge. Thank goodness, I paid attention in class."

Her eyes twinkled. "They were all there, virtually alive on the pages: the old lord; his prodigal daughter, Regan; the old man's young bride, Elspeth, forewarning him of the dangers of taking in his wayward offspring; the mysterious d'Argents; and, of course, the nearly mythic Brenna."

The name chilled David again. *Bren, hexe!* ricocheted through his brain.

"Are you all right?" asked Eleanor.

"Uh... yes."

"You paled so."

"I'm fine," said David. "What did the priest say about Brenna?"

"He called her rebellious, questioned her paternity, referred to rumors of witchcraft. But his favorite word for Brenna was *temptress*." Eleanor pursed her lips. "If you ask me, he was attracted to Brenna in ways that Roman priests aren't supposed to be. Perhaps some of Brenna's wickedness was merely a reflection of the sinful ideas she aroused in others. She was reputed to have been quite a beauty."

David sipped his tea in silence.

Eleanor continued, "One thing which caught my interest was the priest's description of a visit from Brenna's maid. The girl, Mairin, claimed that one of the d'Argent's on the island had acquired some powerful book of spells, and a witch had come to Moryn Castle in search of it."

"Brenna," supplied David.

"No," said Eleanor. "That was the curious part. According to the servant, Brenna was trying to keep the witch from finding the book by using some sort of talisman. The priest concluded Brenna was using Mairin as a pawn to forward her own evil designs. That very day, he wrote to a higher authority, as a precursor to trying Brenna as a witch."

"And the fires saved him the trouble?"

"Perhaps. The rest of the journal is blank."

* * *

That afternoon, the nearly deserted inn smelled of roast pork and ale. David sat down on one of the straight-backed, wooden chairs and ordered some of both. Across the room sat a lone woman, staring out a window. Perfect skin belied the touch of gray in the dark upsweep of her hair. David had not seen her before.

"Here you go." Beth, the innkeeper's buxom, young wife, set the steaming plate in front of him. "Will there be anything else, Handsome?"

"No thanks." David did not think of himself as handsome. That image had disappeared as his hair thinned and threatened to recede. It made no difference to Voy. She found him attractive even though he was twenty years her senior. He worked at it. He had the body and muscle tone of a much younger man.

Beth, too, was younger than the pot-bellied innkeeper she claimed to have married only two months before, but there the similarity ceased. They were the strangest newlyweds David had ever encountered. In the three days since his arrival, he had nightly witnessed Beth flaunting outrageous flirtations, and otherwise ignoring her husband. The innkeeper said and did nothing.

The pork was tender and flavorful, but the potatoes were dry. David washed them down with ale. What was it about the woman at the window? Something more than physical beauty. Something deeply compelling. Before he fully grasped his own actions, David found himself, mug in hand, standing by her table. "An excellent view of Moryn Keep."

"Yes."

"I suppose we're the only guests at the inn," he heard himself saying. "Mind if I join you?"

"If you wish."

Am I trying to pick her up? he thought. *That's nuts. I love Voy.* But he did not retreat. He pulled out a chair and extended his hand as he sat down. "David Schoenburg, American."

"Patience Ward, also American," she replied, placing her delicate hand into his. The touch sent a quiver to the depths of David's soul. An unaccustomed awkwardness slipped over him. He was unsure what came next.

Her steel gray eyes gazed steadily into his. "What brings David Schoenburg, American, to Penmorven?"

David wrapped both hands around his mug. "I wish I knew."

"A strange answer."

His throat felt suddenly dry. He drew deeply from the ale. "You'd think I'm crazy. I do."

Her lips curled with just a hint of a smile. "Then, the telling should relieve the monotony of the afternoon."

David's chest tightened as always when he thought of the dream. The vision careened through his head: His lover burning before his eyes--the vow he made to her, unfulfilled. *What had I promised?*

He pushed aside the question. "I've had this recurring dream."

"About Penmorven?"

"No. Some place in medieval Germany. That's the strangest part."

David downed the last of his ale. "The dream haunted me so much, I decided to look for the location. I've had this idea it was somewhere between Bremen and Hamburg. But when the travel agent asked me where I wanted to go, I said, 'Penmorven.'"

David looked out the window, but he was not seeing Moryn Keep. He was remembering the expression in Voy's dark, Cambodian eyes when he told her he was going, but could not tell her why. "I didn't even know such a place existed."

The half smile returned to Patience's lips. "So you picked a destination you'd never heard of and which has no apparent connection to your dream."

"I warned you it was crazy."

"But you came."

"I came. Now that I'm here, I don't know why I'm sticking around." *Why did I tell her?*

He changed the subject. "What brings Patience Ward, also American, to Penmorven?"

"The bonfires. They're rare. Most places have given them up in favor of television and other modern pastimes." Patience sipped the remnants of her tea. "It used to be on Midsummer's Eve, people throughout the country would burn fires on the hills to keep away evil spirits."

"They're not building them on the hills," said David. "These bonfires line the coast."

"Penmorven's evil spirits come from the sea--from the castles off shore." Once more she gazed out the window. "These villagers have been burning their bonfires on the shore for nearly six hundred years."

Beth appeared with a serving tray. "Surely, you're needin' this by now?" She set a fresh mug before David. "More tea?" she asked Patience.

"Please."

As Beth served the tea, David and Patience lapsed into conversation about the ghost of Moryn Keep. "I've heard these tales," said Patience, "but they really don't make a lot of sense. If Brenna caused the fires that destroyed the old aristocracy, why did she die there, too?"

Overhearing, Beth chimed in, "I asked me Harry the same question. I married me way into Penmorven, you know." She placed both hands on her hips. "'Twas Divine Retribution,' says he, 'for the murder of His priest.' You know, the priest disappeared the night of the fires."

David remembered the journal's blank pages.

Momentarily, Beth's expression was solemn. Then she flashed a smile. "Enjoy yourselves. If you're needin' anything else, just ask Harry." Beth took off her apron and shouted to her husband, "I'm goin' out!" She slammed the door behind her. The innkeeper stared, silently.

"Perhaps, we'll see the ghost of Brenna tonight," said David, making conversation.

"I hardly think so."

David smiled. "You don't believe in ghosts?"

"I don't believe in the ghost of Brenna ni Ruairc." Something deep in her eyes danced darkly.

Once more, the image of the blackened corpse erupted into David's consciousness. His fingers tapped nervously on the table. *Dreams and portents. Ghosts and...* "What did they do with witches around here?"

"Witches? They burned, hanged, and drowned a lot of innocent people," she replied. "A real witch would not have been so easily handled."

"A real witch? That sounds as if you believe in them."

"I keep an open mind."

In hushed tones, David told Patience about the priest's journal and his plans to try Brenna as a witch. Patience's eyes widened as he described the book of spells, the talisman, and the servant girl, Mairin.

"That might cast a different light on some of the tales," she said. "But, of course, the priest assumed Mairin didn't know what she was talking about."

Patience leaned closer. "I've heard of Druid legends about a talisman with great power. Long ago it was divided lest the whole make the wearer too formidable. Among its powers is the ability to blind a witch to the true nature of whatever it touches. Such a talisman could conceal such a book."

Melodramatically, David raised his eyebrows. "And when the witch couldn't find the book, she flew into a demon rage, destroying the object of her quest and herself, as well?" His mouth turned up at one corner. "As you suggested, that hardly seems an effective solution."

"If that's what happened," she said.

"The villagers say Brenna's ghost haunts Moryn Keep."

"Whatever haunts Moryn Keep is neither Brenna nor witch." Patience rose. "The witch's spirit walks not the halls of the dead, but within her body, still alive."

"She'd be over six hundred years old."

"At least." Patience turned and ascended the stairs.

David stared after her. *She's crazier than I am.* He sat in silence until the sound of sirens dragged him from his thoughts.

Outside, a commotion arose. He was drawn into the crowd and funneled down the street. Firemen worked furiously. Flames leapt from windows. The thatched roof blazed. Even at a distance, the intense heat reddened the faces of onlookers.

David's cheeks and forehead flushed hot, but a deep cold enveloped him. From within the inferno engulfing Priest's House, came a scream of pain and terror.

Eleanor!

* * *

The tide was out. A narrow strip of rocks connected the remains of Moryn Castle to the mainland. Squarely in front of it, a huge mound of logs stood silent guard. A steep, rocky footpath passed beside the inn and descended to the very spot.

Earlier, the sun had warmed the countryside; but as the orb dipped toward the horizon, the earth cooled. One could barely see the keep for the mist and the darkening sky.

David stood by the window where he and Patience had sat. Eleanor weighed heavily on his mind--a sense of responsibility, unsubstantiated by facts. No one had suggested foul play. Yet, Priest's House had burned right after he told Patience about the existence of the journal.

His imagination was playing tricks. Even if the journal was valuable enough to kill for, why should he connect it to Patience? Surely, the idea was ludicrous. But so was his presence in Penmorven.

Soon, people filled the inn. Some told ghost stories to wide-eyed listeners, but most talked about the death at Priest's House, the rapid spread of the fire, and the enormous extent of the damage. But, the more the drinks were passed around, the more the talk shifted to bawdy jokes and laughter. David found comfort in the racy songs and the clink of the ale mugs. Someone had brought a fiddle, and a group was singing loudly and off key. Suddenly, a man jumped on a chair and shouted, "It's time to light the fires!"

The villagers milled through the door, still in a state of noisy revelry. A few had tabs to settle with the innkeeper. In one corner of the room, a man extended his arms against the wall. Between them, Beth smiled invitingly.

David started to follow the crowd; but Patience appeared at the top of the stairs, transfixing him. She wore boots and a long, black cape that brushed the stairs behind her. Each step revealed a flash of red beneath the cape. Raven tresses cascaded down her back.

He waited.

Flashlights in hand, David and Patience traversed the steep path past cottages draped with garlands of St. John's Wort and marigold to the shore. All along the rocky beaches and on the cliff above, bonfires danced. Some of the braver youth had built fires at the bases of the castles. The flames cast eerie, flickering light upon the stone skeletons.

The largest bonfire burned in front of the peninsula. Villagers were tossing a myriad of items into the flames "to break the witches' power": herbs, a new cut oaken sickle, a broomstick. Wire frames packed with rags and other paraffin-soaked combustibles were attached to long wire ropes. Young people lit these "fireballs" and, in no small feat of dexterity, swung them in blazing arcs around their heads.

Patience marched past the bonfire onto the peninsula. David followed-- confused. "I thought you came for the bonfires."

"I did, but there's something I must fetch."

David felt cold beyond the chill of the misty air.

They walked until Patience stopped and pointed toward a cluster of rocks rising out of the sea. "Raoul died there. He had given the book to Brenna."

Given the book to Brenna? What is she talking about? Frost crystallized along David's nerves. He turned his eyes from the rocks to the castle. Even in the dark, he could discern the glowing shape hovering above the keep. "My God!" he croaked. "Brenna's ghost!"

Patience ignored him. She strode toward the keep and called loudly, "Mairin!"

"Patience, come back!" David charged after her.

Patience paused, cupped her hands, and called again. The specter turned--brightened--then dived rapidly, straight for them.

David gasped, stepped back, and threw up his arms before his face. When he opened his eyes, kneeling in front of Patience was the form of a girl in medieval dress. The wraith spoke. He understood, rather than heard. "Mistress Brenna, ye hath returned at last!"

David's heart strained within his chest, but his blood was ice and would not flow. *Mistress Brenna?*

Patience asked, "Didst thee as thou wast bid, cailin?"

"Aye, Mistress."

"Show me."

The ghost led Patience across the rocks to the narrow opening of a cave, which would be covered when the tide was in. David followed. Patience lowered herself into the treacherous entrance.

David's legs failed him. His right knee shook. He leaned back against a jagged rock and held on. *This can't be real. Patience and Brenna--the same?* Waves crashed. Spray pelted his face. *Patience knew the ghost wasn't Brenna, because Patience is Brenna. She's the witch.*

Patience emerged, carrying a large, ancient text bound with a chain. *She has the book.* David mustered his strength and thrust himself between Patience and the route back. The ghost shrieked. Something inside David sickened. On the shore the revelry stopped. Some of the villagers were pointing. "I can't let you have that book!" he challenged.

"Fool!" Patience shouted. "You think I'm the witch?"

"You're the one who said the witch is still alive."

"Then you should know I can't be she." Patience moved closer. "You watched me die."

Thunder rumbled in the distance. Images from the dream sharpened. Focused. The dream was more than dream. The dream was memory. In that life, he had loved Brenna. It was Brenna lashed to the stake--Brenna, burning.

Patience spoke in third person. "Brenna's mother, Regan, possessed one half the talisman, but half was not powerful enough to destroy d'Argent's evil acquisition. They used the talisman to hide the book. When Elspeth could not find it, she cursed both households and summoned the Hellfire."

Thunder rumbled again. "But Brenna did not die that night. She and two cousins had already left the castle to search for the rest of the talisman. They journeyed deep into the European continent--into the feudal states of medieval Germany. Elspeth's curse followed. One by one, each of the three died by fire--Brenna at a stake near Hamburg."

Patience's eyes narrowed. "*I* burned at that stake. *You* watched."

Guilt raged through David anew--guilt born of his impotence to stop the deed, guilt for living while watching her die. Behind the keep, blinding streaks ruptured the sky. Thunder roared.

"I have come to destroy the book," Patience pronounced. "The witch who seeks it is powerful. Even fire will not harm her. Should this book fall into her hands, there will be no limits to her power. She's killed for it before. She won't hesitate to kill again. Now, get out of my way before Elspeth realizes what's happening."

"Elspeth?"

"The witch--the young slut my grandfather took as bride. Many times she has returned seeking the book--this time as the innkeeper's wife."

"Beth?" He moved aside and Patience passed by. "Beth is a six hundred year old witch?"

"She's the reason you're here. Keep her away while I burn the book." She drew her cape around the volume and started back toward the bonfire.

The ghost hovered nearby.

David followed. "If you couldn't destroy it before, can you now?"

"I hope so."

"You hope so?" He stopped, then hurried to catch up. "You hope so?"

"Tonight is Midsummer's Eve. Special powers abound this night. I must try!"

Panic had spread among the villagers around the bonfire. Some had run away. As David and Patience approached with the ghost hovering near them, the fireball swingers began to fling their blazing orbs in their direction. David and Patience hastened out of the target area. The ghost retreated.

"The ghost spoke to you!" shouted one of the villagers. "What did she say?"

Patience ignored him. "Hurry!" she said to David. "Make certain she doesn't come down."

Confused, David raced to the inn. Unsure of what he should do, he took a moment to catch his breath; then, he walked to the door leading to the innkeeper's quarters, knocked, and lamely asked, "Is anyone here? I thought I'd have some ale."

He heard the innkeeper's voice through the door. "Go sit down. I'll be right there."

"I haven't seen your wife. Is she...?"

Before David could finish the question, the door flew off its hinges, barely missing him, and crashed loudly against the opposite wall. Beth stood in the center of a pentagram framed with black candles. The candlelight dancing across her face evoked memory. He had seen that smirking face in flickering light before--among the crowd around the stake.

David's doubts vanished. He stared at the splintered wood of the door jam. "I simply asked for some ale."

"You came to keep me from the bonfire!" Beth's eyes blazed. "Thanks for the warning, Love. I had not intended to go." She started for the door.

"No!" David threw both arms around her. He prided himself on his strength, but she flung him against the wall without effort. He slid to the floor as she rushed from the room.

Gasping for breath, David struggled to his feet.

"Don't be a fool!" Beads of perspiration covered the innkeeper's face. "You can't stop her! You'll die!"

David pushed through the door and stumbled after Beth. Well ahead of him, she stormed down the path toward the great fire, where a number of the villagers still gathered. David saw Patience edge closer to the blaze. Her scarlet dress peeked from under her cape. She stood erect, cradling the book. David's dismay multiplied. *Why hasn't she thrown it in the fire?*

Beth shouted, "You're a fool, Brenna! The book is mine!" She flung out her arm forcefully, her fingers pointing directly at Patience. In rapid motion, Patience made an arc with one hand, as if fending off something and casting it abruptly aside. In the direction her fingers stopped, a large rock split noisily open.

Gasps and screams issued from the villagers. They scattered. Only then did Patience heave the massive tome to the top of the great, fiery pile.

Beth and Patience now stood face to face, almost nose to nose. They circled each other until they reversed positions. "Meddlesome brat!" Beth shouted at Patience, who appeared the older. "At last, the book is mine! Did you really think you could just burn it?"

"Then, fetch what is yours, witch, and be damned!"

By the time David reached Patience's side, Beth had made an about face and climbed into the blaze to retrieve the book. Her clothing burst into flames, but her flesh remained unharmed. Triumphant, clothed in fire, Beth bent toward the book.

Whispering in an unfamiliar tongue, Patience removed her cape and tossed it into the fire. "*Bren, hexe!*" she added. The cape ignited, enveloping Beth in an eerie, blue flame. Beth screamed.

"Get back!" Patience shouted to David. She grabbed his hand. They ran for the path.

The bonfire exploded. Giant, superheated flames, stretched toward the heavens. One last, piercing shriek echoed along the shore, then--silence--except for the sounds of the sea and the tiny impacts of droplets as rain began to fall. Only embers remained of the bonfire, and nothing of Beth or the book.

The innkeeper came out of hiding and inched closer to David and Patience. "Is she...?"

"Dead?" answered Patience. "Yes. At last."

The innkeeper fell to his knees. With tears in his eyes, he brought his hands together as if to pray. "Thanks be to God!" He wrapped both arms around Patience's legs and cried like a baby. Patience absently stroked the sobbing innkeeper's coarse hair.

"I don't understand." David rubbed his shoulder--only one of many parts of his anatomy that still ached. "She said the book wouldn't burn. You weren't sure."

"Elspeth--Beth--believed what you believed," Patience said to David. "She could read thoughts. That's how she learned of the journal at Priest's House. She probably didn't want the villagers to learn about the book."

In the dark recesses of David's mind, Eleanor screamed. He shuddered.

Once more, Patience slipped into the past. "I feared that as I searched the continent, Elspeth might follow. Too far from the protection of the talisman, she might discern the book's location--if I knew it. That's why I asked Mairin to hide the book." She lowered her eyes. "Poor Mairin did not understand that as long as she was near it, the talisman would protect her."

"Beth believed the book wouldn't burn," repeated David.

"It wouldn't have--not without the complete talisman. A couple of months ago I located the second half. It protected me from recognition, my thoughts from her awareness. I used it to summon you. I could have destroyed the book alone, but I needed your doubts to destroy Elspeth." She paused. "After all, you had promised."

A memory stirred in David's soul. *Fool!* He chastised himself. *I promised to help Brenna destroy a witch. Instead, I watched her burn as one.*

Patience continued. "Tonight, I sewed half the talisman into my cape. The other half remained chained around the book as Mairin had left it. With both halves in the flames, the book burned--and Elspeth with it. Her own curse aided the talisman. She cursed our household to die by fire. The final victim of that curse was Elspeth, herself--the last bride of Moryn Castle."

Two of the village men cautiously approached and led the innkeeper away. The rain had stopped. The meager remains of the bonfire smoldered.

"Tonight, we vanquished a powerful and evil creature," said Patience, "but it's not finished. I have yet a service to perform."

She returned to the peninsula with David behind her. Intermittent waves lapped at their feet. The tide was coming in. As they neared the fortress, Patience again cupped her hands and called, "Mairin!"

The girl materialized beside them. "Ye have done it, Mistress! The witch is dead! Now we can live without fear!"

Patience stood very close to Mairin--almost touching. She spoke quietly, as if to a child. "Remember the night I gave thee the book?"

"Aye."

"What didst thou?"

"I hid the book as ye bade me."

"And then?"

"I was afeared. I went to the priest, but he would not help me. I heard Mistress Elspeth coming. What if she knew my thoughts?" Her ghostly eyes widened. "I climbed to the top o' the tower. I... I..." She moaned. "Oh, Sweet Savior! I jumped! I am damned!" Mairin wailed mournfully.

"Nay, cailin," Patience hushed the spirit. "What thou didst, thou didst for the sake of others. Look round. Seest thou a light?"

"Aye. A bright and beautiful light--yonder."

"Go to the light, Mairin. Thou hast served well. Be thou released from this place."

The specter faded.

Patience stood quietly for awhile, then turned to leave. With a start, David realized the land had vanished. Between them and the shore swelled an expanse of water.

Patience stepped in. David followed. It was not deep, but the current hit David behind his knees. He stumbled. With a deafening crash, the heavens brightened and released a torrent, drenching them both. Struggling to keep their footing, they managed to reach the shore.

The rain had molded Patience's scarlet dress to her every curve. Long dead emotions awakened within David. He reached out and gently caressed her cheek. For a moment, she placed her hand on his. He leaned forward to taste her lips once more, but she stepped back. "You've kept your promise, David. It's time to go home."

Fighting conflicting emotions, he watched as she picked up a long stick, dropped by one of the revelers. She fished among the dying embers of the bonfire and retrieved two halves of a disk, each attached to a separate chain. She crossed the rocky shore and rinsed them in the sea. Unaffected by the intense heat, ancient markings gleamed.

David gathered his sensibilities. He started for the inn. At home Voy was waiting--warm and loving. He tried to visualize her face; but suddenly, that deep chill gripped him again. Patience's words echoed in his mind: *Long ago, it was divided lest it make the wearer too formidable.*

Shivering, he looked back. Spotlighted in the frenzied dance of the lightning, Patience stood by the lapping waters, her wet dress still clinging to her form. Around her neck hung the talisman--glimmering and whole.

The Pledge

by Bethany Valles

"Like I wanted to hang out with your scrawny, Hollister-covered asses anyway!" I shouted at the door that just slammed in my face. The sound of laughter faded away from the other side, and I knew that Candy, or Bunny, or Muffy, or whoever, was enjoying herself.

I turned and headed for the sidewalk. On either side of me old, stately mansions were crammed next to each other, each one filled to bursting with the daughters of rich men, and fancy Greek letters adorned every doorframe.

I hated this street.

I hated the mansions.

And I really hated Greek.

But I needed to join a sorority.

I kicked a rock because my dear mother wasn't around to abuse. This was all her fault.

* * *

My mother's face as we arrived at my dormitory, Fester Hall, floated through my mind again. It had almost cracked my resolve to attend college halfway across Texas from her. Then she dropped her bombshell.

"Now, Amy dear, don't get mad. But I talked with your father..." she paused, because I groaned loudly at that phrase, which has never precipitated anything good or pleasant. "And he agrees that while we are so proud that you got a full scholarship, we won't pay for your books."

I'm not an ingrate. I know how expensive college textbooks can be, even used. I busted my ass all through high school to maintain my valedictorian status so I could earn a full ride to college so my parents wouldn't have to pay. I spent two years studying for the SAT, and earned a

1590 as a result. And they wouldn't pay for textbooks. I felt my jaw tighten, and couldn't do a thing to stop it.

"Now, don't set your jaw at me! It's for your own good!"

Right. "Can I ask why?" I replied, in a very reasonable tone, I thought.

"I'm glad you did," she smirked. This couldn't be good. "We won't pay for your textbooks, *unless*, you join a sorority."

I was right, it wasn't good. I've always hated the idea of a sorority. Paying dues to a group so that you can call the other members friends has always sounded pathetic to me. I'd never needed anyone before. Why should I start in college, when I've legally earned my independence? And any "friend" I've ever had only wanted to use me. From third grade, when Sherri next door hung out with me as long as she could use our trampoline, to ninth grade when two girls wanted to partner with me for a science project and made me do all the work.

But a sorority, a whole group of girls waiting to use my talents for their benefit? No. My work, my talent, and my effort are mine alone. The only mental image I could muster of sorority girls looked like something from *Legally Blonde*. My stomach clenched at the thought of sitting around in pastel cardigans, (I shuddered and pulled my black, skull-patterned hoodie tight around my shoulders,) discussing mundane things like who should organize the next near-topless carwash. It almost had me in tears.

Or it would have, if I ever let myself cry.

Mom stayed with me the rest of the day and I waited for the subject to be brought up again, but I knew she was buying time before attacking. It was one of her favorite tactics. I knew a false sense of security when I felt one. I marshaled arguments while she prattled on about buying university merchandise to decorate my corner of the dorm room and reminiscences of her own college days.

I decided, while perusing the university bookstore, my best shot would be to remind her that I'm a serious student who needs to study, and that my new part-time job at the library could either cover books or food, but not both.

Sure enough, she opened the subject again as we strolled past the Commons, an area set aside for either student demonstrations, funds drives, and most ominously, pastel-clad blondes standing behind card tables decorated with glittery Greek characters on bright neon poster board.

"So, what do you say?" Mom asked, with an unusual gentle quality to her tone. I took a deep breath, about to recite my case. She interrupted me. "I know you're a serious student, honey. I also know that your part-time gig at the library won't be enough to pay for books. I know you've worked hard in high school to make sure you father and I weren't burdened by your tuition, which was so very thoughtful it hurts me to blackmail you this way."

I stopped walking and stared at her, shocked at her admission to blackmail. She stopped with me, looking around at everything that was now my new life.

"I also know you well enough to be sure that you plan on spending four years locked away in your dorm room, studying and messing around on the internet. It's what you did in high school. I can't bear the thought of you doing that in college, too."

"So this is all about my social life?" There was a note of challenge in my voice I couldn't keep out.

"Of course it is. I couldn't force you to be around other people in high school, but I've found a way now." She started walking again. I followed her, chewing on my tongue to keep from shouting at her in the middle of a crowded area.

We walked back to her parked car and Mom began going through the list of things moms say when leaving their offspring, always adding her own twist to them.

"…and don't be afraid to let your hair down every now and then," she finished as we halted at her driver's side door. I'd been thinking things over, and realized she had me trapped. I had no choice.

"Let me know how it goes!" she yelled through her open window as I waved goodbye. Then she put the car in 'Drive', and was gone.

* * *

So there I was, standing on a street I loathed, with houses I loathed filled with people I loathed, trying to make friends. *Well, at least I can try to make her pay for a shrink when I'm good and traumatized from this later,* I thought, feeling the corners of my mouth stretch into a vindictive smile.

I looked up and down the street, trying to remember which houses had already rejected me and decide which one would reject me next. I knew I was going about this the wrong way. I had a vague idea from the nauseating posters I'd seen that a party was involved. *When Hell froze over,* I thought. Being surrounded by these people and submerged in their music would be more than I could bear. I might stand a chance in a one-on-one situation.

And then it hit me: I was surrounded by people who hated everything about me, from the punk tracks on my iPod to my faded black tee shirt and inky black hair. They hated me as much as I hated them. Their institution was formed for the express purpose of excluding those like me.

This was pointless.

Without books I might as well drop out before I even had a chance to start. Mom would have to help me move out. If justice is done, she'll seriously hurt her back in the process. I sat on the curb, surrounded by the embodiment of everything I hated, and fought back tears.

Several deep, calming breaths later I stood up, brushing my behind off. I would not be run out of college by a bunch of rich, pseudo-ambitious, soon-to-be methamphetamine   addicts. To my left were the houses I'd already tried, to my right, infinite opportunity! I turned right and started again. Walking up the sidewalk to the next house I noticed two or three peroxide blondes peeping out of the windows. I stopped at the door, squared my shoulders, and knocked.

No one answered the door. I rang the doorbell with the same result. I yelled, "Hello!" as perkily as I could, and heard amused giggles through the door. I left. The next house on the street actually closed the curtains as I walked up their sidewalk. I turned around and walked back to the street.

I stopped for a moment and wiped my leaking eyes. Across the street from the last house was an empty stretch of property, or at least empty of houses. Nature had reclaimed this abandoned parcel of land. Grass must have grown thick and tall at one point in the past, though now it was yellow. Trees had been left to grow amid their many descendents, creating one giant thicket.

I liked it.

I liked it even more when I thought of how it must irk the people dwelling in the mansions on either side of it. I wanted to explore the woods, but something about the dusky quality of light underneath the trees raised goose bumps on my arms and sent a shiver down my spine.

I approached the stretch of sidewalk in front of the woods and stared into their depths. There was a sense of wildness about it, an untouched quality suggested by the age of the trees. And when I looked more closely there was no evidence of a drive ever leading into it. The university grew around this plot of land without ever swallowing it. Now I held a deep respect for this stretch of untouched nature.

And I shuddered. What could possibly be on this land that a large public university and its economy have never claimed it? I might like and respect it, but didn't want to venture in. I stood there, staring at insects fluttering in the golden light coming through the canopy of leaves.

Then I saw something staring back.

An indistinct figure seemed to be peeking out at me from the shadow of a particularly large Spanish oak. I thought I imagined it at first, and then I saw the shape again, walking further into the gloom of the woods. There was another shape moving with it, a dog.

I blinked, and both were gone.

I made the decision without thinking about it. I followed. Surely whatever I encountered in this seemingly sacred place would be better than the public humiliation I've endured so far. I stepped away from the safety of the sidewalk and sunshine and into the shade of the first trees. I looked all around to give my eyes a second to adjust to the new light and spotted what looked like a narrow deer track. Any path was welcome, and I followed it.

The path was mostly straight, never changing direction unless to avoid a tree or particularly dense section of brush. The goose bumps came back in force, my hands balled into fists. Though there was no obvious threat, I tensed for a fight. The deer track itself unsettled me; it was unnaturally straight for a path made by wild animals.

So if it wasn't a deer path, whose path was it?

I was about to turn back, or run like hell, when I saw the shadowy figure again. This time two dogs accompanied it. It was too dim under the trees to see features, but I could tell the figure was a girl and I knew she was looking at me. She turned and continued on, her dogs following her.

I hastened to catch up now that I knew what I was dealing with. Maybe she walked her dogs here frequently and knew the area. She could tell me why this land remained untouched in the middle of a city. I glanced at my watch to see how long I had until the bus ran again.

I'd been chasing shadows for almost thirty minutes. How was that possible? Shouldn't I have seen a neighboring fence by now? How big was this place? I knew these questions were all very important and deserving of thought, but I pushed them aside and focused on finding the girl again. A glint of bright red, low to the ground and somehow shiny, caught my eye. I hurried to investigate and retreated several paces when I reached a crevasse, or gorge, easily forty feet deep. I stepped forward again more carefully and peered over the edge.

The red I'd seen was the girl's ponytail. I held an immediate respect for anyone who dyed their hair a primary color, and her particular shade could be found in a box of crayons. She moved quickly, almost skipping down the side of the gorge, with one dog leading and another following.

"Hey!" I called, tired of playing hide-and-seek. She paused and her head snapped toward the sound of my voice. She eyed me for a moment, which gave me an opportunity to evaluate her, too. She wore some kind of dark patterned tights, a dark skirt, and a red tee shirt that matched her hair perfectly.

I still couldn't determine features, so I didn't understand her at first when she replied. "If you can follow, you can join."

"What?" That made no sense, so I must have misheard her. She took off, skipping again, faster than before. Her bizarre behavior only piqued my curiosity. I swallowed my squeamishness over the height and followed.

The way was easier than I expected. A sort of path wound down toward the bottom, where either a large creek or a small river ran. The way wasn't smooth, and soon I was leaping instead of jogging. I had to move quickly to catch up, but I noticed the distance between us shortening. Soon I was within fifty yards of her. I almost hailed her again, but I figured she wouldn't talk to me unless I could catch up to her. That must have been what she meant earlier.

I closed the distance to about twenty yards when the path leveled out. More confident now, I jogged to catch up to her and the dogs. Instead of heading to the creek like I expected, she turned sharply into the densest thicket I'd seen yet. There seemed to be no break in the overlapping branches, yet she moved into them like they were only curtains.

I paused to assess the situation.

I'd followed a complete stranger down into a gorge. I'd never seen anything like this in the brochures about the university, or even the city. I was supposed to be finding a sorority to hate, and I was wasting time. Most importantly, I had no idea how to get out again. My only hope of escaping this place and getting back to the sanity of my dorm room was the redhead who just mysteriously melted into the brush.

Nice.

I turned away from the undergrowth. The creek was pretty, shallow with a rocky bed, and the gurgling noise was peaceful. I heard nothing but the creek and the birds and bugs. All the sounds of the city couldn't reach this pristine picture of Texas wilderness.

A rustling made me turn around. There in the brush, just where the girl disappeared, was another dog. Only closer I saw it wasn't a dog at all. It was dog-like, but wilder. The word "wolf" popped unbidden into my head, but there are no wolves in Texas. Coyotes, sure, but not wolves, and this definitely wasn't a coyote.

I was petrified. The animal gazed at me with unmistakable curiosity, and I stared right back, too terrified to take my eyes off it. It made a huffing noise through its nose and turned around. I let the air out of my lungs, unsure when I started holding my breath in the first place. It looked back at me over its shoulder, then turned to face forward again. I thought it was debating whether or not to eat me..

It looked at me again, and I knew I was dead. My muscles locked down, and I felt adrenaline course through my system, urging my stiff body into flight. It didn't work. The wolf stared, sniffed, then rolled its eyes.

Wait…what?The wolf turned again, facing into the woods. Again it glanced at me over its shoulder, and this time it jerked its head toward the woods.

It was an invitation.

A nervous, high-pitched giggle broke through my lips, and I smiled despite the situation. Nervous breakdowns in college weren't unheard of, but didn't they usually come after classes actually start? Then I thought, *why the hell not?*

"Sure," I said out loud, surprising myself. I sounded calmly amused. I must be nuts. "Lead on, Lassie."

The wolf growled, but led the way. I followed. Where I thought the girl had disappeared turned out to be nothing more than a trick of the light. The branches crossed, closely packed, but not all the way to the ground. I had to crouch, but I made it. The wolf kept to my slow pace and stayed about four feet in front. I could see only about a foot in front of me, so when the dense brush ended I was caught by surprise. The wolf waited in a clearing for me. And in the middle of the clearing was a house.

It didn't look anything like the mansions surrounding this area of town, but then again, it didn't feel like I was in town anymore. It reminded me of a quaint farmhouse, badly in need of a paint job. At one point it might have been yellow. It had three stories and a deep wrap-around porch. There were wolves everywhere.

Naturally, the animals got my attention first. This wolf must have lured me in to be dinner for the rest of the pack. Kudos for strategy. Then I noticed the girls. College-age girls were peeking through the windows at me. Not the way the sorority bimbos had earlier, these girls just looked curious, and some looked excited.

I turned on the spot, taking it all in. The wolves were mostly the color of the dried grass, tawny to light brown. The girls were as different as girls can be. My cursory examination revealed Goths, a few punks, and a nerd or two, but most were plain ordinary.

I turned to find the wolf I followed in, but the girl with the unnaturally cool red hair was suddenly right in front of me.

"I knew you'd find us!" she squealed, obviously delighted. It was more natural for me to scowl at such enthusiasm, but I couldn't help returning her smile. She was just so happy to see me.

I don't get that a lot.

As I smiled at the red haired girl, my face getting red from being stared at, someone else strode forward from the old house. She looked older than the other girls, and held herself with a confidence I could only dream about. She had dark, mahogany hair and equally dark eyes, but all this was secondary to the warm, welcoming smile she wore. She held out her hand to me and I responded automatically, holding out my own.

"Hi, I'm Anne. What's your name?" She gripped my hand firmly.

"I'm Amy," I replied shyly, still shaking her hand. "I hope I'm not intruding, I just wanted to see the woods, and I followed her," I nodded my head to the red haired girl who was still beaming at me, "and then I lost her..." My voice died as I considered the wolves around us. While my attention was diverted, they had moved to form a loose circle around us. The girls from the house were standing behind them. It almost looked formal. Anne no longer shook my hand, but she kept hold of it.

I got a little panicky. "What is this place?" I whispered to her.

"This is place is the *Gren*, and we are the *Vargynja*." Still holding my hand, she began to lead me around the circle of girls and wolves.

"And are y'all way out here to keep away from people who might not want wolves kept as pets?" I asked, in what I hoped was a very non-judgmental way. I knew some people in Texas were wild about keeping exotic animals. A story in the news a few years ago popped into my head: a man who made a lot of money developing software decided he wanted a pet tiger. It was going well until the tiger eviscerated his wife. Better not bring that up.

"No, the wolves are not our pets," Anne answered in a very definite voice. "They are our sisters."

Okay, I'd wandered into some sort of commune, or pagan cult. I felt my muscles tense, my body deciding before my mind that flight was a good option at the moment. Unfortunately, Anne noticed, too. "Let me explain. Let me show you." She stopped our stroll around the ring and I felt her grip on my hand tighten.

Suddenly I knew I really, really didn't want to be there anymore. I would rather beg entrance to the mansions back in the real world. I began forming an escape route in my head, seeking a weak spot in the ring. There wasn't one.

"Daviah?" Anne said, apparently talking to a dusky grey wolf. A vision of me being forced to go hug the wolf, and then eaten by the wolf, plowed its way to the fore of my mind. My breaths got shallower as images of this wolf pulling me to pieces began to play in my head. The wolf named Daviah trotted toward me. Anne's grip on my hand was almost painful.

"Please don't eat me," I whispered to the wolf. Daviah cocked her head. I closed my eyes. I didn't want to see it happen. I felt my breath creeping toward hyperventilation but there didn't seem to be anything to do about it.

Then I felt hands grip my shoulders. I opened my eyes.

A naked girl was standing in front of me, a look of deep concern on her face. "Anne, is she okay? She's not breathing right, and she's gone all pale. She's sweating, too."

"Amy, it's okay. I know, it's a bit of a shock. But you're safe here, I promise."

None of this made any sense. I wasn't dead. I wasn't even bleeding. Though the naked girl was right, I was sweating a lot. I felt clammy.

"This is just cruel," I heard another girl say. I looked to find her, to see what why she objected, when something more startling caught my attention. There were no more wolves. Instead, there were clothed girls, and naked girls.

"She needs to sit down. Let's take her inside," someone else said.

Now two sets of hands supported me as I was led to the house. My head was full of cotton, and my mind rang well above the situation. I knew I should be concerned with the presence of naked women, and the sudden disappearance of the wolves, but I couldn't make myself care. I protected myself with apathy.

They, Anne and the first naked girl, led me into a sort of parlor. Squashy armchairs, overstuffed sofas, and little tables filled the room, all comfortably arranged for small conversations. They took me to one of the sofas and set me down gently. Someone pressed a glass of water into my hands and I immediately drained the whole glass. For the first time I felt the dozens of pairs of eyes that must have been watching me since the naked girls appeared.

"What is a gren?" I asked. There were lots of questions floating around in my head at that moment, but this is the first one that came out of my mouth.

"The *Gren* means 'den'," Anne said.

"And varg-whatever? What does that mean?"

"*Vargynja*, it means 'she-wolf'."

"That's old Norse, right?" I asked, because I wanted time to think about everything that just clicked into place in my head.

"Yes, very good!" Anne said, delighted. I felt rather than saw the tension leave the room. Apparently, everyone really was just concerned over my well-being. That was…sweet.

"So, what you're saying… everyone here is…a…." I couldn't frame the question. It was so stupid.

"A she-wolf. We really don't like the term 'werewolf', though I guess that's accurate too." Anne's words had a practiced tone about them. This was not her first time to go through this. "We all attend the university, but we live here together."

"Of course." I leaned over and rested my forehead on my knees. It seemed a good enough position to assume for a mental breakdown. "All I wanted to do today was join a sorority so my parents would agree to pay for textbooks." I said to my knees. "And instead I end up chasing a *vargynja* through the woods to her *gren*." My head shook as I spoke, and I knew they didn't understand what I was moaning about, but really, could I have gotten more sidetracked today?

"You don't seem like the sorority type," the Crayola redhead said.

"I'm not. I'm the outcast type, but my parents want me to be socialized." Why was I spilling my troubles to people who obviously had their own issues to deal with?

Anne leaned back and looked at me like I was a pair of shoes she couldn't make up her mind about. When I was about to get uncomfortable with the weight of her stare she stood up and turned to her, uh, pack.

"She's in," Anne said. Then she turned and smiled at me. I blinked, and instead of a smiling Anne, there was a wolf with a dense, rusty coat standing on a pair of jeans and a tee shirt.

She bit me.

It wasn't a lunging and snarling affair, but the shock was immediate. The urge to scream was overpowering as Anne locked her jaws around my calf and held me. I felt the pressure in her bite building and realized she hadn't yet broken the skin. Two girls were holding me still for the procedure.

"It's okay," said a familiar voice, and I saw that one of them was the vibrant redhead. "Anne's the best. She knows what she's doing. Oh, I'm Victoria, by the way."

I wanted to respond to Victoria, but I was biting my own lip to avoid yelling and to keep from thrashing. Victoria noticed the lip-biting.

"You're doing very well. Sheila and I are just going to keep hold of you in case it gets too hard to be still. We don't want you to hurt yourself, or Anne," Victoria said. I tried to feel good about this, but Anne's long teeth had just broken through. I felt a moment's pain, and then the pressure on my leg left.

"Flu shot," I said. It was the only thing I could compare it to.

Victoria laughed. "Something like that, yeah." She and her companion, Daviah again, released me. I had been rigid in my seat with the effort of holding still, but now I relaxed into the back of my chair. I felt flushed, like a fever I didn't know I had just broke.

"She needs to drink some more water," Anne said, pulling on her pants.

Someone said they'd get more water, and I heard footsteps receding. The crowd around my chair was silent, except for a giggling Victoria. Three of the others glared at her. "I'm sorry," said Victoria. "I shouldn't laugh. But you looked so shocked! Did I look like that?" she asked around.

"Everyone looks like that," Anne's calm voice said from somewhere behind me. "Except you, Vic, were hyperventilating for the whole experience."

I felt the need to defend myself. "To be fair, I had no idea you were going to bite me. Or make me into one of you. That's what's happened, isn't it?" I may have sounded accusatory, but I felt I had the right.

"You followed us here. No one could do that and not want to join. Right, Anne?" Victoria sounded unsure.

"You can't know about us, and not be one of us," Anne answered, "That's not how it works. And, your ability to go into danger when all your senses are screaming at you to go back means you are predisposed to be *vargynja*."

"Predisposed? *Predisposed?* I was bored! I was angry! I didn't want to be on Greek Street anymore! That makes me predisposed?" I meant to make a point, not shout. But I was really not feeling like myself anymore. I felt like I was folding in on myself, like wadding a tissue up before you throw it away.

I was scared. My body wanted to do something I didn't want it to do. I didn't know what would happen if I let it. Nothing happened to me without my express consent. I'd planned my own school wardrobes since kindergarten. I'd made my own lunch since second grade because I didn't like the way Mom cut my sandwich. I'd always done things myself because I couldn't trust anyone else to get it right. And now my body was yearning to be something I had never planned for it to be. I couldn't trust my own body.

I whimpered.

"It's starting," I heard someone whisper.

"We'll talk about it later, Amy." Anne said, patting my forehead. "Vic, you help her."

"Okay. I'll be with you, Amy. It'll be okay."

I felt a deep spasm. A muscle I had yet to learn about contracted deep within me, and it squeezed tighter and tighter until I was on the floor. I was in a full-body Charlie horse. I couldn't scream. The muscle pulled my diaphragm and vocal cords with it. My breaths became pants. My knees were in my eyes.

"Let it happen, Amy. It's okay. You're fine," someone reassured me.

But I couldn't let anything happen. I felt the need to yield, but I couldn't. I wouldn't. What would happen if I didn't fight it? I hadn't planned for any of this.

Suddenly Anne's wise eyes were all I could see. She was kneeling over me, forcing my attention upon her. "I know, Amy. It's scary. You didn't tell your body to do this, and it's doing it anyway. But I promise you you're safe. We're here now, and we'll always be here." Her eyes, I noticed, were gray and very moist. "You must trust us, Amy."

I shook my head. How can I trust these strangers? They lured me here and bit me! I was in charge of me, no one else.

I came to this point the same moment the unknown muscle tried to relax. But I was wise to it now. I wouldn't let it. I kept myself in the unnaturally curled position the muscle left me in.

Misplaced trust in my mother put me on the same street as these accursed woods.

Misplaced trust in these girls brought me into their home.

Misplaced trust in Anne specifically had gotten me curled in a fetal position on the floor in agony.

I would not trust this.

"Amy, we will be your family. We will support you. We will always be here to help you. In us, you have found people who will be in your life until your death." I shifted my eyes to the speaker. It was Victoria. "None of us had anyone stable in our life, Amy. I was shifted through so many foster homes I lost count. A lot of us were," Victoria cast her eyes around looking for people to corroborate her story. I saw heads nod all around.

My new muscle flexed again, this time my knees jerked violently, smashing into my eyes. Again, I understood I should yield to it and let it have its way. I wanted to. I wouldn't let it.

Tension filled the room. I shut my eyes tight and listened to the stillness around me.

"Amy, you must let it come," Anne, this time.

"What will happen to her if she doesn't?" I heard an unknown voice ask.

"I don't know, I've never seen this before," another answered.

"I haven't witnessed it, but there were stories. None of them end well." Anne's bleak tone supplied more information than her words. "Her body wants the change, but her mind is rejecting it. She can continue on like this for days, until she's too tired from lack of food and water that she dies."

"But no one's ever died, right?" Victoria's voice.

"Of course they've died. Just not anyone in the past century," Anne sounded hopeless. If I could've spoken, I would have sounded pretty hopeless, too.

So I can choose to let my body do something beyond my control or reason, or I could die trying to prevent it. I tried to put the rigidity of my body out of my mind, so I could think rationally.

Make a pro and con list, my rational mind reminded me. I've used this trick for decision making since I was at least four years old. I used it last when choosing which university to attend.

Pros first, I thought. Well, I would satisfy my mother's requirement of social activity, so I would have books for my classes. If I got lost, I'd have people to call for directions, or maybe even a ride. I've never been able to do that before. But then, I've always committed maps and directions to memory so I wouldn't be lost.

Okay, so I have one pro, and one non-issue. Now cons.

Well, I'd be a dog. *For how long?* My mind kept asking. That's the real issue here. How long would this last? Could I ever control it? I have to control it.

"…remember screaming," someone was saying while I gathered my thoughts. I paid attention.

"I do, too. And I know Vic screamed," someone else added.

"Everyone screams. Everyone except Amy, here," Victoria said. I wondered why they sounded worried that I wasn't loud.

"I think," Anne said, "it all has to do with control." Wow, ten points to Anne. "Look at her clothes. She's a punk. But check out her nails, her skin, her hair. Punks never look this healthy. Her skin is clear with no makeup. She takes care of herself way more than any punk I've ever met.

"So she likes the punk look, but not the punk attitude," someone else said.

I was so tired of being talked about. But I only knew one way to stop them talking about me: to let this happen. To Change.

I took a deep breath.

The next muscle spasm came, sharp and insistent, and I relaxed.

The sensation was complex. Simultaneously, I was being balled up and stretched out. Imploding and exploding at the same time. And then it was over.

I shuddered, and then opened my eyes.

Things looked…wrong. There was no color, and yet everything was almost blindingly clear. I could smell the dust in the carpet, the polish on a girl's toes, the rubber of cheap flip flops, an oak tree…

I don't know how, but I could tell I smelled oak trees. The grass and weeds had a different smell. And I could tell them all apart. Not to mention the rich smell of the earth, sunshine, and the creek… I couldn't even describe the smell of the creek.

What did I just do? I leaned to put my head in my hands, but smacked my head on the floor instead. Oh, right. Dog arms don't bend that way.

I shuddered again, and an imploding-exploding feeling came with it. I didn't fight it; I just closed my eyes and waited for the feeling to stop.

When I opened my eyes everything was back to normal.

"Wow, that was really fast," Victoria said.

"Very impressive," Daviah added, smiling.

"It all comes down to control," Anne said.

"Now what?" I asked. I felt odd, but not bad. I felt…used. And now I had no choice in the matter. I had to hang out with these girls, and probably do their term papers too. And to top it off, now I was naked in front of strangers. I gathered my clothes and began dressing myself.

"Now dinner!" someone said, and soft chuckling filtered through the crowd.

"Yeah, I think it's time to eat. Amy? How about you, can you eat?" Anne asked. I hadn't thought about it before, but now I was starving.

"Sure," I answered. "I'm angry, used, tricked, and hungry. In that order. The least y'all can do is feed me before I start on your term papers." I'm sure that didn't make much sense to them on the surface, but they got the point.

"Whoa…" Victoria started, but I didn't let her finish.

"That's all anyone's ever wanted from me. Do this, Amy, and I'll be nice to you. Let me use this, borrow this, give me this, and I'll be your friend," I could tell I was on the verge of screeching, but I just didn't care. "I wasn't going to let that happen to me again! I was going to be independent! No one to owe anything to, or to let me down when I needed something! I had a plan!"

This time when I put my head in my hands, it worked. "I am the stable one. I've always been the stable one, Victoria. I wanted to be the stable one on my terms, for once. 'No mandatory group projects in college', that's the one thought that made me the happiest about coming here. You've stolen that from me." I was sobbing now, and I didn't care that my nose was running, or that I was hiccupping while I talked, or that they probably don't even know what I'm talking about. I just wanted them to know I was upset.

Not that it would matter. It never had before. I still did the homework, loaned out the notes, bought the lunch for the kid who spent all his money for the week on chips by Tuesday, and never so much as a thank you in response. Never mind returning the favor.

I felt calmer. I'd shouted myself out, I guess.

"My point," I said, and noticed for the first time that I could hear a pin drop, "is that I had plans. I was going to finish school in four years, work for a graphic design firm for three years, and then start my own company. Now I have to rethink all of it." My voice trickled to a stop. I didn't think I had any energy left to make them understand how badly they'd messed up my life.

"Amy," Anne began, a peculiar tone I couldn't identify in her voice, "do you think that we made you a *vargynja* because we thought you'd be a good asset for us?" I still couldn't decide what her tone meant.

"Sure. That's all I've ever been, and apparently all I'll ever be." Even to me, I sounded sad. The silence stretched uncomfortably.

Anne finally broke it. "We made you one of us because Victoria could tell you were like us already. We can sense when a new *vargynja* is near. We made you one of us because you were already like us: hard-working, practical, and let down by the world. We all are. In your case, it sounds like you've been taken advantage of too many times to count. So have we, in different ways. But you're smart, Amy. What does a 'pack' mean in nature?"

I thought about it. "A pack ensures survival of the familial group through nurturing young and protection through numbers." Geez, I sounded like an encyclopedia.

"Exactly, we nurture each other, we protect each other. And we certainly do not use each other." Anne sounded fierce, and fiercely maternal. "Because you're new to the *gren*, you are like our young. We'll protect you, watch your back, and help you whenever you need it, whether it's with a class, someone bothering you, or just missing home. We're a family, Amy. And if you want to, you can be our sister, too."

Oh, now I had a choice? That sounded so good in my head, I said it out loud. "Now I have a choice?"

"Of course, we won't force our company on you. Every now and again, a girl does decide to be a lone wolf. That's okay, but we're not family. They're outside of our protection."

I thought about that. I was already sort of a lone wolf. I took care of myself. The label didn't sit well with me, though. 'Lone wolf' implied a certain degree of loneliness, of lost-ness. I was tired of feeling lonely.

"What would change?" That question really did need answering before I could consider anything else.

Anne answered gravely, "Nothing has to change. You can still live in your dorm, if you want. Where are you now?"

"Fester."

A collective shudder ran around the room. I squirmed in my chair. I wasn't thrilled about it either. Sharing space with five hundred of my closest friends didn't appeal to me. And the shower situation reminded me of a prison.

"Well, if you really want to stay there, of course, you can. But there are twenty-five rooms here, and only twenty of them are occupied. You could have a room to yourself, if you like. Each room shares a bathroom with its neighbor. It's a very comfortable house." Pride colored Anne's last remark. "We all split cooking detail, and cleaning."

"How would I even get approval to pick up and move, though? I mean,

I was assigned a room, and three roommates. Don't I have to apply for a change, or something?" The logistics kept getting in the way.

Knowing glances and smirks crossed the girls' faces. Victoria answered, "We have a deal with the registrar's office. It's not a problem."

"Wow." Not a brilliant reply, but it fit.

Another wolf trotted noisily through the room, its claws clicking each time a paw touched the wooden floor. It clicked all the way up some stairs to my right and out of my view. All eyes were on the stairs for a minute before pounding feet, definitely only two of them, announced her return.

"Okay, it's all cleared. If she wants, we can move her stuff tonight. Whoa…" she ended as the atmosphere in the room hit her. Her hair was naturally blonde, and she was a bit on the pudgy side compared to the rest of the girls. "What's wrong?"

"Amy is a bit suspicious of our motivations," Anne blushed. "It's completely understandable."

Cool, confident, pretty, fierce Anne actually blushed. And I understood. They weren't taking from me. They were offering to me. This situation was unprecedented.

I cleared my throat and felt, rather than saw, faces turn toward me. I looked around and met their eyes. Each pair held a mix of apprehension or sadness. Already, my feelings mattered enough to them to make them sad. I cleared my throat again. "Okay, so y'all will help me move?"

Anne let out a breath and grinned at me. She surveyed the room. "Girls, is there anyone here who doesn't want to help?"

The room was immediately filled with dashing bodies and whirling hair as they rushed to get ready to move my things for me.

Wow. I have friends.

* * *

The phone rang once before she answered.

"Amy? How was your first day? Did you meet anyone?" she asked in one breath.

"Calm down, Mom. And yes, I did meet some people. I joined a sorority." I waited for the auditory explosion on the other end to stop.

"Oh, you'll have so much fun! How was the Rush? Is that the right term?"

"It was real informal. I had a bite with them," I paused to quiet Victoria, who was hovering over me and giggling at my inside joke. "They're really nice. And I get to live in house with them, instead of Fester."

"Oh, Amy I'm so happy for you, dear. I knew you'd find a group you'd like. Who are they?"

Uh oh. I hadn't planned on what to tell her for this.

She wants to know the name! I mouthed to Victoria. She grabbed a notepad and started scribbling.

"Amy?"

"Yeah, Mom, sorry. Someone was talking to me..." I reached for the paper Victoria pushed to me. "It's not Greek, which is why I like it. It's called... *Vargskinn*," I read from the paper. "It's Old Norse. That's why I went there, the name was so cool."

"Well, you sound so happy..." I could hear my mom's voice getting thick with suppressed emotion, and knew it was time to end this conversation.

"I am happy, Mom. Don't worry about me. I have a whole pack of friends now."

Chemistry Lesson #One - Opposites Attract

by Barbara A. Higgins

I.

On the first day of his senior year in high school, Andrew Fleming pushed open the inside entrance door, slipped, and fell on his keister. In that position, getting up required help.

After that humiliating event, a procession of trust fund troglodytes, Gordon Gekko wannabes, and self-proclaimed assholes either stepped over him or tried to kick him out of the way, in their hurry to avoid tardy slips.

Many of his fellow students had a wisecrack, joke or epithet to unleash as they passed over or around him, but none offered Andrew a helping hand. They all knew him as "that crippled kid" who earned a perfect score on every test or assignment, thereby eliminating the need for grading on a curve. Before long, the halls went silent as Andrew still struggled to right himself.

The warning bell rang its last peal as Stephanie Feldman cautiously climbed the stone steps to the outer doors of her new school. Arriving late on the first day sucked, but couldn't be helped. Her dad was such a putz. He managed to get lost following the simple directions given by their hotel manager. Heaven forbid he should do the same at his new job. Shuddering, she envisioned moving back to Port Chester by the end of the week, without ever realizing the fresh start this transfer offered.

Luck held Stephanie's hand when she pushed the outer door open seconds before the automatic security locks engaged. Now, no one entered without a passcode or by convincing the dragon lady at the main office to buzz them in. Finding the inside right door ajar made no sense to her until the floor spoke.

"Hey, sweetheart, could you do this guy a favor and give me a hand? I've fallen on my good leg, you see, and this brace is hard enough to maneuver when I'm standing."

Stephanie recognized the hint of desperation in his self-mocking comment. She sounded the same when lost and seeking guidance in a crowd of clear-sighted people. "Well, short-stuff, I'll hold out my hand and, if you can reach it, we might get this herd of turtles out of here. I believe the Old Testament contains a parable for our situation, something about the blind leading the lame."

"I wouldn't know, princess. My religion pretty much ignores that part of the Bible."

"Holy crap, you mean I'm holding hands with a mackerel snapper? A hundred years ago my Temple shunned this deviant behavior, and your Diocese offered no less than excommunication."

"Spare me the antique melodrama, lady. This floor is freezing my software."

Blushing, Stephanie pulled on his hand. As floor boy rose to eye level, she gasped in surprise. At one foot away, his features cleared to a lovely, soft haze, as if this whole episode had evolved into a schoolgirl's romantic fantasy.

Pulling herself back to reality, Stephanie teased him, "You know, whoever you are, with that thick crop of dark hair and hazel eyes, all you'd need is a yarmulke to pass for a Jew, or maybe even Hasidim if you glued on a couple of ringlets. Obviously, you're pale enough, but the size of your brain remains a mystery."

Andrew flushed, both from the exertion of standing upright and the jolt of familiarity when their eyes met for the first time. Her gaze affected him like no feel-good drug ever could. Colors brightened, an angel's voice caressed his ears, and the movement of her glossy pink lips mesmerized as she spoke. His blood raced, warming those previously cold places that only felt this hot during a bath. Every square inch of him glowed, like the banked embers of a summer campfire, tamed but ready to ignite with the slightest encouragement.

This short-sighted temptress's last comment finally registered on Andrew's scrambled brain, forcing him to drop her hand and look away. She smiled serenely and, he hoped, remained unaware of her full-frontal assault on all his senses, even the sixth.

He had to know who she was before they separated, so offered an introduction. "Hi, I'm Andrew Kaiser Fleming, the last and probably the least of six siblings, but a shoe-in for valedictorian of the class of 2000 at this institution of privileged education." Again, he extended his hand her way. "And you are . . .?"

Awkwardly reaching for his right hand, Stephanie grasped his forearm instead and shook it so that his fingers brushed back and forth across her right breast. Andrew clamped his jaw shut and closed his eyes to keep from shouting out victory like a Viking warlord.

His beautiful samaritan did the screaming when his right knee gave out from all the excitement. Grabbing him around the waist, she whispered in his ear, "I'm Stephanie Josephine Feldman, your competition for top dog in this pack of back-biting yuppie puppies. So nice to finally meet you, Andrew."

Stephanie marveled at how her father's mistake had put the one boy she'd hoped to meet right into her arms the very first day. She'd studied the school's roster of high honors students and decided Andrew Fleming fit the mental, physical, and emotional profile of her perfect match. That he was gorgeous as well added extra frosting to her already perfect confection. Her whole body quivered and her pulse raced when she imagined discovering the full extent of his vanilla with chocolate icing yumminess.

Dear God, please let him be an inquisitive, adventurous virgin like me, she silently prayed.

Interrupting her reverie with fidgeting and the rattling of his leg and arm brace, Andrew voiced the obvious, "If we don't get to class shortly, they'll mark us absent. I don't know about yours, but my mother will mobilize the National Guard if this school calls to report me missing. Her co-workers have always called her 'the general'. Thus, her child-rearing methods contain a strong military component I prefer to avoid whenever possible."

"A regular Patton in petticoats, is she?"

"No, more like Hitler in high heels." Shocked by Andrew's angry tone, Stephanie changed the subject back to their immediate problem.

"Tell me which way to the elevator, please. I need to get to AP chemistry on the third floor."

"Grab my left arm, Miss Feldman. You're going to be my new lab partner, since everyone else has paired up by now. Follow me to the land of OZ, as we are off to see Mr. Neely, a.k.a. the Wizard."

Stephanie dutifully obeyed Andrew's silly command. Males, after all, needed to demonstrate their control and superiority. *May he never discover what scholastic contortions I've undergone to make our class schedules almost identical,* she thought while assuring herself that really, this was not stalking, just efficiency.

II.

Her chemistry and trigonometry courses challenged Stephanie the most. She understood them, but had a problem studying since those textbooks weren't available in large print. She was legally blind, not totally devoid of sight, so had no knowledge of Braille text.

Four years ago, she'd gone in for a routine eye examination when her near-sighted glasses no longer cleared the distance. Leaving her optometrist's office with a diagnosis of Stargardt's macular dystrophy devastated her entire family. Every descendent of Eastern European Jews worried about tay-sach's affecting their children, but this autosomal recessive disease never crossed her parent's minds.

Stephanie needed a competent study buddy to guide her and check her work for any vision related mistakes. Andrew offered to help her out before she could work up the courage to ask him. Life didn't get any better than this, at least not in high school. A boy she had the hots for didn't give a crud about her defects, just as she considered his cerebral palsy a minor problem. Their disabilities complemented each other. Together they became one whole person.

By the end of chemistry class, Andrew stood in awe of Stephanie's mind as well as her quirky personality and myriad physical attributes. Her legs, light brown hair, and eyelashes went way beyond long. He pictured touching all three of them with suave sophistication rather than his usual seventeen-going-on-twelve-year-old-guy clumsiness. But mostly, her pale amber eyes bewitched him with their sparkle and challenge, even when they laughed at his blatant lack of skills.

Every one of Andrew's siblings had experienced love (and all the chemistry and physics that went with it), but not him. Most girls refused to touch him, in case his condition was contagious as well as just plain creepy. His lower body often danced without the presence of music, so he wore one of his brother-in-law's new MP3 players plugged into his ear and hummed whenever his leg went crazy in public.

Playing spin the bottle at Melissa Beckman's twelfth birthday party marked the only occasion a non-family member had kissed Andrew. He often prayed not to have that remain his only experience with the opposite sex. How could someone so smart in school be such a dummy about girls?

Until Stephanie – she didn't terrify him. She complemented him, like a burger and fries or movies and popcorn.

Contrary to the most prevalent rumors circulating around school, Andrew and Stephanie did not jump each other's bones that first week. A lamentable circumstance, he thought, though absolutely necessary as they both remained deaf, dumb, blind, and crippled when it came to sex. Andrew had to admit, however, that to everyone else they did appear to be a couple living in each other's pockets like furry pet gerbils.

Stephanie thrived in a constant state of euphoria when she and Andrew stuck together wherever they went, like cheese on a pizza. They held on to each other for support as well as for the thrill of it. Subtle displays of affection between them were deemed both appropriate and necessary by the powers that be. You had to love the Americans with Disabilities Act, she concluded just before entering Mr. Neely's chemistry classroom their fourth week of school.

While waiting for Andrew to arrive, Stephanie thought about her transition from a large prep school in western Connecticut to this relatively small private school in north Westchester County, N.Y. Her former campus, being on the National Historic Register, had a harder time accommodating disabled students than this relatively modern facility. Plus, she'd been a much smaller fish in that piranha-filled, golden pond. Here, she stood out, both as a freakishly clever force of nature, and as the girl who made everyone notice that Andrew had a heart, a wicked sense of humor, and needed to be loved as much as the next dude. Together, they'd thrown off their wounded nerd personas and transformed into an A-list power couple.

That should have propelled their star-crossed virgins' story to a satisfying, happily-ever-after conclusion, except when Stephanie finally snapped out of her glowing reverie, she sat alone. Andrew never returned to school that week or made any attempt to contact her. On Friday, the school counselor distributed a memo reporting Andrew Fleming's survival of yet another surgery and encouraging students to send get well wishes to his home in Ossining.

Stephanie choked on her own saliva as the urge to vomit reminded her to swallow and breathe. Her feet fought her head for dominance. They demanded to run all nine miles to Andrew's location. She convinced them their chances for survival would be greater in a cab. After raising her hand for the key to the girl's lavatory, she alerted the teacher of her queasy stomach's volatile mood.

Fifteen minutes later, Stephanie waited in the nurses office for the taxi that would deliver her feet, stomach and aching head to their new house off Scarborough Road in Briarcliff Manor; a mere ten minute run to Noel Drive in Ossining.

III.

Andrew plotted his mother's demise with the cunning and precision of a special-forces operative. He lacked only the necessary heartlessness and brawn to execute this flawless plan. Plus, there existed irrefutable evidence that some female members of his family had come back to haunt the living. Fear of an eternity suffering his mother's revenge made him re-think.

Though pushing Mom down the elevator shaft from their home's fourth story would bolster his wounded ego, he doubted Dad would survive her loss. True love is pleasantly myopic, so Andrew's father rarely noticed his wife's tyrannical obsession with their second son's imperfect body.

Being a twenty-five year medical professional, Olivia Fleming stayed on top of the latest medication or surgery for the treatment of cerebral palsy. Andrew had been an unwilling guinea pig his entire life, but Mom persisted in torturing him. Rarely did her efforts offer the promised relief for his suffering or for her monstrous guilt. She faulted herself for his condition. He blamed the Fleming Family Curse.

Back in 1844, a grief-stricken gypsy woman with "second-sight" and anger management problems, cursed every Fleming male but the seventh son to end up either disabled, crazy, or dead by middle age. Mrs. Fleming refused to even acknowledge the possibility of such powerful mind control.

Andrew believed.

Everyone in the family knew how to break the curse. A daughter of the seventh son only needed to fall in love and marry a male descendant of that gypsy. Then they must produce a male child to replace the innocent grandson she'd lost by the hands of Fleming men.

Andrew's father was the seventh son of a seventh son. His four daughters held special powers prophesied by the gypsy woman, as well as the ability to finally break the curse. When that blessed event occurred, Andrew knew his CP would be history. Until then, nothing his mother tried would improve his condition, or her attitude.

"Mom, I need to get back to school. You put my class standing in jeopardy when you take me out for a week like this."

"Which is more important to you, Andrew, being valedictorian or walking across the stage without assistance to get your diploma?"

"You already know the answer to that, Mom, or you wouldn't be so defensive. I'd prefer having complete control of my own body. You've tinkered with it for the last time."

"Since when does a seventeen year old get to veto his parents' decisions?"

"Just one parent's idea, Mom. Dad fought you on this surgery harder than I did. He and I contacted a lawyer on Tuesday, after yet another risky procedure failed to improve my right leg. I'll be an emancipated minor before you can inflict any more unnecessary pain with your malignant guilt trip."

"How will you ever take care of yourself without help or pay for that private school you love so much, Mister?" His mother got right in his face, her fists on her hips.

"Your not so loving daughter, Claire, bought me a condo in Tarrytown and limo service whenever I need it. I've retained a live-in companion/bodyguard should you accidentally discover my whereabouts and need to be shown the door."

She growled and threw up her hands in dismay. "I should have seen that coming. Claire still refuses to forgive me for trying to derail her wedding two years ago."

"Mom, please, let it go. Your children are too much like you to put up with your crap. I'm the last one to say, 'enough already'. Stop attempting to fix your worst mistake and biggest regret. Blame it on the curse like the rest of us, and let me move on with my life."

"I can't lose you too, baby boy." She caressed his face with her right hand. "What will it take for you to change your mind?"

"At least, Mom, make nice with Dad. He now has six empty bedrooms to choose from, should you continue to piss him off." Andrew turned away and hobbled out of the room to begin packing. The limo driver expected him out front at 6PM. After a relaxing weekend in his new home, he'd return to school and Stephanie on Monday.

The front doorbell chimed, distracting Olivia Fleming from giving her son a sample of the tantrum she wanted to throw in his face. The ungrateful little smartass had way too much brain power, but not nearly the experience required to navigate his medical needs or make decisions about his future. She'd give up control when he could walk away from her without assistance.

The person at the door grew more insistent as Olivia descended the three sets of stairs from the top floor to the foyer. With every step her annoyance level rose until she would happily eviscerate the cretin standing on her porch. With any luck, it would be a pair of those crispy black and white Mormons. She loved scaring the bejesus out of religious zealots.

After opening the door in full combat mode, Olivia froze from shock. The female child in front of her represented an entirely different category of worship from what she'd expected. When, she wondered, had Jews started going door to door?

Stephanie's anxiety level ratcheted higher with every minute that passed while standing on Andrew's front porch. As her left hand twisted the chain on her Star of David, the right tortured the doorbell until it screamed nonstop. How could it take this long for him to answer the door when he had his own elevator? Hopefully, he hadn't fallen on the way there.

Stephanie didn't mean to be such a pest, but Sabbath started in three hours, and for the first time, she was in charge of tonight's sader.

In her mind, love would always trump religion, except when tradition and promises were involved. Two of her unbreakable rules of conduct: 1. Don't ever go back on your word and 2. Never reveal a confidence. Tomorrow she would be at Temple all morning and with family the rest of the day. Stephanie had to see Andrew right now. Her heart refused to wait until next week.

When a towering blonde woman with fiery gray eyes answered the bell with a ferocious look on her face, Stephanie regretted her inability to turn and run. This had to be "The General", Andrew's mother. His maternal hostility made a lot more sense to her now. This was no Mrs. June Cleaver; more like belligerent Bertha Battle-axe or Cruella De Ville sans puppies.

Stephanie winced and rapidly muttered, "Please, Mrs. Fleming, I need to speak with Andrew for a few minutes. May I go up to his room so he doesn't have to come down here?"

"Wait a minute," Mrs. Fleming snapped at her. "Who the hell are you and why can't this wait?"

"Oh, I'm sorry, ma'am. My name is Stephanie. I'm your son's best friend at school, but I haven't heard from him all week. What happened to him?" She struggled to keep her tone polite and submissive.

"He entered the hospital on Monday for a minor surgical procedure, nothing for you to worry about, dear. Perhaps you could return another time. I have a few things to discuss with him myself." Mrs. Fleming's tone gave new depth to the concept of condescension.

Stephanie raised her chin and eyes, stood to her full height of 5'7", and calmly fired her first and only warning shot. "First, I must confer with Andrew right now. We partner on several class assignment that require his input a.s.a.p. Then, I will literally run back home to prepare our family's Sabbath dinner before the sun goes down. I don't have time for a pissing contest with a papist. Either you let me in, or I scream for help until either Andrew or the police come to rescue me from the mad woman harassing a poor blind girl."

Mrs. Fleming sounded amused as she asked, "Do they teach that behavior in your fancy school, or is it inherent in all Jewish American

Princesses?"

"A little of both, of course. Only the ruthless survive prep school and a Jewish momma." Stephanie's next words shot from her mouth with cold precision. "Now let me in so I may determine firsthand whether Andrew survived his mother's love intact."

Mrs. Fleming stepped aside and waved toward the foyer where Andrew stood with his mouth hanging open. She laughed and said, "Go on up, children. Obviously you two deserve each other; and Stephanie… Mazel Tov."

Andrew marched Stephanie back through the kitchen to the elevator before his mother could reverse her decision. No one confronted Olivia Fleming and came away unscathed.

His girlfriend rocked! "Remind me never to wander away from your light side, Ms. Feldman. When you go dark, even an atheist would attempt praying."

"You call that dark? I'd barely worked up to pale gray in an effort to remain polite. I save dark for my own mother."

"Whatever, I'm still impressed. Hearing you give Mom a verbal knuckle sandwich warmed the ventricles of my heart. I may swoon."

"That's nothing, boy. When we get to your room, let me show you the difference between vasovagal syncope and euphoria. Unless you'd rather I use this incredible tongue for talking only."

"Damn, woman, don't tempt me knowing our time is super limited." He tore open the elevator door and dragged them both over to his memory foam mattress.

Stephanie held up her hands for him to wait. "First, you tell me what's going on."

"Fine," he grinned happily. "I'll do all the talking while you do that other thing you mentioned. Deal?"

"No way, buddy, I can't do that and concentrate at the same time. Munching on you makes my ears buzz." Andrew stared at Stephanie without blinking. Sucking in a deep breath, he slowly exhaled to calm his racing heart and boggled mind. Before long, he regained the ability to speak. Albeit, at an elevated pitch and speed.

"Okay, here's what you need to know. I'm moving out on my own tonight, to a condo less than a mile from school. I haven't had time to work out the logistics of how this will impact you, me, and the rest of the school year. I've legalized my freedom from micro-managing mommy dearest and I'm running with it. If you'll help improve my frazzled mood, we can work these things out together."

Stephanie grabbed his head, kissing every inch of his face, until Andrew pushed her back on the pillows and took over. After all, this was his room, his fantasy, and his seven minutes in heaven… finally!

IV.

Andrew spent the first five minute in his new home on his knees, purposely, not accidentally. He got down and prayed his mother would never find this totally rad haven from her incessant meddling.

Claire had furnished the place with all the latest electronics in every room, including built-in speakers for that ultimate surround sound. Andrew shared his older sister's love of music and movies, especially the classics of both cinema and rock-and-roll. You wouldn't call them purists or elitists, however.

Neither of them cared much for black and white films or vinyl records. This was, after all, the age of technology, the eve of the twenty-first century. Also, Claire's business specialized in promoting artistry of most every kind and the latest gadgets available to enhance the experience.

Of course, they forgave *The Wizard of Oz* its colorless segments, which only emphasized their point that color brought more definition and depth to movie watching than shades of gray.

Sitting back on the sofa with his feet up on the coffee table, Andrew reminisced about spending just about every one of his birthdays watching *Scrooge* the musical with either of his two favorite sisters, Claire or Evie. Claire took over when Evie married and joined the Marines with her husband. They had trained for years to become the eyes, ears and lifeline for special-forces teams moving "off book" in enemy territory.

Evie possessed a very unique skill that had been Andrew's own salvation when his pain became unbearable as a child. A few moments in her arms had him forgetting his limitations and the suffering they caused. Her surrogate mothering kept him alive.

Evie's special warmth and love couldn't cure him, however. He'd barely survived her loss until Claire's near fatal accident had the two of them doing both physical and mental therapy together. The mother who gave him life resented all three of them for succeeding where she had failed.

A loud knock on the front door startled Andrew out of his reverie. Then a banging sound followed by fluttering, squealing, and the smell of carnations preceded the sensation of being smothered. Having his face smashed between two tall willowy blondes was like coming home to his childhood.

While Andrew shifted his head so he could breathe, the set of boobs over his right ear spoke. "Hey, Drewster, how's it hanging little bro?" Evie used to call him the Drewster because the hair on his head stood up like a coxcomb when he woke up in the morning. "Hug me back, baby boy, or I'll put sand crabs in your bed tonight. Remember you were always afraid of them crawling out of my duffle and pinching your Willy Wonker."

"Evie, you've obviously been hanging out with Marines way too long. You have all the finesse of a street walker," Claire teased. "This sweet boy has finally dragged his scrawny ass out of the reach of Mom's poisonous tentacles and deserves a little respect. Today he is a man."

"Amen and halleluiah, Andrew, because now is your time to shine." Evie kissed the top of his head and wiped the mist from her eyes.

"Thanks for the group hug, ladies. I'm the luckiest brother in the world, because you two are generously allowing me to pick tonight's movies." They groaned in unison until he whipped out *When Harry Met Sally.*

After one movie, two bowls of popcorn, and three boxes of gummy bears, they all craved a change of venue. Even a classic movie could be a bore if your body refused to sit still that long. Andrew hoped to explore the exercise set-up in his spare bedroom before relaxing in the bathtub later tonight, but worried about offending his sisters if he refused to tag along on their next adventure.

Claire, noticing the spastic twitching of Andrew's right leg, commented. "I just had this place exterminated, so I know you don't have critters in your Calvins, Drew. What do you say we check out the toys in the back bedroom while Evie uncovers that six-seater spa on your patio and whips us up some brandy malts?"

Andrew's eyelids disappeared as he stared raptly out the French doors to his fenced patio. Then, with eyes closed, he started bouncing up and down on the sofa chanting "I have my very own hot tub", until he lost his balance and everyone landed on the floor in a fit of giggles and wheezing.

Another hour passed before the three siblings abandoned the spa and dressed for bed. Claire and Evie would spend the night before driving into Manhattan in the morning. Andrew looked happy but exhausted.

Claire had noted Andrew's feeble, closed eyed attempt at staying awake in the water. No doubt the fear of death by underwater snoring was likely the only reason he remained upright. She debated whether to let him sleep or finally initiate him into the Fabulous Fleming Females shared mind control.

"Andrew, honey, there's something important we need to discuss with you. How would you like to travel with us or wherever you like without any interference from your CP?"

Andrew's eyes popped open. He appeared wide awake now as he explained. "I assume you're talking about what you call floating."

Claire felt her own eyes and mouth open wide this time. "How would you know about floating, little brother?"

Guilt flooded Andrew's conscience, constricting his heart to the breaking point. He couldn't refuse to answer without reinforcing Claire's worst fear. She never wanted her secrets revealed unless she did the telling, and would assume the fact that he knew meant someone she trusted had betrayed her. He decided a total confession of his sins against the sisterhood was his only hope for forgiveness and inclusion in that exclusive society.

"I beg the pardon of the 3-F Sorority for being a nosy baby brother who spied on three of his sisters while one attempted to teach the other two to float. You were making so much noise, I couldn't resist coming downstairs to watch you. I swear I saw nothing that would scar me for life, although Lilith blistered my ears with some language I can't forget."

"So, you already know the mechanics of floating. Does that mean you've tried it?"

"I have."

"Did you succeed?" Claire persisted.

"Well, remember I was only twelve when that happened. My emotional immaturity prevented achieving any kind of launch until about two years ago."

"But why not come to us when you figured it out? Floating is a crapshoot without someone to teach you the shortcuts." Claire took both his hands in hers. "I would have been proud to show you the numerous tricks I've learned over the years."

"Claire, think back to the problems you faced two years ago. I just couldn't add to the chaos in your life back then. You needed help, not me." Andrew watched her expression turn blank for a minute and then resume its compassionate smile. She winked and started shaking her head.

"This day just got so much better. Wait till I catch you up on the tricks you probably haven't discovered."

"I mastered only the basics, Claire. That's enough when you're all alone."

"But you have Stephanie now. That opens up a whole new dimension to the experience."

"She's not part of the curse, so how could she participate?"

"Didn't you know that floating existed even before the curse? Fleming women rocked long before the men screwed up."

V.

Stephanie practically had to pull an all-nighter cleaning up after her first solo sader. Like a meshugener, she'd insisted on doing everything herself. Never - ever - again, at least not with half the extended family in attendance. If being married meant doing this every Friday, she'd find herself a nice reformed Jew after finishing medical school. Or, better yet, a gorgeous lapsed Catholic.

She missed Andrew even more now that they'd finally practiced a little mouth to mouth resuscitation. Without the Sabbath deadline, who knew what liberties she'd have allowed yesterday afternoon? Maybe they were both better off knowing bupkis.

Stephanie's only goal today after one hour of sleep, two hours in Temple, and five hours at Uncle Jacob's, involved many more hours of booming delta wave, deep sleep with lots of REM activity starring Andrew Fleming. Oy vey, that sounded wonderful, she thought as oblivion descended.

Andrew never got to thank Claire and Evie for their extended tutorial in the wee hours of Saturday morning. They'd worn him out and then left him sleeping off the high, without a by your leave.

He may have blushed when the lessons started, but now he understood things he never knew existed. That kind of power was nothing to be shy about. Andrew intended to share this wealth of information with a certain doe-eyed young lady as soon as she fell asleep tonight.

Just to be certain of his welcome this evening, Andrew called Stephanie's house after dark, but she'd already gone to bed. Her mother insisted he not wake her. Hanging up his bedside phone with a silly grin on his face, Andrew pulled the covers over his head and a few minute later, floated over to Scarborough Road.

Stephanie woke briefly, remembering vague, almost nightmarish dreams of Passover, Yom Kippur, gfelte fish, potato latkes, and not a single gentile in sight. Really, did the universe have to subconsciously point out that in fact, she and Andrew shared very little common ground?

Intellectually they meshed perfectly, and they both had type O negative blood. Chemically speaking, people with matching blood types have a stronger sexual attraction to each other. Doesn't that count for something?

Stephanie had to polish her arguments for being with Andrew, once her parents understood they did more than study together. She'd already blown it with his mother. If their two moms ever got together, Stephanie would be at the epicenter of a mini holocaust. That would almost be funny, in a Texas chainsaw bloodbath sort of way.

From the size of her last yawn, Stephanie expected sleep to overtake her momentarily. Instead, she felt an oppressive weight cover her from hair to toenails. Breathing ceased as the pressure on her body became unbearable until... poof!

It disappeared. What the frog was happening to her? Then a small voice in her head said, "Hey, Stephanie, can you hear me?" She sucked in a deep breath, preparing to scream, and the voice grew louder.

"No, babe, don't alert your parents. It's me, Andrew." Hearing that, she hollered even louder than intended and brought both parents running into her room within seconds.

Andrew whispered, "Tell them you just had your worst recurring nightmare about getting a B+ on a pop quiz."

"No, this can't be happening," she whimpered. Her parents assured her it was only a bad dream, and she almost believed them until her head began laughing, and she started to cry.

Andrew now realized he should not have sprung this on Stephanie without warning her. She'd never be a "just roll with it" kind of girl like his sisters. That constituted a large part of his attraction to her personality – she reacted to life in a big way. There were no namby-pamby, whatever responses from her.

Her freaking out he could handle, but this silent sobbing crippled him inside instead of out. Without the ability to touch her, he remained helpless, in spite of his newly found freedom.

Already knowing what the sound of his voice would do to her frayed nerves, Andrew resigned himself to declaring this evening a total washout and prepared to make a silent exit, until he heard Stephanie clearing her throat.

"Andrew, are you still there?"

"Yes. Would you prefer I left you alone, sweetheart?" Crap, now he felt like crying.

"Please, please don't go yet. Hearing you in my head convinced me I'd finally lost what little sanity remained up there. That scared me, not you. I just need to make you understand my reaction had nothing to do with you and everything to do with old insecurities and neuroses. I'm a hot mess, and you stepped in it right up to your eyeballs, or mine, I guess."

"Does that mean I can stay for a while? No doubt you've been too preoccupied to notice how amazing this feels with the two of us together in one body. I can feel you surrounding me like a soft, sexy pillow."

"So far, Andrew, you come across as a mild case of non-kosher indigestion."

"That feeling will go away when I show you some moves I learned recently. Right now you should start using your internal voice to talk, or your parents will come back to investigate."

"Okay, can you hear me now?"

"Like you were right next to me, Stephanie. Are you ready to take our relationship to a level that doesn't even exist in the real world? Let me teach you how to leave your body and its blindness behind. Then we'll only need to think about a place and we're there, instantly."

"Whoa, Superman, explain the hows and the whys before we tackle the wheres and whens. Are you saying you're not just a voice in my head, your whole body rests inside of mine?"

"No, my body can't do that when it's home in bed. The part of me that eats, sleeps, poops, and limps got left behind. The part that thinks, dreams, loves, and questions the universe; that's parked inside you. This is not the *Invasion of the Body Snatchers.*"

"Wow, I had no idea minor surgery could perform such miracles. Can you also part the Red Sea, or do you just walk on water to get to the other side?"

"Funny girl, why would I walk when floating is so much faster?"

"All right, then, Andrew. Let me officially welcome you to my nightmare. Either I'm in dreamland, or I'm several noodles short of a brain stroganoff. Please, don't bother to wake me until Monday morning."

"That went well... not." Andrew whispered to his sleeping host. He'd so hoped to show her what a half-gainer or a jackknife felt like. Or, vicariously enjoy a steaming hunk of bread pudding as she consumed each bite.

Andrew released a frustrated groan as Stephanie dreamed of them exploring each other. Time for him to head back and re-think his approach to sharing this amazing activity with her. He would need a solid, scientific explanation to sooth her insecurities; one a lot less scary than a 155 year old curse.

Stephanie used the upset stomach excuse to spend all day Sunday in bed. Both her mental and physical exhaustion had sunk bone-deep. Now nothing registered but the pain of knowing she'd rejected Andrew as if he meant little more to her than a head full of white noise. She'd happily hit rewind or re-do buttons to start this weekend over again.

Funny girl? Not anymore. When would she learn to keep her smart mouth zipped shut? What really frightened Stephanie more than her surreal possession by Andrew, amounted to the fact that in their dynamic duo, she appeared to be the normal person. How warped was that concept?

Monday morning, 8:00AM crept up on her while Stephanie rehashed the past thirty-six hours in her mind. She'd never be ready for the moment Andrew stepped out of his stretch limo and approached the bench she sat on. Her brain lay frozen under an avalanche of regrets. He might forgive her disloyalty and rudeness, but would he ever trust her again?

Blinking away what had to be her last available tear, Stephanie opened her eyes to find Andrew's face no more than three inches from hers. In two seconds, he'd closed that gap, held her in his arms, and kissed her until she smiled. Then he invited her to come by after school to check out his new place and meet two of his four sisters. Sometimes being a neurotic Jewish girl wasn't so bad.

VI.

Andrew had to sit on the sidelines squirming while Claire coached Stephanie on the art of floating. So far only one other person not related to the curse had mastered the process. If Stephanie succeeded the way Claire's husband had, then perhaps the future would see many more people going on no-cost, luggage-free sightseeing vacations.

Having Claire explain her ability as the result of a traumatic, near death experience, put Stephanie at ease with the craziness of it. The less she knew about the family curse, the better. If only an equally benign explanation existed for the other surprise they had planned for her.

With her 20/200 vision, Stephanie would never qualify for a driver's license. Andrew just needed a specially equipped vehicle to obtain his. He wanted her to have that freedom. Once the curse ended, he expected to be perfectly normal, while she would still be handicapped.

Andrew had visions of Stephanie breaking his heart under the guise of allowing him to find a normal bride. Whoa! Cart before the horse Freudian slip. How did that word end up in his pre-frontal cortex?

Andrew crossed himself thinking, *Baby steps there, buddy. You just got this filly calmed down. Don't let that M-word out of its dark cage until you've mastered the L-word. Shoot for 2005 or beyond.*

Okay then, as soon as he stopped hyperventilating, they could take care of the body Stephanie left behind when she floated off with Claire. The lightest touch on her closed eyelids should reduce her from legal blindness down to 20/40 best corrected vision in each eye.

Stephanie's eye doctors would be talking about this minor miracle for the next decade. All she needed to believe was that floating sometimes caused happy side effects, not that some members of his family have been cursed with super powers.

Andrew didn't feel any guilt whatsoever about telling white lies when Stephanie returned, opened her eyes as she rose from the sofa, and informed him his coffee table needed dusting.

"I can still see! Oh, Andrew, my eyes saw every tiny detail while we floated around London, in the dark! But now, you look marvelous, by the way. There are individual leaves on the trees, not one big multi-colored blob."

"That's amazing, Stephanie. Didn't we tell you to expect something awesome?"

"I can read the tiny print on the back of this DVD. Wouldn't life be perfect if this never went away?"

"My life would be perfect if you never went away." *Oh shit, why did I play that card six years too soon?* "Um… that didn't come out the way my brain intended."

"I understand. Loving you puts my mouth in high gear and my brain on cruise control. Anything's liable to pop out uncensored, like hurry up and kiss me before Claire comes in for a landing."

"Did Claire teach you to be a demanding little nympho as well as a fabulous floater?"

"I've always had an aggressive streak. You've brought it out now that I see what a handsome hunk you really are." Stephanie pulled him closer and wrapped her arms around his neck.

"That's a terrific start, my dear, but where do we go from here?"

"You mean after the mind-blowing snogfest?"

"Yeah, that works for me."

"I'm thinking later tonight you pick me up and we'll visit the Holy Land. After a couple of days rest, let's do Vatican City and Rome to balance things out. Next week you decide where we go."

"With such a great big world out there, this could take a very long time. Are you ready for that kind of commitment, Miss Feldman?"

"Ready, willing, you name it boy and I'm there."

"If that's your attitude, then let me tell you about a little twist I've been working on but haven't quite perfected. Together, I think we can make my theory work, but first, pucker up."

Andrew and Stephanie are still working on his theory that floating can be done in space as well as within the earth's atmosphere. Therefore, they should be able to incorporate time travel in their adventures. Because floaters cannot interact with the physical world, they could do no harm in another time, or even another dimension.

The Fleming curse remains unbroken, so Andrew's leg is still a problem. However, Stephanie's aggressive streak keeps them both extremely satisfied, with or without bodies.

Púca Dawns

by Patricia Flaherty Pagan

"Ghost playground? Ha-ha. Dumb boys. Who would haunt dead grass?" the pale, brown-haired girl with bruised legs wearing a clean, gingham dress asked the gnarled tree on the edge of the overgrown lot.

Maeve thought that fear was like electricity: it buzzed around behind things, but usually you couldn't see it. Maeve wouldn't step on a crack in case she broke her mama's back, she wouldn't play with Ouija boards, she wouldn't eat grasshopper pie, just in case, but only one man made her feel hold-your-breath scared. So she went to the abandoned playground that Tuesday as afternoon shadows began to reach for the sun. It didn't look scary. It looked like a good place to fall down.

Walking across the brown grass, Maeve hummed the Scooby Doo theme song. Then she climbed on top of a boulder perched atop a small hill and rocked back and forth on her heels. "One… two… three…"

Curious, a hazel beast serpentined his way through the undergrowth inching closer, ever closer, to surprise her.

Yet she faced away from him, unmoved. "Richard? Jay? I know that one of you is there. You double-dared the entire class to come here at night. Now push me off. I won't tell."

The púca reared his tall, ram-like horns upwards and revealed his furry face. He pulled from the fading day's heat a booming voice, "Richard I'm not, but push you I shall!" His hoof gently tapped her shoulder blade. Then the púca snarled with glee as the little girl tumbled off the large rock and down the small hill to the dirt below. Thud.

Rising slowly, the girl checked her knees for new scratches and felt along the hem of her dress for rips. She found several.

"I really did fall and rip my dress. I did. Thanks, Jay. Don't tell any-"

Her blue eyes rose to meet the púca's ones and the relief deserted her voice. He rubbed one hoof across his bearded chin and smiled.

Maeve gaped at him.

"The pleasure's all mine, tumbling girl."

She ran. Dazed, the girl raced home, refused supper, and apologized to her mother for falling, ripping her dress and bruising her legs.

"It wasn't real," Maeve whispered as she wrapped herself in a cocoon of purple cotton sheets that night. Then she surrendered to a fitful sleep marked by dreams of black horses with glowing eyes.

One week later, he sensed her on his land and sang her to him with a lullaby from the age before language. "You haven't brought me a carrot, Maeve."

The girl started, dropping her small, brown paper bag. "Who's there?" She gasped.

From behind a sagging and diseased oak, a gray rabbit the size of a German shepherd dog emerged. Maeve said nothing but stared at the patches of dirty and matted fur on his back and his long ears lined with peachy sheen. Her hands trembled. His earthy, foul scent enveloped her. Fascinated, Maeve smelled burnt cake and fresh mud mixed with her grandmother's allspice.

"The swings have long since fallen down," the rabbit-spirit waved a paw at the lone metal pole, listed over by years of January snows, that remained on the former playground. "Who are Richard and Jay, and why do you cross my fields?"

Maeve frowned. She braided and unbraided one of her pigtails. "Richard's in my class. He picks his nose. Jay is his dumb friend. But rabbits don't talk. Except in movies."

Two prominent buckteeth shown as the púca flashed a mad grin. "So what am I then? And what will I do?"

The little girl pursed her lips and straightened the collar of her pink blouse. With his bulging eyes, the púca saw that the blouse had been buttoned incorrectly, so that a lone button waited at the top, forlorn. Her purple cotton skirt and pristine white tights looked new. Indeed a small tag peeked out from the waist of the skirt. *Strange child.*

"I don't have carrots. But if you're hungry, I have fudge. Ya want some?" Maeve retrieved her paper bag. It jangled. She withdrew from the bag a small, wide, white box that smelled faintly of brown sugar and peanut butter.

As he nodded, the rabbit's long ears bobbed. His cotton tail swayed. Maeve tossed the box at him and ran. She sprinted off, her red Mary Janes hitting puddles and casting drips of mud onto her white tights as she went.

Sweet. He chuckled, letting her go.

The next Tuesday, and the next Tuesday after that, she returned, carrying with her a faded copy of *The Voyage of the Dawn Treader* peppered with ripped pages. The púca allowed her to walk one yard further into his fallow playground each time.

One night, he wanted her coins and candy. Horned and half obscured, he crouched beneath a deflating, moss-coated climbing tire and held out his hairy palm. "Women's children speak riddles. You come here to fall down. Then you go to see Mr. Gile whom you say snaps at you like a ferret. If you're a bad girl like he says, Maeve, why does your tutor give you presents?"

She bit her lip. "I donnu. He wears fake red hair that smells funny. But Mama says he helps me with my reading and he tutors out of the goodness of his heart."

Famished, the púca –- in the form that night of a small, goat-headed pony –- tossed her three chocolate Tootsie Roll Pops into his maw, wrapper, sticks and all. With the toe of her white Keds, Maeve dug into the dandelions and dirt by the edge of the tire. Beyond that, taller and taller weeds choked the field in the gathering dark.

"You should be afraid."

"Of Mr. Gile?" She blushed.

"Of me. But you're not."

Above them a cloud shifted, and the only star that Maeve knew, Cassiopeia, burst into view in the summer sky. Crossing her arms and puffing out her cheeks she declared, "If you eat me, no one will bring you money and lollipops." But her voice betrayed her by rising at the end, so the hungry spirit knew that it was a question that Maeve asked herself.

"You are a wise girl. Strange, but wise."

"Thanks?"

"It is night now. Go. A child's mother will worry."

Maeve considered his yellow goat eyes. Suddenly, she smiled, waved and skipped away on the path through the brush that she had marked the week before.

The next Tuesday came and went. No children dared to cross the fetid mud ringing the deserted grasses that had attacked the former playground. By day, hawks circled. By night, owls hunted. Nearby motorists imagined that they saw shadowy mares racing along the shoulder of Concord's roads. Mothers smelled garlic and dreamed of thunderstorms.

Maeve was sitting on her front steps looking with red-rimmed eyes at a new copy of *Number the Stars*.

"Where are you going, or not going, my friend?" The whiny voice of the squat, big-nosed hobgoblin in his hat of tree branches made Maeve jump half a foot in the air.

Wobbly, she landed at the edge of the middle stair. "Is it you?"

The wee, grinning bogeyman in the pointy shoes -- carrying what appeared to be a small bundle of wheat -- made a dancing bow. "Indeed!"

Maeve produced one plump, red delicious apple from the pink, checked bag on her shoulder. "Sorry I didn't... Here you go!"

As the child tossed her snack, the púca saw the spread of purple bruises across the child's right hand, knuckle and fingers.

In one swift motion, the spirit stuffed the entire fruit into his wide mouth and chomped it to bits. Maeve studied her frilly socks. One fat tear escaped her eye.

He watched her.

Sniffing the air, he trotted around the house and regarded the empty driveway with concern. He closed his eyes for ten seconds, searching. Then, racing back in his long pointed shoes, the púca hopped up onto the step next to Maeve. "Your mother starting taking an accounting class after work on Tuesdays, so Mr. Gile is coming here now."

Maeve nodded. She pointed above them to the blue ruffled curtains of the second floor window of her bedroom. In his mind's eye, the púca could see her blue and purple polka dot bedspread and her collection of silver bracelets and rings embellished with jumping horses.

"He wants to read upstairs." Her tears fell in earnest.

A rusted green Chevy pulled around the corner and drove slowly down the block.

"He's coming," Maeve sobbed.

"Don't read the wheat or eat the greens!" the goblin sang. Then he threw his hands wide and sheaves of wheat flew about in every direction, seeming to multiply in the wind that suddenly roared for miles and miles. People were temporarily blinded by whirls of grain all over town.

Thunk! Mr. Gile's Chevy crashed into her neighbor Mrs. Petticer's freestanding, cast iron mailbox.

With a loud cackle, the púca goblin vanished in the grain twister.

When the echo of her friend's laughter faded and her eyes cleared, Maeve saw Mr. Gile hop out of his car, adjust his slipping auburn toupee, and yell curses into his cell phone. Then wrinkled Mrs. Petticer strode out her front door into the still blowing annual grasses and demanded to know what her mailbox had ever done to him! And furthermore, who was teaching men how to drive these days?

Maeve laughed, whispered "Thank You" into the air, bounded into her front hall, and locked the front door behind her.

The following evening, a midnight-haired horse galloped across the town while cicada sang. As he moved, tiny seeds of wheat trailed from his velvety, dark mane. He came to a stop on the outskirts of the abandoned playground. In the moonlight, his silver eyes saw a small girl wearing white cotton pajamas with embroidered pink flamingos on them and a too-big Boston Red Sox cap spread a plaid blanket on the ground. On it she laid out a rotisserie roasted chicken, two baked potatoes and a bag of Chips Ahoy cookies. When she finished setting out the feast, Maeve ran away barefoot.

After his supper, the púca lay back and rubbed his gray, furry rabbit belly.

"One good turn deserves another," he said to the clover and weeds on the ground. "An insidious garden grows across town." The rabbit spat, and dandelions withered and blackened all around him.

Devils live in unremarkable houses. Sniffing and scrunching his nose, the rabbit caught no maleficent odors streaming from the back kitchen window of house number thirty-six Curland Road - just a whiff of macaroni and cheese left stuck to the bottom of a pot on the stove's burner. While rabbits lack a tapetum lucidum, the púca saw the sleeping Mr. Gile through the golden tapestries of his thoughts. Gile snored.

A moment later, a low sound flitted past Gile's ears, causing him to toss and turn in his squeaky bed. Groggy, he sat up and rubbed his bulbous, hairless scalp. The scents of charred bread and allspice filled Gile's room. Again the low sound darted by him. Perhaps water coming out of a hose? Perhaps nothing? Gile blinked and lay his head back down on his sweaty pillow.

An image flickered behind his eyelids as sleep reclaimed him: a huge hare dancing about in Gile's vegetable garden, tramping on the peas and spitting at the tall vines of his tomato plants. An enchanted bow played a fiddle. Gile's snoring cut through the rousing tune.

Without witnesses, the púca kissed one withered, green tomato on the vine and then vanished into a school of fireflies swimming across the sky. The sun began to rise.

After a bologna sandwich lunch the next day, Maeve's mother broke the news about poor Mr. Gile's unexpected death. Maeve counted the pink stripes on her favorite shorts so as not to smile.

"I knew it."

"Knew what?" Her mother asked, appraising her lovely girl. "What's got those wheels in your brain turning?"

Maeve dropped her gaze to her Mary Janes. "Some tomato plant leaves are poisonous. I saw it on TV."

"If only he'd known not to eat them. He studied so many books but misread his garden." Her mother mumbled as she cleared the table and downed a gulp of coffee. Then she led her daughter out into the yard for a game of badminton.

Maeve never saw her púca again but she often dreamt of him at daybreak, in the moments right before waking, when dreams feel alive.

The Stolen Key

by Rebecca Nolen

The sky was the perfect brown of the underside of a boulder, which is what it was made of if one were being picky about description. Being miles below the earth's surface had its advantages. There was less noise for one thing. Kreech Koodytot needed to hear anything following them. His soft paws made no noise, but the humongous beast next to him was such a clodhopper. Really, the slob, Smat, was getting on his nerves. Kreech glanced around the clearing in the Yugg-Drasil woods. The Yugg-Drasil trees of the forest reached to the sky where many grew through to the outer earth. He'd never understood it. He was here now because he had a plan to take Queen Tosia's most precious possession just as she had robbed him of his. Nothing would interfere, he'd seen to the preliminaries. He had been thorough. The imbecile he had with him might cause something to go wrong but that possibility was covered unless the ugly lizard made a mistake *before* the deed was done. A problem afterward? Well, he didn't need to worry about the afterward.

Through the sticky forest undergrowth of nettle and weed, reptilian scales glinted in the half light of the Fifth Sun. The sudden peeping caught Kreech's attention. Those pesky snippins! Once he had Smat's attention he gestured for him to follow. He ran and leapt across the cleared space to the hole beneath the lone tree. Smat tumbled down the hole after him. Kreech ground his teeth and whispered the password to get them through the quicksilver curtain. Except for the slither of Smat's hide against the interior stone of the entrance, they moved silently into a long hall. Despite the flaming torches that lit up the opalescent walls as they passed, no one challenged their purpose here.

They came to the throne room and Kreech leaned toward Smat to speak in a low whisper. "I got us this far without a problem, now it's down to you."

He leaned away and held his breath so he wouldn't have to smell the raw liver odor that got worse every time Smat got nervous.

Smat was the ugliest of dragons, from his mottled eggplant and orange scales to that great quivering belly of blubber. Globs of blue stuff rolled from the folds in his skin. And just what was the reason for the protrusions above his eyes? The blue mucus was pooling at Smat's feet. If they didn't get in and out quick they would drown in the stuff. Kreech muttered, "Hurry up!"

"I go in and grab the key, right? But Kreech, the guards won't be happy with me."

"Look at them, Smat. Asleep on the floor. I put sleep-root in their tea. Go!"

Smat started bouncing. The blue stuff poured down his scales to the floor. The smell was horrendous. "This is a fun trick we are playing, right Kreech?"

"Yes. Yes. A great trick."

"Queen Tosia is so beautiful. Will I get to see her? Will I? I heard she wasn't well."

"She's well."

"I heard she's still mourning Sereptra's defection."

"You would believe anything." Kreech muttered, barely able to hold his fury in check at the mention of Sereptra's name. "Go in there, get the key, and give it to me!"

"Don't get mad. Smat hates when you get angry at Smat."

"Then go!" Kreech felt the fur ruffle at the base of his neck. He'd kept his water rat shape in case they met someone. Both Smat and Kreech were Neelons. Neelons could change shape at will but each only possessed a few shape choices. He had finally discovered his true shape after Tosia destroyed his beloved Sereptra's hopes. He would change into his new shape when they were well away from Tosia's castle.

He had planned everything so well. As a water rat and Tosia's trusted advisor, no one would question why he was there with another Neelon. Not until afterward.

Smat snuffled and smudged away a tear as he stepped across the prone bodies strewn across the throne room floor. The stone pedestal was highlighted by the light-catcher above it. Water streamed across the floor, deepest at the pedestal. Smat sloshed through the ankle-deep water and yanked the key from its slot. He turned and galloped back to Kreech. Just before he reached Kreech a sudden blaze of light exploded from one side of the room.

Kreech hadn't counted on that. But he still had his plan. He yelled, "Smat! Give it to me!"

Smat tripped on his own feet, the clumsy cow. The key went flying. Kreech caught it. He turned and ran toward the outside. Smat was soon at his heels. They made it out and up the stairs, across the clearing and into the woods. The peeping sounds were all around them.

Smat fell again. He wailed, "Wait! I can't catch my breath. Poor Smat."

"No waiting, fool! That light was the Golden Guardian. I had no idea he was there. I thought he was a legend."

"But you said Tosia would like our tricky ways."

A spear of bright light burst from the palace entry. Smat hardly had time to scream before he blew up, raining a thousand smelly pieces to the ground.

Kreech didn't give it a second thought. He was fast but not faster than light. He had to get away. The backup plan had worked like a gem. All he had needed was a large, fat something between him and whatever Tosia had used to safeguard her key. And Smat? The universe didn't need any more dumb.

He had to get to the other side of the forest. His tracks would hardly make much difference amongst the other tracks in the sand. The important thing was to get away with the key. He had it! Oh, how Tosia would suffer now.

He scrabbled his way through the ancient Yugg-Drasil forest, he swam across many streams and even the Big River before coming to its edge, something that the water rat shape did well. The only thing the wimpy water rat shape did well. The Fifth Sun gave no warmth and only dreary light. Degrees of shadow defined the Penumbran landscape. He gazed across the expansive valley to the mountain range beyond. On the other side his true love waited for him. If Sereptra knew he had the key she would come back to him. She would love him again.

He just had time to change to his dragon shape to fly across the unclimbable mountains. Kreech had always viewed the shape-changing as a curse, like a disease with no cure. Until he discovered the dragon within. Today was the first glorious day he no longer had to hide his true nature.

He concentrated – hair to scales, soft paw pads to dangerous talons, blunt rat teeth to sizable fangs, and flimsy rat ears flattened against his now angular skull. Though his eye color would not change from red, the pupils grew from round to fine slits – perfect eyes for a dreaded dragon. Lastly, his neck and tail grew long and muscular, capable of dispatching weaker creatures.

Whew! All this stealing and running and changing was exhausting. He had never been more tired. Should he take a short rest before the flight over the mountain? He was camouflaged well, and he only needed a respite, for just a moment – a brief moment.

Minutes later, he was fully awake. He had a sense of sweet on his tongue. He sniffed the air and found a peculiar sweet corn scent that he remember came from a type of bug he had not seen in ages. He glanced around. Yes, he was alone beneath the canopy of the mattress-sized Yugg-drasil leaves. What did this bug scent mean? For the moment his brain refused to come up with answers. He had the niggling feeling that something was amiss.

His insides churned. Perhaps his brain needed fuel? His favorite meal was all around him; he could hear their obnoxious peeps. They were the Queen's spies. For such a mighty dragon, the snippins made a lovely snack. His stomach growled as he imagined a squiggly, delicious snippins sliding down his throat. They were irritating, hairless, squirrel-shaped creatures, always leaping about in the branches, talking backwards and forwards, informing on him. There were such a surplus of them, they needed eating. He'd dispatch a few before flying across the mountain. There were no snippins on the dry side.

He paused and raised his long snout to sniff the air. He caught that sweetcorn smell again. Could it be? No, Drina were a rarity even in Penumbra. Wait! He felt for the key. That's odd. He patted the ground around where he was sitting. He'd left it next to him. He patted some more and felt only sand and sprigs of noodle-grass. Where was it?

He scrambled up and tore at the earth, flinging sand and grass, ripping at everything he could reach. No! Where was that ridiculous key? His thick tail whipped back and forth, wiping out the underbrush and uprooting small trees as he paced. How had he lost it? Curses of despair escaped his lips and his talons tore at unseen enemies. What had happened?

He had smelled the bug. That was it. There was only one bug that carried that scent so strongly when acting for Tosia. A Drina! Rare or not, it had been a Drina, those stickle-backed skinny-legged child-protectors who worked for the Queen. They used trickery to cast sleep on innocent dragons. He knew that sudden tiredness had not been natural!

Aauurrgh! He twisted an invisible scrawny neck.

Kreech was supposed to hand the key to LeVane. How could he stall for time? LeVane would grind his bones for beetle fodder if he didn't get it to him.

Now was the time to plan again. He would follow its scent trail, it wouldn't be hard. He would find it, and there would be one less Drina. He would destroy the Drina, get the key, and take it to LeVane. It shouldn't take longer than one sun rotation, two at the most.

First, to be on the safe side he would search the forest. It was unlikely that the Drina had stuck around knowing Kreech would be onto him, but he had to be sure. Next, he would go to the surface world. They hang out there with their supposed "missions" for the Queen. They hide behind human-like skin and clothes, though it is only a disguise, not an honest shape-shift. They tend to stand out as tall and awkward without the ability to speak human correctly. They had nothing on the Neelons for shape-shifting.

Yes, he would go to the surface world as Nogard. If he didn't get the key, he might be able to momentarily appease LeVane if he brought back more children. Yes, they could always use a few more.

Death Hires a Stylist

by Mandy Broughton

Ever since the apocalypse, Myrtle always kept her Death-Be-Gone spray by the door. Sitting next to the plant insecticide, it stood ready to be used the next time Death came knocking.

"There he goes again!" Myrtle grabbed her spray bottle. Tossing her cane aside, she swung the door open and pumped the handle. Mist sprinkled the front porch.

Death threw his cloak-covered arms over his face to shield himself. Alas, failure, so he fled.

Myrtle tried to slam the door shut but something caught.

"He dropped his scythe again, clumsy fool." Clutching the doorjamb, she eased herself down to grab the wooden handle. "He'll be back."

"He always comes back," Vern kept reading his old newspapers and leaned back in his recliner. Myrtle felt like giving Vern a squirt or two.

Leaning Death's instrument against the doorjamb, Myrtle's vertebrae crackled as she straightened up. She studied the spray bottle in her hand. "Sooner than we think. This is my plant insecticide."

"Insecticide doesn't work against Death. What're you thinking?"

"I was thinking I'd like help." Myrtle placed the insecticide next to her Death-Be-Gone concoction. "Bad enough we survived the zombie apocalypse but now we have to put up with Death knocking on our door every other day. And I'm the only one who bothers to run him off."

"Try using the right spray for a change, woman." Vern shook his newspaper, rustling the pages. "That might help."

"Why'd he run off because of insecticide spray?" Myrtle shuffled to the kitchen. "Maybe he's getting a bit touched in the head."

"Don't you go underestimating him." Vern wagged his gnarled finger at her. "He's still got a few tricks up his sleeves."

Myrtle stopped in the kitchen doorway. "Hate Death. Hate zombies. And those werewolves — they leave fleas everywhere."

"Enough about the fleas, Myrtle!"

She snorted. "Dirty fleas. I'm tired of cleaning up after them." Her joints popped as she eased into the kitchen. "Dinner's ready, old man, come eat your grub."

Vern readied himself for the five-minute trip to the kitchen table. "Smells like pickles. Again."

* * *

Death was tired of everyone running when he came around. It made it quite difficult to collect souls. He had decided he needed a new image, one that invited people in instead of running them off. So his publicist sent him to a most famous stylist. Excited, Death found himself in a chair facing the makeup maven.

"Mr. Grim Reaper, you are my most famous client so far." The stylist circled Death, gathering ideas. "Those vampires I recreated will be nothing compared to the new you."

Death nodded, pleased.

"The cloak has got to go, along with the worms and maggots. You have to have them? Hmm, maybe we can bedazzle them. Make them sparkly." Manicured fingers waved their magic in the air. "And your name, it just does not spell fun."

Right then, Death knew this new image would help him gather the souls he wanted.

* * *

"Who's Sparkles?" Vern held the gold invitation at arm's length, squinting to read the shimmery embossing.

"Ferdinand had a dog named Sparkles. No, wait, Peaches. Its name was Peaches." Myrtle's head blocked Vern's view as she read the invitation in his hands. "A party?"

"You dragged me to a party last year." Vern tossed the paper in the trash.

"Maybe Sparkles is a friend we thought was dead but isn't." Myrtle fished the invite out of the can. "Whoever he is, I'm sure it'll be a great party. I clean and cook for you. The least you could do is take me to a party."

"Kind of hard to do since we can't travel at night." Vern lowered himself into the recliner. He opened the newspaper, rereading old news.

"And we can't go during the day since the vampires took to roaming the streets in their SPF 3501."

Myrtle flattened the invitation on the table, smoothing the wrinkles. "I think my black evening dress still fits. And your tux, I don't suppose there's a dry cleaner left?"

"I'm not going to any party."

* * *

"We leave an hour before sundown," Vern locked the door.

Myrtle patted his arm, giving him an "Of course, dear."

With his other hand, Vern dragged his machete along the road. The rusted steel grated against the crumbled concrete. Vern sniffed the air. "What's that smell?"

Hanging her cane on her arm, Myrtle opened her pocketbook and pulled out a sheet of paper. "I found it in an old magazine. Do you like it?" She rubbed the sheet on her neck, attempting to put more of the smell-em-good onto herself.

"Smells like pickles." Vern tugged at his bowtie. Bowties -- *the easier to noose yourself*, he thought.

"I used vinegar to bring out the perfume. It's an excellent preservative." Myrtle returned the perfumed sheet to her purse.

They meandered along until they reached Old Pepper's place. Myrtle remembered bringing Ima a casserole. Vern thought of old man Pepper taking out thirty zombies and smoking a cigar to celebrate. He missed the old fart, almost as much as he missed cigars.

The geriatric partygoers mounted the steps. Music? The Beach Boys could have deafened the dead.

"Someone's already dancing on the table." Vern popped his dentures into place. "Drunk. Who's still got a stash?"

"He's sparkly," Myrtle said.

Vern pulled eyeglasses from his jacket pocket. Fumbling, he finally got them open and in place. "That's Death on the table!"

Death danced. Gold rings and necklaces glittered in the light. Sequins and rhinestones covered his cloak. And a tiara topped his hood-covered head. As he spun, maggots radiated outward.

Myrtle tried to dodge but her dodgeball days were past. Bedazzled worms fell to the floor. They inched off, leaving trails of glitter.

Vern raised his machete. "That's not natural."

"Sparkles is Death?" Myrtle stared at Death and his dazzling dirt nap bugs. "He invited us to a party?"

"I think the old boy's tricked us." Vern pushed Myrtle to the door, being mindful of her weak hip.

Death stopped spinning. He grinned his lipless grin and then launched himself at the post-centenarians. Vern swung his machete but only connected with the tiara.

"He looks so nice on the outside." Myrtle ducked behind Vern.

But Death grabbed Myrtle's ankle, knocking her cane to the side. So she whacked him with her purse. Vern swung again. His machete turned the pocketbook into a spent piñata. Coins, three colors of lipstick, two bottles of empty lotion along with papers rained to the ground. Myrtle kicked Death in the face and her heel caught the perfumed sheet, shoving it up Death's skeletal nose. He jumped back trying to remove the offending item, but couldn't so he ran out the back door, putting as much distance as he could between him and the card-carrying AARP members.

Vern tugged Myrtle out and away from Old Pepper's place. As they hurried home, bones creaked with every step. "Good thing he didn't like your perfume. I never dreamed the old boy had good taste."

"It wasn't the perfume." Myrtle wished she had worn more comfortable shoes. Each step was a pain in the bunion.

"But he ran-"

"I see that same reaction every other day when I spray him with Death-Be-Gone."

Vern frowned. He then uttered a sentence that had never crossed his lips before, "I don't understand, Myrtle."

She smiled, her ill-fitting dentures out of place and crooked. "Preservatives keep Death at bay. My Death-Be-Gone? It's just vinegar and water."

The Witch's Child

by John D. Payne

Timberlen was not a bad girl. So when her little cousin Jayni told her about the monster she had seen, deep in the woods where she was not supposed to be, Timberlen scolded her. All the children knew– they had been told by their parents, often– not to go into the woods so far you could not see your way back out. And Timberlen knew how dangerous the woods were, because she had been in them more, and farther, than any of the other children on the farm.

After Jayni looked properly chastised, Timberlen said she would help. She would go back in the woods with Jayni to find the monster, and slay it if necessary. And if it was too big, they would go tell Sakeda, the hired man.

Timberlen sent Jayni to go get apples and cheese for them to eat in the woods. Then she fetched Stuart, because he could help protect them from the monster, and he would not boss them. Bertram noticed Jayni sneaking apples and followed her too, because anything someone else wanted to hide must be worth taking or breaking. Ellspeth was always watching Bertram, because he was always being wicked. So the five of them went into the woods together.

They were just coming into the glen where they liked to play when Jayni saw it again. She shrieked in terror, dropped her baby doll, and ran screaming from the glen.

"You dropped your baby, baby," Bertram called after her. He was the oldest, and he was mean to everyone, including Jayni, even though she was his sister.

"Be nice," Ellspeth said. "Jayni thought she saw a monster."

"She did see a monster," Timberlen said quietly. Timberlen thought it was stupid how children always complained that their parents never listened to them - because they never listened to each other, either.

"Have no fear," Bertram cried. "I'll save you, good ladies!" He took his leather sling and a blueberry-sized pebble out of his vest pocket, and began to twirl it around.

"Be quiet," Timberlen said, "you'll scare it away."

Then Ellspeth saw it. She made a noise like a shriek coming in backwards, and ran out of the glen after Jayni.

Bertram saw it, too, and he dropped his sling. "Devils!" That was profanity. "Devils' toes and Allfather Wodne's hairy backside!" That was blasphemy. Grandmother would beat Bertram soundly if she ever caught word that he had been using such language. Bertram was lucky Ellspeth and Jayni had already run away.

The monster was hiding in the bushes on the other side of the glen, so she could not see it clearly. It would be stupid to get too close, but the creature was no bigger than a chicken. Too small to get Sakeda or one of the uncles. And despite all the noise they were making, it was not running away. Maybe it was deaf. Bertram's father had a deaf dog. Bertram was cruel to it.

"A monster..." Stuart said slowly, seeing what the other children had seen. He did everything slowly. He was only eight, more than a year younger than his cousin Bertram, but he was head and shoulders taller. Whenever the boys played at fighting monsters, slow Stuart always had to be the giant. The soldiers always beat the giant, once they got enough soldiers. And Stuart usually got beat afterward, too, for fighting with smaller boys.

"You're the monster, you big smelly ogre," Bertram retorted. He picked up his sling and another pebble, and began to spin it around again.

By now, Ellspeth and Jayni had returned to the clearing, but both looked to be on the verge of bolting again at any moment. Timberlen, on the other hand, stood beside slow Stuart and regarded Bertram thoughtfully. "What are you doing?"

"I'm going to kill a monster, by Wodne's teeth." The sling continued spinning, but without releasing the rock it held inside.

"I don't think you should do that," Timberlen said. "If you do, I'll tell Aunt Enna."

"Go ahead, tell her," Bertram said in a loud whisper. "I don't care if she gets mad, because Father won't punish me. He'll be proud of me for killing a monster." With a final flick of his wrist, the sling discharged its projectile. There was a cry of pain from the bushes, echoed by smaller cries from Jayni and Ellspeth, who clung to each other.

"You hurt it!" Jayni cried.

"Of course I hurt it," Bertram said, as he pulled another rock from his vest pocket and placed it in his sling. "I'm a hero. And it's a monster."

"Maybe..." Ellspeth began. "Maybe we should talk to someone grown-up." She looked from Bertram to the bushes and back again. "My brothers are back at your uncle's farm. I'm going to get them," she offered.

Bertram grinned cruelly and began to spin the sling again. "Go on then, if you're afraid. I'll take care of this myself."

"No," Timberlen said, "I'll take care of this." She stepped out from behind Bertram and walked to the bushes-- and the monster.

"Looks like I'm going to take care of two monsters today." Bertram spun his sling again, and a rock flew over Timberlen's shoulder, narrowly missing her head.

"You could have hit her!" Ellspeth said.

"I'm going to tell momma," Jayni said. "I'm going to tell her you tried to hit Timberlen. You're going to get it for sure!"

"Lots of little monsters in the woods today," Bertram said with a smile, loading another rock into his sling.

Then Stuart stepped forward and shook his head. "Don't."

"Get out of my way, stinky."

"No."

"Out of the way!"

"No. Leave Timberlen alone."

Bertram swung his sling, slowly. "I don't want to hit you with this, but if you don't move you're going to be sorry."

"If you hit Stuart with a rock, we'll all see it, and everyone knows you're a liar," Ellspeth said, "so you better put that away."

Bertram kept swinging. "Make me."

"I'll tell Poppa!" Jayni shouted.

Stuart reached for the sling, but Bertram danced away out of his bigger cousin's reach.

"I'm just playing! I'm not going to hit anyone. Devils' teeth!"

Stuart followed his cousin around the clearing until Bertram put the sling and rock away in his vest pocket.. Meanwhile, Timberlen had gone into the bushes and come out with a little rag-wrapped bundle in her arms.

"Look what she found," Jayni said, crowding in to see. "What is it?"

"It looks like a little tiny goblin," Timberlen said. "I think it's a baby."

"Oh, a baby!" Jayni cooed. Then she looked at the bundle. "It's ugly. Its face is all squashed up."

"Just like Timberlen's," Bertram said in a nasty voice. "I think it's her baby."

"You stop, Bertram Miller!" Ellspeth said. "You have been so mean today. I think you should tell Timberlen you're sorry for trying to hit her with that rock."

"Yeah," Stuart said.

"And you should apologize to Stuart, too."

"I wasn't trying to hit anyone," Bertram replied, "I was trying to keep her away from this witch's brat."

"What are you talking about?" Timberlen asked.

"You're a witch, and this monster is your baby."

"Timberlen is not a witch," Stuart said, "and that's not her baby. It's a goblin, like she said. People can't have goblin babies."

"Don't you know anything? Father told me all about goblins." Bertram lowered his voice to a dramatic whisper. "He says they're witches' children!"

"It's true! Poppa says so," Jayni chimed in.

Bertram nodded solemnly. "That's right. Father says that there were never any goblins around these parts before that old witch showed up."

"What witch?" asked Timberlen.

"You know," Bertram said.

"You mean Momma Seeget?"

"See! You knew," Jayni said.

"As soon as that old witch got here," Bertram continued, "people started seeing goblins in the woods. They'd never been seen this close to Garmartten before, but wherever a witch goes, there's always goblins– witches' brats."

"Well, witches are supposed to be old ladies, right?" Timberlen questioned. "So, how are they supposed to have all these babies? Everybody knows when you get to be old like Momma Seeget, all your children are grown up and you don't have any more babies. So how are all these goblins getting born from all these old witches?"

"They're not all old," Ellspeth said timidly. She blushed when everyone looked at her. "Some of them are very young," she mumbled.

"Aunt Meggan," Stuart whispered. Timberlen shot him a furious glance, but he already looked frightened.

"Everyone says she was a witch, Timberlen," Jayni said snidely, "and that's why she disappeared– on her thirteenth birthday. The other witches took her so they could teach her about curses, and making spells, and drinking cats' blood . . . and every bad thing!"

"Like laying with devils," Bertram concluded.

"Watch your mouth, Bertram Miller!" Ellspeth said.

"That's how you get goblins," Bertram said smugly, "from witches laying with devils. I can say it because it's true."

"It's not true at all," Timberlen said. "Momma Seeget is the nicest old lady I know. She gives all the little children honeycomb to eat when they come to her cottage. And she helps sick people. She helped Aunt Ester get well when she had that fever last spring, and she helps all the ladies when it's time for them to have their babies. And if you think she's a mean old witch who lays with devils and has goblin babies, then you are even stupider than I thought, Bertram Miller."

"You're a witch, too– just like your aunt Meggan."

"She's your aunt, too. You're part of this family."

"No I'm not. I'm a Miller. My mother left your family when she married my father. She's not one of you any more. You Hunters are strange. You let that stinking Shibenji monkey-man live with your family. They're the enemy! We fought a war!"

"What do you mean, we fought a war?" Timberlen smirked. "I didn't fight a war. You didn't fight a war. Uncle Aber fought in the war, and it's his house, and if he thinks it's okay for Sakeda and his family to live in our home, then it's his business. Why should you care, Bertram– you or your father? He didn't fight in the war, did he?"

"Shut up!"

"I'll shut up when you answer me," Timberlen said angrily. "If your father wants to fight the Shiben so much, why didn't he want to fight when there was a whole army of them around?"

Ellspeth tried to conceal a giggle behind her hand.

"Stop laughing!" Bertram demanded.

Ellspeth stopped.

Bertram turned to glare at each of the children in turn. But he saved his angriest scowl for Timberlen. "At least I have a father," he said to her at last. "At least I know who my father is. My father loved me and he loved my mother. Your father didn't even want to see you be born– whoever he is."

Timberlen said nothing. She just turned to go, with the goblin child in her arms.

Bertram continued to shout as she walked away. "Go on, then! Go back where you came from, witch-girl! You don't belong here anyway. You Hunters are all witches and goblin-lovers and wicked women like your mother!"

Timberlen kept walking, too angry at Bertram to let him see her cry. As she left the glen, she heard Ellspeth and Jayni reproving Bertram for his ugly words. She also heard heavy footfalls behind her, so she was not surprised to see Stuart fall into step beside her. They walked in silence for several minutes, with the warm light of the sun occasionally finding its way down through the forest's many layers of new spring leaves to play gently on their faces.

"I can help," Stuart said finally.

"What?"

"I can help carry," He held out his arms.

Timberlen gently handed him the baby goblin, and Stuart smiled as they continued to walk through the woods. He never said another word. He didn't even ask where they were going, although he looked a little scared when they reached old Momma Seeget's cottage. One of the horses from the Hunter homestead was tethered outside, and a thin trail of smoke leaked out from a hole in the roof. Timberlen walked up to the door with Stuart and the baby trailing after her, and knocked firmly.

"Momma Seeget? Are you at home?"

"Yes, child, come in," a grandmotherly voice came from inside the cabin.

Timberlen opened the door and walked in. Stuart followed her, carrying the baby goblin. The cottage was a small, one-room affair, full of dried vegetables and herbs. Seeget, a plump, white-haired woman in her fifties, stood by a small stove, pouring tea into a wooden bowl held by a black-haired man in his mid-thirties, sitting on a small stool.

Timberlen curtsied. "Hello, Momma Seeget. Hello, Sakeda."

The man inclined his head and bowed from the waist. "Good day to you, Timba-chan. And to you, young Stuart."

"Yes, a good day to you both," Seeget said, "but what's that you're carrying, Stuart?"

Stuart stepped toward Seeget and held out the bundle in his arms, so that the old woman could get a good look. The creature let forth a pitiful whine as Seeget pulled the rags back from its face.

"Merciful Wodne," she breathed, putting a hand to her lips. "That's a goblin child. And it's hurt." She looked accusingly at the children.

"We found it out in the woods," Timberlen offered. Seeget frowned at her. When Timberlen saw that this was not enough explanation, she continued, "We went to the glen past the brook to play, but when we got there, it was in the bushes and we all saw it and then mean Bertram Miller hit it with a rock from his sling! I told him not to."

Stuart nodded.

"Fine, fine, fine, child. We'll hear more of that later." Seeget took the goblin baby out of Stuart's arms and laid it on her bed. She began bustling around the room, gathering herbs, bandages, and the like. Timberlen sat down on the floor next to the bed, where she could see the goblin child. Seeget nearly stepped on her as she hurried about. "Sakeda," she called over her shoulder, "there are too many people in this house for me to work. Will you take Stuart back to Aber's place? Ester is probably wondering about her little boy, especially if the other children are back from the glen."

Timberlen looked up at the two adults, but it appeared that she was not going to be likewise banished.

Sakeda grunted an acknowledgment, and hopped up from his stool, setting down the wooden bowl. He took Stuart's hand and led him out of the cottage. Before he stepped out the door, he turned back for a moment. "Should I come back again?"

"Yes, by all means," Seeget said, busily unwrapping the goblin child's rags. "I will be needing you shortly."

Sakeda bowed low, and Seeget absently waved a hand to dismiss him. All her attention was focused on the wounded infant in front of her on the bed. "Timberlen, child, fetch me that bowl of tea, will you?" Timberlen sprang up and grabbed the bowl, careful not to spill any of the hot tea as she carried it to the bed.

"Thank you," Seeget said without looking up. "Put that down right here, will you? Now, put your finger here for a minute while I tie this knot. My hands aren't as nimble as they used to be. Good girl."

Seeget continued her work, clucking to herself as she tended to the creature's bruises and scrapes.

"Are you a witch?" Timberlen asked.

"Well, that's a fine question for a well-behaved girl to ask, now isn't it?"

"Are you?"

"Do you think I am?"

"If you're not a witch, then why do so many people call you that? Did you used to be a witch, before?"

Seeget said nothing. She poured some oil in a large wooden bowl, dropped in some dried leaves and began crushing them into the oil with a stone pestle.

"I think you are a witch," Timberlen said.

Seeget set aside the bowl with the herb poultice. "One thing you'll learn as you get older, child, is that most men– although there are rare and beautiful exceptions, but most men, mind-- don't like for women to have a lot of power."

"Power?"

"Yes, power. Prestige, influence, intelligence, courage, strength . . . "

"Men don't like women to be strong?"

"Not all men, child, not all men," Seeget said. "But many men– and women, too!– don't like women to be strong. Strong-willed, particularly. Confident. Independent. They don't like that, no they don't. They like a woman who does plenty of this–" Seeget mock-curtsied and bowed her head respectfully. "A well-behaved woman, a woman who follows the rules– that's what people like."

"You told me to be well-behaved," Timberlen said.

"Did I?" Seeget asked. "Well, it's bred in the bone, I suppose. Hard to escape it, child, hard to rise above. But some of us try. And those of us who do, we get called . . . one of three names. Of those three, I prefer 'witch,' thank you very much."

"What are the other two?"

"I'll tell you when you're older."

Timberlen thought about that while Seeget applied the poultice to the goblin child.

"Momma Seeget?"

"Yes, child."

"I'm older now. Will you tell me what the other two names are?"

Seeget cackled with laughter. "Older now, are you? Well, indeed you are child, indeed you are." Timberlen waited for the answer to her question, but Seeget was busy shushing the mewling baby goblin and trying to rock it to sleep. Timberlen frowned and thought some more.

"Momma Seeget?"

"Yes, child."

"I think I want to be a witch, too."

"What, right now?"

"No. When I am older, I think."

"But you're older now, aren't you?" Seeget asked, and erupted into laughter again. This caused the little goblin to squall all the louder, which got Seeget busy shushing again. Timberlen made up her mind right then that when she was a witch, she would not poke fun at little girls who were being serious.

Seeing the look on the child's face, Seeget dried a few tears of laughter from her eyes and straightened out her smile. "So," she said, "you want to be a witch."

Timberlen nodded solemnly.

Seeget grunted. "Well, it's a lonely profession, child– as you can no doubt see. Most witches are unmarried. Men like to be the strong one, the protector, all that sort of thing. And so it takes an awfully strong man to be a witch's husband."

"I know someone strong," Timberlen said quietly.

"Oh, child," Seeget sighed sympathetically. She set the tiny goblin baby down in the center of the bed, wiped her hands off on her apron, and knelt down to give the little girl a hug.

"Now, Timberlen Hunter, you listen to me. Stuart Farmer's a good boy, but I don't think he's for you." She searched Timberlen's eyes, but found no agreement. "You like him because he's not loud and rash like that nasty Miller boy. But quiet doesn't always mean thoughtful. Your head is full of thoughts, and you'll want someone to share them with. Do you understand me, child?"

Timberlen didn't want to answer. So she turned away and looked at the goblin child, whose wheezy snores made it sound like its head was completely full of mucus.

Seeget patted her kindly. "You have too much of your grandfather in you to listen to wise counsel. And too much of your mother, too, I fear. But you're not a bad girl."

Timberlen smiled, pleased. Then she remembered what Momma Seeget said about well-behaved women. "I don't need to be bad to be a witch, do I?"

"No," Seeget said. "You just have to be comfortable in bad situations."

"Bad situations?"

"Sometimes we face difficult choices," Seeget said. "Like this morning with the other children. You didn't want to leave this poor creature to die, but you knew that if you brought it to your parents, you would be scolded for being where you oughtn't to be. So, you came here."

Timberlen nodded. "Stuart was scared, but not me." She felt a surge of pride at the recognition of her cleverness and leadership.

Seeget smiled, sadly. "That's the end of the problem for you, but only because you passed it along to me. The difficult choices all still need to be made."

Timberlen looked back at the little goblin baby, now still and quiet. "Are you going to take it back to its parents?"

"They won't want him back," Seeget replied. "That's why you found him out in the woods. Goblins abandon babies that are sick or weak-- and healthy ones, too, if there's not enough food to feed the adults in the tribe."

"But maybe it was an accident. Maybe he just got lost."

The older woman shrugged. "Goblins don't trust humans, and for good reason. Now that he's got our smell on him, they would never take him back. They'd kill him."

"No!"

"Yes," Seeget said. "I've seen it, more than once. And heard their chief laugh at me afterward, believing that they had foiled some clever scheme of mine." Her lips twisted up as if she had a mouth full of bitter melon. "No, we won't be taking him back to his people."

"So are you going to take care of him yourself?" Timberlen asked.

"Humans don't trust goblins, either," Seeget said. "Or them as cares for goblins."

Timberlen couldn't help but remember what Bertram had said about witches and the origins of goblins. A woman that everyone called a witch behind her back would have an awful hard time explaining a real live goblin baby to people like that.

"Say I keep him here with me." The old woman's gaze flicked over to the sleeping goblin. "It won't stay secret. People in the village-- and yes, your kin among them-- will drive me away before I could nurse him back to health. It's hard to care for a healthy human baby on the road, let alone a sick goblin baby. He'd most likely die before I could put a roof over our heads."

"But maybe not," Timberlen said, hopefully.

"Maybe not," Seeget agreed. "Maybe we'd both live long enough to get driven out of some other village." She smiled wryly. "But I would certainly lose my home, and might not find another one. And the people of this village would certainly lose my services, and it might be years before they would find a good witch again."

Timberlen mulled it over, but no other solution presented itself. "That's a hard problem."

"Yes."

"What will you do?"

"I already did it," Seeget said.

Timberlen glanced over at the goblin baby, lying silently on the bed.

"What do you mean?" she asked. "What did you do?"

Seeget sighed. "I eased his pain."

Timberlen rushed to the bed and picked up the tiny form, holding its ugly face next to her own. It made no sound, and did not move. It was not breathing.

"You killed him! That was poison!"

"It was medicine," Seeget said. "The medicine he needed."

Timberlen stared at the old woman. "You are a witch," she said. "And I hate you."

"You wanted me to make your problem go away," Seeget said. "I don't blame you. But you need to know that when you shy away from a terrible choice, that burden just gets passed to someone else. Or so it might seem, to them as labor hard to preserve their ignorance. The wise know that a burden as heavy as this one can never be passed off clean. It can only be . . . shared." She smiled, sadly.

Hot tears streamed down Timberlen's face. "You want me to feel guilty. But you killed him, not me."

Seeget shrugged. "Tell yourself what you want. You're too clever not to see the truth. This curse will be with you all your life. Make your peace with it how you can."

Timberlen bolted out the door fled and into the woods. No matter how far she ran, she couldn't get away from the memory of that ugly little face, still and cold and peaceful.

Stuart and his father found her in the forest the next day, not far from where they had first heard the little goblin's pitiful cries. They asked her many questions, but Timberlen had no words. So they took her home to her mother and her grandmother.

They hugged her and bathed her and put her in bed. When she wouldn't sleep, they got something Sakeda had brought from Momma Seeget to help calm her down. The more Timberlen screamed, the more they insisted that she needed it. In the end, she could not keep them from giving it to her.

As she choked it down, through bitter tears, she couldn't help thinking that it didn't taste bad at all.

Booly

by John Fritz Schwab

"It is dangerous to burn on the wrong day," said the old great-grandfather. He lived the first half of his life in the Far East where they had such beliefs. But he should probably just be quiet now and not chew his gum so noisily either. *Smack, smack, smack, smack*. He knew he irritated them. Besides, they could blame him for their ignorance.

Because he started it all by marrying a white woman when he moved to California. His half-Asian son further diluted the heritage by marrying a white woman, too.

And so it went. The half-Asian son and his fully white wife made a terribly white daughter, and it was she who slept with her white and tattooed boyfriend and became pregnant as a teenager. She was the one who just died, still unmarried, a year and a half after the birth of her child. Could there be any faith left after all these washed out generations?

The motherless toddler also carried no color, except when he ran about for too long or cried too loudly, at which times the knobs of his broad cheeks became flushed with heat. But, though pasty white, he was not weak or sick. "Come here, my chubby American," the great-grandfather would say, and the sturdy little child would rush to him snorting and giggling with much silly life. But that was before the untimely burning.

The parents of the deceased girl visited the funeral home and arranged for her cremation without consulting the old man. They no longer paid attention to what he said about anything. They thought him strange in his old age, and they didn't like the way he blurted things out. They said his mind seemed to have spun back to its earlier days, and that everyone found him either crude or ridiculous.

"Then at least leave the bastard child with me," the old man demanded the morning of the ceremony, smacking his gum as he talked. His son and daughter-in-law would have yelled at him for insulting the little boy, had they not already been so distraught over the death of their daughter.

"You know you don't watch him very well, Pops," his son said. "You let him run all over the place, until he knocks into something and hurts himself. Too many bruises and cuts he's gotten while you sit there in your corner and dream of homemade noodles. He's going with us. He needs to see his mother off to heaven. We would have you go, too, but it will mean a lot of moving about. You know how those cranky bowed legs of yours are. Anyway, there will be too many people for your liking."

Just then the hefty child ran up to swat his great-grandfather on the knee. The old man, with a reflex from the past, snatched the child and wrestled him onto his lap. The tubby boy twisted and squealed delightfully but could not get loose.

"Let him go, Pops," his daughter-in-law said. The old man could tell she was annoyed. "Just let him go, or we'll reconsider putting you in a home – a good Christian place." Her husband looked uncertainly at her as she said this. He went to the old man who was his father and pinched him under both arms until he was able to pry the boy away.

And though the great-grandfather didn't go to the ceremony, but sat in his chair in the corner – not thinking of noodles now, but of a time in the old country when he was five or six and sad because his kite broke from its string and was carried away in the wind – even so, he later imagined what happened.

* * *

The rest of the family was in attendance, there at the funeral home, along with many friends. As for the eulogy, kind words were found to describe the young mother. Her father cried out that she was a good daughter, who often helped out around the house, sometimes even without being asked. She'd been a good student, too, sobbed her mother, and planned someday to go back to high school and graduate. Her evening job at a handbag shop in the mall was just a small step on her way to becoming a fashion designer. And others said how much she loved her robust *bully boy*, whom she laughed with during the day. She angrily defended his little honor against any sarcasm.

Later, the disposable coffin containing the dead mother was brought out of the chapel. It was rolled through the back of the parlor, into the room with the incinerator, where only employees were allowed. Family and friends were asked to remain in a carpeted waiting area, furnished along the walls with decorative urns similar in design to pottery from Arizona. The mourners formed a semicircle and held hands. One of the older women, the great-grandfather's younger sister, recited a translation of an Eastern proverb. And those who knew it began saying the Lord's Prayer, while others just mumbled something along. The child was also part of the human chain, and everyone dropped pitiful tears as they looked down upon him. He was still angry about not having been allowed to run in after the big box, and he did not understand the chant, just as he had not understood the words spoken by the lady with the heavy brown face. He looked all about now in a look of watery terror, and cried suddenly for his mother. His cries became more and more congested and unintelligible as the reverberating roar from the fiery retort grew louder and louder. The knobs on his cheeks turned red, and his skin became damp with perspiration. He seemed overwhelmed, boiling.

During the escalating bellow from the chamber – at a point where there seemed a climatic rumble, as that which happens in a symphony mimicking the sounds of a storm – the child's breath was suddenly drawn away. He gasped horrendously, and everyone thought the poor child was attacked by asthma. All eyes watched, but no one appeared capable of motion. They saw the boy struggle for air, every molecule from his lungs dissipating, his stubby throat thoroughly constricted. His eyes rolled, his sturdy little legs buckled, and he staggered a few steps forward, a few steps backward, before collapsing on his rump. The plop to the ground slammed his eyes shut. He was a big boy now and wore no cushioning diapers. Sitting there like a plump, resting doll, he at last regained the ability to breathe. It was a while longer before his eyes reopened, and when they did, everyone could see they were not the same.

* * *

One week after the cremation, the toddler's cousin, a girl he used to run up to and call *Caffy*, began coming over to the house while the young grandparents were off at work. The girl was twenty years old, simple, and could not get a job anywhere else. Still, it was better that she looked after the boy. The old man was feeble and had to struggle just to make it to the bathroom in time. He, too, refused to wear plastic, padded underpants.

The girl cousin soon found it enjoyable babysitting and playing with little Booly – for that's what she thought his mother had called him. He didn't run wildly about as he used to, colliding into things and slapping people on the leg. Nor did he cry or squeal or chuckle. He didn't call her by name anymore, either. He seemed to have lost any desire to speak whatsoever, although his grandparents claimed he mumbled in his sleep at night much like his great-grandfather. But he was perfect for playing tea and dress up. His cousin would laugh every time as if it were fresh.

"His spirit has been pulled," said the old man, whenever anyone expressed dismay at the child's unresponsiveness. "The mother was too weak to carry all of him – or he was too heavy. What would you be like if your spirit was pulled? Damn my son and his wife. They let my granddaughter burn on the wrong day. I told them and they would not listen. Damn them both. The little bastard is now only half here."

And it was true that little Booly seemed to be missing something. Physically, he grew taller and squarer, and looked much older than he was. But he walked without any self-guidance, only coming-here and going-there as directed by his cousin or by one of the grownups. His appetite seemed fine, if one only casually watched him. He ate and drank whatever was placed before him, dropping or spilling nothing. But studied more carefully, he did not appear to either enjoy or detest. He stopped only when his plate, bowl, or cup was empty or taken away.

One morning the boy sat in a sturdy dark wooden child's chair, placed next to the old gray chair of the old man. The two of them, the great-grandson and the great-grandfather, often sat there together in silence, regretting the loss of happier days. His cousin, who still hadn't grown tired of him though he was almost three years old now, called him into the kitchen to come eat. The boy rose when his cousin called, not hurriedly and not belatedly, and walked into the cramped kitchen, intending to pass just to the side of the stove on his way to the table. This was as he had been trained. His cousin, though, didn't see him coming, and when she whirled around in her reckless, unthinking way, she brought a scalding pot of oatmeal in full contact with the side of the child's neck.

The girl shrank back immediately, but it was too late. So thorough was the scorching that the great-grandfather, following behind the boy, heard the hiss. The child's skin sizzled. Booly squawked and threw his hands up, wafting the charred odor, which the old man realized was that of the overcooked oatmeal and not of the boy's flesh. Whirling in pain, Booly spun into the kitchen table, where he knocked over two out of the three glasses of milk that had been set. He hooted and hopped and dashed headlong into a plastered wall, which cratered and sent forth a chalky mist. The cousin and the great-grandfather helped the boy up from the ground. Dusting him off and pulling white bits from his hair, they saw the chaos in his eyes. They stared at each other but said nothing.

A few days later, when it seemed the boy had settled back into his usual placid state, another incident occurred. Booly and his great-grandfather were again sitting in their chairs, which someone had drawn a bit closer together than usual. Neither one talked, but the boy had a little sporadic twitch happening on the right side of his mouth, while his grandfather accompanied his own inner thoughts with the snapping of his gum. From the adjacent kitchen came a tuneless hum, along with the clanging of dishes and the smell of toast. There was a pop -- metallic and plastic -- and the repeated sound of mechanical springs being compressed. The cousin passed through the room with the idle males, and just as she disappeared into another part of the house, the boy stood up. Hurriedly he moved toward the scent. In a slow, ratcheting manner the great-grandfather stood up too. He heard the toaster release again, and now at the threshold before the kitchen he saw Booly standing on his tiptoes removing the half-burnt bread. It was too late for the old man to stop the boy, who now dove both hands into the two vacated slots. A long moment passed while the boy cooked his fingers. It seemed to the great-grandfather that time was stilled. Withdrawing his well-grilled flesh at last, the boy threw himself about, pitching out a high-toned, ecstatic squeal of pain. Cathy, the cousin, returned and gasped silently in guilt and horror. She grabbed the wild child and carried him to the sink where she ran cool water. The old man fetched butter from the refrigerator -- but not for the toasted bread. Even after the two adults had managed to grease and bandage the blistered fingers, they noticed there remained a brightness in the boy's face, a purposeful focusing of his formerly vacant and motionless eyes.

Later, when the boy's grandparents came home from work, they spoke harshly to the cousin. This was the second time now that she'd let the boy get hurt. But the old man rose and in a monstrous voice resurrected from an earlier decade defended the poor girl.

"It was I who didn't watch him. The girl had to go to the restroom. Can't anyone go to the restroom without being blamed? We did not purposely let him burn himself. And, anyway, it was on a good day and he will quickly recover. Don't speak to me or to anyone else about letting people get burned!"

After that, the great-grandfather and the cousin were vigilant. They prevented the boy from entering the kitchen unsupervised. The boy gave up easily and slunk back into his previous torpor. Even a small fire on the stove didn't stir him from his little chair in the next room.

But as weeks went by they relaxed. The cousin hummed unattractively and let herself get distracted. The great-grandfather fell asleep in his chair. One afternoon a knock on the front door failed to awaken the old man, but drew away the girl – not before she hurriedly removed a broccoli casserole from the oven. Except, in her haste she hadn't turned back the dial, and some cheesy spillage now burned on the bottom coil.

The great-grandfather woke up thinking he was in a smoky dream of the past. He was back in the old country, in his old house, where an open fire burned in an old stone stove. The smell became so strong that even the cousin, who stood at the door denying to a young candle salesman she had any money, should have been alerted to it. And now something clanked on the kitchen floor. The old man, realizing this was no dream, raised himself and hurried toward the kitchen. Something clanked again just as he entered.

The two racks from the oven lay discarded, scorching the yellow linoleum. The boy had removed them with his bare hands and was now in the process of crawling in head first.

The old man was already in motion and with his quick hands could have grabbed the boy in time.

But the great-grandfather's feet froze as though in a nightmare. Wavering at the threshold to the kitchen, two thoughts began ticking in his head, back and forth like the long hand of a hesitant clock. *Why am I standing here like a useless bowlegged old man?* Then: *Why don't I have faith and let the boy do what he has to do?*

And so the old man simply watched. Not with dread, but with understanding.

He was still standing there, watching and understanding, when the girl rushed up from behind and shoved him out of the way.

* * *

Booly, his grandparents, and his great-grandfather sat at the kitchen table eating their supper. This was about a year after the boy was treated for his intensive burns. The old man did not want the casserole the others were having, but instead helped himself to a little dish of fish, with a pasty dab of Chinese horseradish, which he had prepared himself. Wasabi, the horseradish was called, and it was especially potent today. Inside his mouth a satisfying flame rose and opened his sinuses, and the tears in his eyes were pleasant. He smiled and thought now to glance at the boy, Booly, who sat dutifully eating the bland casserole.

The boy's grandparents left in the morning. They had fallen back into the same routine, because everyone needs to work and earn money, especially when there are medical bills to pay. The old man went into the kitchen.

From a big jar he kept in a cabinet he took several pieces of bubble gum. He proceeded to unwrap them. One by one he popped them into his mouth, chomped them till they were soft, before spitting them into a bowl. He kneaded the wads together and mashed them flat with a wooden spoon. From the refrigerator he took out a fresh root of the wasabi, which he shaved with a thin-bladed knife, allowing the slivers to flake over the paddy of gum. He used his fingers to fold the two ingredients together. He took another knife now and cut the mixture into bite-sized pieces.

And after breakfast, after the boy had eaten the cold cereal that had been placed before him, the old man invited him into the sitting room. Booly plopped into a chair inches away. The great-grandfather held out his palm and the boy took the offering and placed it in his mouth.

Booly's nostrils widened and his eyes watered. In no time at all he became animated, talking much too fast. Soon he was bouncing around the room. The great-grandfather made him return to his seat, however, and after the boy calmed down they both sat about just chewing and chatting, like two old men. After a while the boy tired and the old man did most of the talking.

The great-grandfather looked not at the boy as he spoke but toward the window, which opened up into a view of the small back yard and which had growing and beating against its pane a solitary flourishing stem from an otherwise worn down rose bush. But his words, if not his gaze, were directed to the boy. He began telling a story from his youth, pausing frequently to *smack, smack, smack, smack*. The boy, meanwhile, didn't understand much of what his great-grandfather said. Or maybe he did, for he seemed to nod reflectively just at the right moments, chewing in rhythm.

The story from the East begins when the old man was fourteen. His older brother, whom he much admired, had for no clear reason become hostile toward him. Often, the older brother would approach the younger one in a sudden rage and violence would ensue. The older boy knocked the younger child down on the ground, kneeled on the smaller one's chest and screamed vilely into his face. This happened several times before the younger boy, now Booly's great-grandfather, began going off on long walks after finishing his chores. He walked all about the village, without any other purpose than to avoid his older brother. He did this for many weeks, until one day, while on the side of the village closest to the mountain, a brilliant big-bellied blue-green bird flopped down from a roof and landed right in front of him. It cocked its long neck and displayed its many eyes.

"I stepped back at first," said the old man to the boy, "but then I laughed. I laughed like I hadn't in ages. You see, my chubby American boy, a peacock is good luck. He is reborn by fire, like they say here of the bird called phoenix. First, a part of him dies – with you it was your mother – next, the rest of him must burn. But you know how that goes. Yes, he is good luck, and it is said that luck repeats. Right then I went home, and *my* good luck was that my brother put his arm around me and told me he was sorry for bullying me. He had decided to become a soldier and would be going away. He said that I could take his bed and that he would never forget me."

Upon this conclusion, Booly asked, "Is there any more gum, Pops? This piece is losing its flavor."

And Cathy, the cousin, who had been dismissed from the household but who had since been forgiven and was now back working and listening, hurried in to help the old man out of his chair.

The Bargain

by Claudia Herring

The angel knelt, red wings glowing in heavenly light, splendid as a bird of paradise.

"*The Annunciation* by Petrus Christus." The Marquis gazed lovingly on the top painting of the diptych. "You see all around, the angels." He indicated his opulent gallery and Andras saw that each painting featured at least one if not a host of angels. "Angels speak to men." His Excellency's dark eyes glistened. "Many think this stopped in ancient times, but the truth is, as you know..." The Marquis moved close to Andras, his breath hot and sour. "They still do. Prayer is the thing. Pray enough, listen intently and the celestials answer." He tapped his hand, jeweled rings glowing, against his embroidered sleeve and stared at Andras,

Andras knew he should say something. He took a slow breath as a shiver rattled up his spine, imagining a momentary frown clouding the angels' benevolent expressions. He envisioned the words of men -- prayers, annoying, pleading and begging -- rising up to heaven like dense swarms of gnats. "God's messengers." Andras kept his voice low.

"Praise the Lord." The Marquis shouted and raised his arms in supplication, lifting his face to the high clerestory window where the sunlight streamed down upon him, his eyes glinting like coals in a grate.

Andras startled, but formed his expression to one of acceptance

"The Lord giveth and the Lord taketh away," the Marquis roared, whirled around and stopped in front of Andras. "You are here because of my vision."

Andras stepped backwards, fearing the Marquis might seize him in his agitation. The man shouldn't touch him when he was unprepared. "In truth, I am the messenger and the servant." Andras had grown weary of his tasks.

Years before he had fallen from the grace of his master, and he winced at the memory of flaming swords and other cruel punishments to keep him in control. But his kind were doomed to servitude.

He pondered the name he was given, Andras, *interfering with divine will*, and his newer, more acceptable name, Remiel, *mercy of God*. Perhaps this task would prove both names prescient. He steepled his hands under his chin.

The Marquis focused his glimmering eyes on Andras. Were those tears streaming down his host's cheeks? In the name of heaven, the man was weeping, the trails of tears as luminous as the faces of angels in his paintings. His Excellency turned down his mouth and squinted at Andras' plain woolen doublet with red sleeves, his green hose and his worn lace-up boots.

Andras looked at the paintings, the many angels' feathery wings—red, rainbow-colored, white, and gold. Their silken robes flowed with wondrous folds, embroidered sleeves threaded in gold and silver and studded with precious jewels. Glowing nimbi shone like moonlight around their glossy bright curls. "I am an humble servant sent to help. For even with all his magnificence, the Lord has many sheep to tend and therefore has many shepherds." Andras gave a weak smile. He thought a wink too undignified.

The Marquis stared, scowling. Andras suspected he might send him away, so he opened his arms in a beneficent gesture and undimmed his nimbus for a brief moment.

"By my faith." The Marquis shrieked and jumped back, bending down and pointing. "You *are* His messenger." He dropped to his knees, hands folded in prayer. "I was going to have my sentry take you outside and gut you." He sobbed, blubbery, wet. "I would have been disgraced in the Lord's eyes. Disgraced." The Marquis shot to his feet. "This vision I had. This deed I will do." The Marquis caressed the nearby visage of an angel, the celestial's halo shining in gilt. "You will help."

Andras shrank back.

* * *

The Marquis stabbed his knife into a confit of baked swan. A footman poured wine, another dished pâté of meaux, olives and orange salad onto his plate. His Excellency's young wife and three sons ate quietly at the table, studying their father's guest when they thought he wasn't looking. The youngest closed one eye and searched intently around Andras' head, flushing red when caught. Andras merely smiled, hiding his fear that he might not have succeeded in his camouflage. He had been ordered to fit in and if pressed, to let the Marquis see only a glimpse.

His Excellency sipped his wine and set the glass down with a thump, his furrowed brow and hard stare dark with the fury of a gathering storm. He took a deep breath. His hands shook. As if anticipating his actions, the family grimaced and hunched their shoulders as one, their faces drawn up in the most painful expressions.

The Marquis flung his glass against the wall, the crash summoning a wide-eyed look of fear on the children's faces.

"This wine is off. Remove it from my sight. Bring another." The footmen scrambled, taking the glasses away as a new bottle was opened. A small amount, deep red in shining crystal, was poured and there was a collective holding of breath until...

"Better." The Marquis set his glass down. When it was full he said, "New wine for all," and the family let fall a sigh of relief.

He swabbed a slice of meat in sauce and fixed Andras in his sight. "I am honored. Your Master has been most accommodating."

Andras looked up in surprise. Unusual for a believer, even one of this magnitude, to have no questions. The footman set a new glass of wine by his plate and Andras brought it to his lips, thinking of the Eucharist. The Lord must have spoken clearly to this one.

"My Master is much the perfectionist." Andras forced a smile, raised his glass and the Marquis nodded, his eyes burning with conviction.

* * *

The footman flung the curtains aside to a sky fading from deep cobalt, revealing the mountainous horizon. "His Excellency will meet you on the east portico at sunrise."

Andras remained in bed, covers pulled to his chin until the footman left. Then he leapt up and pulled the bolt across the door. Satisfied he would have his privacy, he bound his tunic tight and put on his doublet, pulling the long sleeves over his wrists, just as beams of golden light broke the silhouette of the mountains. The mirror reflected the glow of his nimbus, which he dimmed as he stepped from the chambers and closed the door. A long red feather floated in the soft rays of sunlight and slid into the shadows under the bed.

The Marquis and one of his sons waited beneath the portico. "You have met Gregorio, my youngest. Perhaps you've been informed of him?" His Excellency fingered the tassel on his hat and looked expectantly at Andras.

Andras had heard Gregorio's name spoken with passion. He nodded pleasantly at the Marquis, then focused on his son. "Good morrow, Gregorio. Fare thee well on this day of providence."

The boy's light brown eyes shifted when Andras shook his hand and he cocked his head with a puzzled look. Andras stifled his surprise—he had reached deep inside to prepare his body for the touch. *Gregorio shouldn't be able to discern.*

"We must be about our business." The Marquis shouldered a leather pack and took to the stairs just as a footman appeared.

"Milord, beg pardon." He thrust a salver holding a parchment scroll towards his master.

The Marquis broke the seal and unrolled the scroll. His face reddening, he left the porch without a word.

Gregorio gazed at the mountains. Amethyst peaks drawn sharply against a soft peach firmament. At a dove's mournful cry he turned his head, the warm light illumining his skin. He stepped nearer Andras and leaned in close. "What is this we are to do?"

"It is your father's place to tell you." Andras kept his tone benevolent. Even he had been appalled at this deed the Marquis had agreed to, but it had been done before, only to different ends. After centuries, even the Lord might repeat himself. The act was thought of as a great sacrifice, but Andras only saw the Lord's greed, his insatiable quest for glory. It would seem that by now, by the same token of repetition, His followers would come to their senses.

The boy rested against the balustrade. Opened his mouth. Hesitated, casting his eyes to the ground. "Father has been . . . disturbed. Messengers, dispatches, day and night." Gregorio jerked his head towards the distant palace. "Mother's eyes are red and swollen in the morning." The boy pressed his lips tight and looked as if he might cry. "I feel a plague about our house."

He took Andras by the hand, eyes suddenly alight with a fervent glow as though he had just experienced an epiphany. "I sense something about you. When you're not looking at me, I see light around you." Gregorio let go the visitor's hand and peered into his face. "Are you a... a guardian spirit?"

"I am a messenger." Andras undimmed himself. The boy gasped and floated from the ground, his feet a finger's breadth off the marble floor of the portico.

"Save us." Gregorio's voice was a whisper.

He had shown too much. Andras touched the boy's arm, bringing him to earth.

"I knew my prayers would be answered." Gregorio fumbled at the neck of his fine woolen tunic and pulled out a gold chain strung through rings on a thin golden cylinder. "A piece of the holy cross inside," the boy's voice hushed with awe.

Andras tried not to show his disdain. These false relics sold for too many . . . darics? The currency of the moment eluded him.

"When I pray, I feel the weight of the cross." Gregorio's eyes shone starry. "I know our Lord hears me."

Andras stared at Gregorio, at the expression in the boy's eyes. Why, he was sincere. He hadn't found anyone that pure since...

Andras had been guided to a genuine, innocent soul. Oh, the quest for these pure souls, so easy to lead, to corrupt. The Gods needed them, but they had become scarce. He was to confirm his discovery and then act.

The boy faced him. "The king is displeased. Our money is gone. Father has done wicked deeds of-"

The Marquis rushed onto the portico. Gregorio sucked in his breath, slipped his talisman into his tunic and stood straight.

"Pardon, the Court rises early." The Marquis smiled, but his eyes remained haunted. He drummed his fingers against his leather pack.

A sensation bore upon Andras as when Helen fled with Paris for Troy, when Genghis Khan united the nomads of furthest Asia, when Tristan set eyes on Isolde. He could see the whole unraveling.

Gregorio descended the stairs to the courtyard after his father. He paused, face shining, and motioned their guest to accompany him.

Andras followed father and son out of the palace walls and up the winding path. As they rounded a stand of cypress, he regarded the rocky summit towering above them and shook his head. *Nothing good ever happened on a mountain.* He remembered Moses and his tablets—caused naught but trouble. But at least the Lord gave specific instructions then. With the passing years instructions and answers had become vague to nonexistent. Was this finally a turning point?

Andras halted, hand on a huge striated boulder orange and green with lichens. He wilted as if a fever ravaged his body. *A pang of conscience? Now?* Enough irony there for a long laugh. But his body was at a loss, laughing only a memory. By the light reflecting from the stone's shaded surface, he could tell he glowed. His nimbus must be in full sight. With great effort, he dimmed it.

* * *

Gregorio stood beside Andras, surveying the valley spread below. Wind ruffled the boy's russet hair. He held his talisman through his tunic and whispered, "Will you make miracles here?"

Andras stiffened, but he smiled at the boy. Oh, the perfect pure innocence of belief. He watched the Marquis walk the short path from the summit towards them. He clutched Andras' arm and whispered, "If you bring a message from your Lord Master, I am ready."

Andras reached into his doublet. "My Lord Master said you know your task. This is a prayer."

The golden seal crumbled as the Marquis straightened the scroll. His brow furrowed and Andras stepped back. He knew what it said, but the contents were likely to change even when the scroll was safely tucked in his doublet.

"Yes, a prayer." His Excellency studied the scroll, his face a mask but for a twitch of his mouth. "You saw that I have two other sons, and my wife is just now with child."

The Marquis shut his eyes for a moment and murmured something about forgiveness. Andras studied him curiously. His Excellency walked to his son, put one arm around his shoulders and pulled him close. Gregorio, the start of a smile on his face, leaned against his father. With a quick, violent motion the Marquis strong-armed Gregorio, forced the boy to the ground and bound his hands.

"Father." Gregorio struggled to his knees. "What have I done?" He tried to stand, eyes scouring his father's face, but stumbled and fell. "Father."

"The Lord will receive you with open arms, my son," the Marquis said through his tears. He unsheathed a dagger from his pack. His tasseled hat blew away and, through a gust of wind, he murmured, "My vision. The gold. The power. All from the Lord." He looked at Andras. "You are to be witness."

Andras froze. This had happened before, long ago, but this time it would be different. The Esteemed One had searched amongst the peoples and had found not a soul, but now there was Gregorio. Andras had been warned, but found himself unprepared for what was to transpire. These things always seemed more righteous in the abstract. If he acted with haste he wouldn't have to face the Lord.

The Marquis stepped aside. "My youngest son for my and my family's salvation, here and in the afterlife." He pierced Andras with his eyes, eyes starved for power, for forgiveness, for redemption. "Your Lord and Master awaits him." The Marquis looked to the heavens, then seized Gregorio by his silky hair, dagger poised at his throat.

They had a wager. Andras didn't think he would dare, but the Esteemed One knew the power of belief. This wouldn't be the first time Andras had lost.

He ripped off his doublet.

His wings burst from the bindings of his tunic. Red feathers spread to the span of ten cubits. The cardinal glow of his radiance reflected on Gregorio's face.

The Marquis, hand unsteady in surprise, skimmed his dagger lightly across his son's throat. With the brush of a crimson wing, the blade sailed from his hand.

A blinding light exploded on the mountaintop. Andras arced his wing over his eyes. The Presence. Could he escape?

He swooped Gregorio into his arms. They soared from the ledge. As he fled from the light, Andras ran his fingers along a line of blood traversing the left side of the boy's throat. The blood vanished. The flesh healed.

Gregorio whispered in reverence, "You saved me. My prayers..."

* * *

Andras set down at the agreed-upon spot, placed Gregorio gently on the ground and untied the boy's wrists. The atmosphere shimmered in the enveloping gloom. The boy clutched Andras by the legs.

At the heart of the darkness, a radiant figure materialized.

"Gregorio, you come to me in all your righteousness." The voice, mesmerizing, rivaled choirs of angels. Out of the shadows, lithe arms reached for him, graceful as a divine dancer. The boy let go of Andras and stepped forward, eyes intent on the cherubic face.

Andras watched for a moment, then bowed his head. How far he had fallen. He turned away, but at the corner of his vision a glint flared from the murk. He stood alert, staring at the boy who fingered his talisman through his tunic. By the saints, he could see a glimmer of luminescence on Gregorio's fingers, as if the boy hid a bright star.

With piqued interest, Andras watched the Esteemed One gliding towards Gregorio, cloth-of-gold raiment flowing over her alluring curves, almost concealing the twitch of her forked tail.

Effa on Fire

by Chantell Renee

"When the sun comes up, I'm going to die." Telling the new generation the truth is as important as knowing it yourself.

"Hava-Custos, you should be thinking of life not death."

The young Infan is correct. But I have been a Custos, attendant for the trials, far too long to not know death is much more common.

"Infan, when we are without our Caretakers we usually go by designation only. So you may call me Custos." In truth, I am able to do all four of the jobs assigned to the young. But it is my thirst for knowledge that makes me a possible candidate for tradesman. The Caretaker post is needed but seeing so many Lilation perish has made me wary of life on the ground. Of course getting a post would only occur if I live, which I won't.

"Thank you for showing me so much Custos, I do hope you survive." The Infan's dark, straight hair is pulled back today, showing off her tilted eye shape. Not many species have eyes like ours, large and solid in color. Our Mother gave us this trait. Most have the shades of our world, blues and greens. My own is mixed of the two sacred hues.

The baby the Infan is caring for has fallen asleep. I help her put the child into its crib. Though we are not that different in height, I notice the length of my arms has changed. A sign that I am ready for the trials, it becomes dangerous if we allow our bones to grow on their own. Death is certain that way.

"Caretaker Hava has said she will let me watch you during your trials. You won't be able to see me, but I will be there." The young female rolls the corner of the baby blanket between her long, pale fingers. She is scared. My group will be the first she truly knows to go through the trials. The young female's mentor, who is a part of my group, must not have said much to her about the trials. Not surprising. We all find it difficult knowing we would each be replaced.

"Our Caretaker has trained our five well. All those puzzles and riddles will definitely work during the burning phase." I touch her small hand, she has just turned six. Odds are she will die during her trials. Only two out of the five live.

The Infan girl must continue with her duties and I must finish passing my post to the new Custos of our group. We say our farewells for now.

As I walk through the settlement, I notice many eyes looking my way. Caretakers and helpers stare from out of their huts as well as the passersby. Even with all the attention, the dry dirt between my toes cools and comforts me, reminding me of our simple lives. These caretakers know me. I have tended for their helpers during their own trials. And though we all live in the same sector of the forest, we are not allowed to socialize. Our way of lessening the horror of losing so many Lilation at such young ages.

"Discipulus." Hava calls to me, stopping my progress to the ceremonial area. My feet stop automatically to wait for her. In our culture your caretaker is almost as important as the great Mother and Father.

When a Lilation makes it to adulthood, you no longer use their post designation when speaking to them. One of the things to look forward to about adulthood, having a real name, I've chosen Effa. But for now, I must answer to my post title.

Hava is twice my height and four times my size, like the other caretakers who walk around us. As she stops in front of me, I feel a tightening inside. I believe the homo-sapien species calls this feeling 'jealousy'. Her body is strong, with thick sturdy bone and smooth pale white skin. Her hair is a lovely dark brown, to her waist and as glossy as our sea. But I know I will never be an adult.

"Yes Hava?" My eyes meet hers without hesitation, just as I have been taught to do for the last twelve passings of my short life.

"I can see you have let death settle in your mind." Hava has always been able to read me, even as an infant.

"I am hopeful ...-but yes, I don't see it like you do." I look at my feet, noticing how much larger Hava's are compared to mine.

"Discipulus, at five you started reading the history of our stars. You are strong of both mind and body. Do not give up just yet." Hava reaches out to brush my long dark hair back. She has been so nurturing, I could not have had a better life.

We part and I continue my journey. Ten beds of straw and brush have already been laid out. One of them is mine, but I will not know which until morning.

"Hava-Custos." The young girl addresses me as I approach. She is my replacement; I have made sure she knows what to do and how to do it. She looks nervous; this is her first trial as an attendant. We have trained for two passings now, she is ready.

"Hello Hava-Custos." I reply. This is the first time she has had someone use the proper designation. I no longer need it, the dead don't have titles. She smiles up at me.

"I have prepared the bed. We don't start the tables until tomorrow." This is odd. Usually we are to prepare everything the day before. But being so near my final resting place, I can't bring myself to inquire about the change.

"That is fine. This is your first trial, our training is complete." I move around the bed and check to see the straw is tight enough to hold together but loose enough to burn. When she doesn't answer, I look at her. She is scared.

"You know what you are doing. I have watched you for two passings of the Milkyway now, and you have a great hand for this." My speech doesn't crack the façade of strength she is trying to show. I know she is afraid simply because she is quiet, which is so unlike her.

"I don't think I have ever told you the story of my first charge."

"No, you haven't."

"Well, she was a wonderful Lila. She came from Caretaker Bita. She lived through the Burning to the Breaking. Her head char and chest char actually cracked." This got the young girl's attention.

"I attended her for a moon cycle."

"Did she live?"

"No. But she was strong. She looked at me before she died. She was ready to meet the Mother."

"Thank you for your tale. I will be as kind to my first as you were." She turned and made her way to the path. That one was tough, but she too knew death was more likely for me.

Although, thinking about my first, I can't help but feel a little hope flare up. If I live my very name will honor her. She'd asked to be named Effany. I remember looking at Caretaker Hava, I was six at the time. She'd come to me after Effany had stopped breathing.

Placing her hand on my shoulder she asked, "What species is the most resilient among the stars?" I hadn't stopped looking at the black and red of the departed Effany. But my Caretaker's voice broke my trance and helped me pull my eyes away.

"Human, though they are not allowed outside their star grid." Tears washed down my face.

"What makes them so tough?"

I thought about her question. Hava moved my hands to start the process of wrapping Effany for disposal.

"They have unmatched intention to live. This is why they are in quarantine. They would be uncontrollable elements that would throw our peace out of balance."

Effany's shroud was complete. Hava stood and picked her up. "You will always remember your first. Go. There are the survivors to care for now."

The ten of us move to the prepared beds. I want to be brave for the young here. I recognize the boy who cares for me, he is Vitzz-Custos. Caretaker Vitzz is one of the best instructors. On the table the boy has readied all the right oils and washes.

I look out at the crowd and see Caretaker Hava. She moves her lips, she is saying 'know you can live'. But the memories of all those I have prepared, not one of whom survived, is all I can think about. Even if I live through this, I will still have weeks before my new form would be ready to move. Whatever happens here, the me I am now will die.

We lie down, and our attendants remove the garments we've worn for so long. The air cools my skin. As one, the Custos start to apply the first oils. All ten of my sisters and brothers, five from Hava and five from Bita, feel what I feel. It is time. When my boy moves up to my chest plate I look at him hoping he'll look back. So many times my charges would look to me as I prepared them. I never wanted to bond; I regret that now. This is the last hour of life for them. As the participant, I find myself longing for that last connection.

He avoids my stare so I memorize his lovely face. He has youthful soft, pale skin, short dark hair and thin lips. His childlike skeletal structure protrudes. Strength isn't always a good sign for the young. The bones may not crack when it's time for them to burn.

"If I live, my name will be Effa."

He pauses, turns his eyes towards mine and gives me one nod before he moves down the other side of my body. How odd it seems I'll finally have my own name.

The needles are next. Kindling fluids are injected to my existing bones to help the new ones push through. I don't cry out until the point pushes into the core of each bone. My attendant ignores my screams. I am grateful for his persistence. As awful as each stab is, dying would be worse. When he injects my facial bone, I smell the familiar chemical and this brings comfort. My eyes and nose start to run, the result of the strong odor.

He pours the last emollient onto my already soaked body. I close my eyes and mouth as he drenches my face. The chest and face are the areas that are vital for survival.

"Let some of it in your mouth, trust, it will help." He whispers. I've never heard of allowing the burning oil inside your body. I realize it could help, so I part my lips and let the oils seep into my mouth. The taste is awful.

"Not too much, just enough to help your head make the first trial, so don't swallow it." He moves away. In my mind I can see my helper slide his working table back and proceed to the next step of the process. Splashing noises of igniter fluids dropping to the ground as he soaks the torch, tell me I was correct. I hear the crackle of the flame. The pain and foul taste of the fluids, pale in comparison to the sound of those flames.

As he waits for the others' torches to catch, the battle inside me to prevail or perish threatens to send me off the table running into the forest. Which has occurred in the past, when we found the runner, they had died from their bones trying to grow. The memory of the bones crushing the organs from the inside is all that keeps me on my table.

The first lick of the fire is on my hair. My thick mane brings the burn to my scalp and face. I want to cry out. I hear the others cry around me, moans of agony, is what I can manage. Even if this is all I have left of my life, I do not want to miss a minute. Over the entirety of my body, the skin is peeling and pulling apart. The flames have already reached my muscles and organs. The agony is manageable; perhaps I can make it through. Somewhere near I hear a shrill scream. Did we all not get lit simultaneously?

The bones of my face are the first of my skeleton to burn, the muscle there being so thin. The fire finds the needle holes and lights up the core of my structure. This is beyond pain. There is no time or place any longer, only the fire. Screams echo in my head, somehow I know it's my own shouts, but it's difficult to think. My brothers and sisters all join in and we become a choir of screeches. If I could only pass out, leave the torture that this reality has become. But my chances of life will increase if I stay awake throughout the burning.

More of my core is consumed by the flame as the muscles are reduced to nothing. My voice is gone, no more substance to make the noises. Here and now is the time to push, if I don't...

"What colors are the Tadakian oceans?"

I don't know how, but I hear Hava's calming voice.

I try to answer but I can't speak.

"Effa, tell me the colors."

"Purple..." The first of the crust is forming on my face. "Orange, not red like it looks from the sky..." The flame has burnt out over my chest and face.

"Silver is the last. It is that color because of the rock bed underneath." The last of the burning ceases. From head to foot I am solid char. I've made it to the crust, now all I can do is wait and see if my new bones can break through.

During training you never understand the agony of growing new bones. I would rather burn again. The boy's idea of the oil in my mouth helped; I cracked my head char two days before the rest. Though I have never heard of more than four surviving, there are whispers around me that all ten of us have made it to the growing.

My boy is good at keeping me informed of my progress and that of those around me. By day six, two of the ten fail the trials of growth and are taken away in their death shrouds. Every day I hear Hava in my mind asking me questions about the stars and places in them. I answer and know it is this that keeps me determined to suffer the shooting pains of bone growth.

When my eyes open, I see the sun is up and the boy is still here. When I breathe, the crackling is gone. This means my chest bones have hardened. I want to move my legs, but if they are not set I could cause a defect in their forming. I watch the boy and stay very still.

He has an ointment used to let the skin stay supple so the growth will be easier and continue without death to me. His hands labor deep over my legs, and I realize the crackling is gone from them too. I wait until he has worked the salve over my feet to attempt movement. He watches and I watch him. We both know I am ready.

"You are the first up. Well done. May Mother and Father be with you always."

The area is empty except for the seven others still on their beds and attendants. Strange, usually there are those who look on for days.

"Vitzz-Custos, how long has it been?"

"One moon cycle, you were ready early." I look down at the child before me, he is tiny. Before the trials we were close to the same size. I have grown four times his height. My bones feel strong. The new skin is shiny with the ointment.

"Thank you." I know there is not telepathy in my race, but in a way, I want to thank Hava for her help too. If she'd not pushed me during my training my mind would most certainly not have made it through.

I walk back to my Caretaker's hut. Hava looks at me as I step inside.

"Effa!"

"I lived."

The End

Now that you have finished Tides of Impossibility, won't you please consider writing an honest review and leaving it on Amazon and/or Goodreads, or any other online sales channel of your preference? Reviews are the best way readers discover great new books. We would truly appreciate it.

About the Editors and Authors

The Houston Writers Guild was founded in 1998 by Roger Paulding with seven participants and has grown to more than 200 active members today. Over its first fifteen years, the Guild sponsored 36 workshops and six 2-day conferences. Roger led the group until 2013, when he passed the reins to Pamela Fagan Hutchins. Pamela announced in that same year her vision to operate the organization on a nonprofit basis with the goal of passing the torch in one year to the next HWG member who wanted to do the same. On September 17, 2014, Fernanda Brady and Denise Satterfield became the next stewards of the HWG. Together they are gearing up to take the vision to the next level, striving to turn HWG into a non-profit organization.

C. Stuart Hardwick, editor, is an L. Ron Hubbard Writers of the Future Contest winning author of speculative fiction. He's also a Baen Memorial Award finalist, a James White Award semi-finalist, a lover of curries and Greek food, and a southerner from South Dakota. Weaned on Black Hills treasure hunts and family lore like pages from a Steinbeck novel, Stuart spent his youth creating "radio shows" on antique recording tape, making stop-animated scifi films, and building ill-conceived flying machines out of parts from the swing set and his mother's garden furniture. A science fair robot led to a career in software and technical writing, including a stint with the creators of the video game, *Doom*, and a chance to write for the journal, *TechTarget*. Along the way, he married an aquanaut, got hugged by a manatee, and trained his Aussie dog to pull a sled.

Stuart has been called a sophisticated, complex writer, but his work often recalls the adventure and optimism of the Golden Age. It's been called original, evocative, poignant, and mesmerizing, and has been compared to Bradbury and Heinlein—fitting, since those are two of his earliest influences. He leans toward hard science fiction, but writes and defends all variations of genre.

Stuart studied writing at U.C. Berkeley, lives in Houston Texas, and has been known to wear a cape. For more information and a free signed e-story, visit www.cStuartHardwick.com.

K.J.Russell and Adrienne D'Agostino met online playing World of Warcraft. Years later, they are married with four cats: Sylvanas, Eomer, Eowyn, and Fish.

K.J. Russell, editor, is the Director of Publications for the Houston Writers Guild. Tides of Impossibility is his second anthology produced in that capacity, with the first being its science-fiction sibling, Tides of Possibility. He leads writing workshops at the Writespace studio in downtown Houston, and can be frequently found on panels at sci-fi conventions as far away as Colorado. His debut e-novella, Absolute Tenacity, released to strong reviews. It has been called a captivating, twisting story that "pops violently with a raw, unexpected ambivalence." His first full novel, The Dusty Man, is set to release in May.

Adrienne D'Agostino graduated with a Masters degree in Aquatic Ecology from the University of Colorado and now teaches science to middle- and high-school aged students in Houston. Raised by a geologist and an artist to see the world from every beautiful angle, Adrienne very patiently explains basic science to K.J. Russell when he gets it wrong, using simple diagrams and small words so that he can understand. Together, they are writing a high fantasy novel based in the world of *Bone Flowers*.

T.J. Akers wants to be a multi-millionaire when he grows up and give his wealth away to his favorite causes -- churches, schools, and animal shelters. Since the millions have been slow in coming, he's settled for working in a public university as a computer technician, volunteering at church and the local animal shelter, doing honey do projects for his wife, and writing stories to entertain people, especially younger readers.

His full-length fiction has been honored by the American Christian Fiction Writers Association as a 2012 First Impressions Finalist, a 2013 Genesis Award finalist, and a 2014 Genesis Award semi-finalist. His short story *Entertaining Angels* was a finalist in the 2014 Writers on the Storm contest sponsored by the Texas chapter of the ACFW. His short story *Necessary Evil* has been published in the science fiction anthology *No Revolution Too Big* (Helping Hands Press - April 2014).

He holds a masters degree in English from Minnesota State University-Mankato and can often be found roaming that university's library on his lunch break, especially the children's and young adult sections. Librarians have always been his heroes.

He lives with his wife of twenty-nine years in southern Minnesota.

Mandy Broughton writes mysteries and speculative fiction -- particularly science-fiction but also horror. She has a trio of middle-grade mysteries but avoids the Grim Reaper when writing for children. Her adult cozy, *The Cat's Last Meow*, does have dead bodies as well as a cat. Rest assured, that cat is almost as bad as Death in *Death Hires a Stylist*. She has published several sci-fi short stories in two different anthologies, *Tides of Possibility* and *Space City 6*. She also has two novels being released in early 2015. One is a historical horror, *Quincey Morris in A Vicious Paradigm*, and, of course, another tongue-in-cheek murder mystery, *Sliding into Murder*.

When Mandy is not writing about herself in the third person, she lives in Houston with her husband and three children. They love to travel, primarily to locations with beaches and water. These beach locales offer the best opportunities for water skiing or scuba diving. She is one of the few people that enjoy the heat and will tolerate the humidity. And she will only travel to places with snow if they possess a chair lift to the top of the mountain and hot chocolate at the bottom.

For the record, while it is true she has spent more money on books than groceries, it only happened once. And due to the great invention of peanut butter sandwiches, her husband did not starve that month.

Visit her online at www.MandyBroughton.com or on twitter @MandyBroughton. She will talk to anyone who will listen in 140 characters or less.

Once upon a time, **Lisa Godfrees** graduated from Texas A&M University with a BA in Anthropology and MS in Genetics. She lucked into a job at a crime lab where she worked for over a decade as a forensic scientist before tiring of technical writing. Always an avid reader, she hung up her lab coat to pen Bible-themed speculative fiction while taking classes at Dallas Theological Seminary.

These days, Lisa wears as many hats as she had majors in college: wife of a rocket scientist, mother to two precious girls, forensic DNA consultant, part-time A/V Tech Director at her local church, and writer. If she's not reading, writing, cooking, or doing laundry at her home in the Clear Lake area, you can find her playing 42 on her computer, studying martial arts, or watching football.

Lisa is the current president of Writers on the Storm, local chapter of the American Christian Fiction Writers. She joined the Houston Writers Guild in 2014. Her short stories include *A Sirius Revolution* in the *No Revolution is Too Big* anthology and *Zero Regrets* in the *Colony Zero* anthology (Helping Hands Press, 2014). *Truegenics*, another Colony Zero story, releases in November. *Shadow Play*, a flash fiction piece, appeared in the September 2014 issue of *Splickety Prime*. Her first full-length manuscript was a 2013 Speculative finalist in the ACFW's Genesis writing contest.

Artemis Greenleaf has always been fascinated by the mysterious, and she devoured fairy tales, folk tales and ghost stories since before she could read. In 1995, she had a near-death experience which turned her perception of the world upside down. She lived to tell the tale (and often does, in one form or another), and went on to marry an alien. She lives in the suburban wilds of Houston, Texas with her husband, two children and assorted pets. She writes novels, short stories, and non-fiction, and her work has appeared in magazines and anthologies. For more information, please visit artemisgreenleaf.com.

Corinn Heathers is a science-fiction and fantasy author living in the San Francisco Bay Area, on a personal mission to expand diversity and inclusion in both genres. She has a deep interest in military science fiction, largely borne from a youthful love for space and science-fiction simulation style video games such as *Mechwarrior*, *Wing Commander* and *Freespace*. Corinn prefers to create universes in which stereotypical science fiction tropes are deconstructed, subverted, averted and stood on their heads before building them back up again.

Corinn also enjoys exploring themes of variant sexuality and gender in her works, typically crafting characters who are persons of color as well as gay and/or transgender characters. Her stories generally contain elements of slice-of-life and non-heteronormative romance set against a backdrop of larger conflict and forces at play that conspire to pull the main characters in all sorts of interesting directions. Artificial intelligences play a large role in both her science fiction and fantasy stories, generally written from a more sympathetic angle than the usual; she's known to often say that her quirky AIs "just want love and hugs and perhaps to bake delicious brownies."

Claudia Herring aspired to be a baton twirler when she was five and an archaeologist at thirteen. When she became a graphic designer and an author of fantasy, she decided she'd hit upon the perfect compromise.

Along the way she worked as a gift wrapper, a server in a Mexican restaurant at an amusement park (where she rode the Black Dragon at midnight—an actual ride, not a sexual allusion) and an illustrator in medical graphics at the Texas Medical Center where they featured videos on wound healing during lunch (yes, hard to stomach).

Her varied experiences feed her work. As a designer and illustrator she formats the written word around visual art. As a writer she weaves words into stories that form worlds. Her novel, *His Master's Bride*, a historical fantasy set primarily in Regency England, won first prize in the Houston Writer's Guild Novel Competition. Next in the *Djinn Chronicles* series, *Ties of Smoke*, is in its second draft.

When she's not delving into the world of the Djinn, Claudia is practicing yoga to go to that hushed space where she imagines and plots her next fantasy novel. You can find more about her books at www.claudiaherring.com.

Ignoring the head of her high school English department's advice to become a fiction writer, **Barbara Higgins** spent years after graduation studying neuropsychology and optometry. Effectively thumbing her nose at school administrators who told her parents she was too dumb to be a doctor.

Those science and math books contained plenty of unsolvable mysteries and a fair amount of paranormal psychobabble, but not a single sizzling romance. What she published back then was the proverbial antidote for insomnia.

As the scope of her profession expanded in more boring directions, the yearning for good literature returned along with a growing curiosity about her antecedents. After hundreds of books, many interviews, and access to Ancestry.com, Dr. Higgins has built a modern framework for the most compelling stories and characters of the past.

With membership in both the Romance Writers of America and the Houston Writers' Guild, those tales have become manuscripts and her writing skills continue to evolve. Although, dealing with mathematical absolutes and the laws of physics was much simpler than navigating the mercurial rules of writing. .

Chemistry Lesson #1- Opposites Attract is the only short story in the Fleming Family series. The first volume covers the history of the 1844 curse that has most of the men in this family crazy, crippled or dead by age forty. The rest is Claire's love story, followed by those of her sisters, Cece and Lilith. The fourth book kicks that curse's butt.

Barbara Higgins lives with her family in Montgomery County, TX.

Patricia Hughes began writing late in life. She has written a series of short stories featuring the mystery-solving characters of Dallas McGee and the ghost of her great grandmother—some of which have been published in *Alfred Hitchcock's Mystery Magazine*. Her short story, *Lorelei Wakes at Midnight*, appeared in the anthology *Appalachian Winter Hauntings*. Another of her stories, *Food for the Gods*, was made into a short film of the same name. She is currently working on her first novel, *Earth Child: The Seeding of Tomorrow.*

Born in Sayre, Oklahoma, Hughes has spent most of her life in various parts of Texas. Currently, she and Herbert, her husband of forty-five years, reside in Brenham, Texas. They have three grown sons and four grandchildren.

She is very active in the Pilot Club of Brenham, one of the clubs of Pilot International, a service club which has nothing to do with flying. Brenham Pilots say, "We don't fly planes; we protect brains." Brain Safety & Fitness is a major service focus.

Hughes's professional background was in education. She has a Master's Degree in Adult Education from Texas A&M University, Kingsville. She was named Teacher of the Year by the Texas Association of Adult and Continuing Education in 1981. She is also a licensed nursing facility administrator and a certified assisted living administrator. She and her husband owned and operated a 104 bed nursing facility for twelve years until their retirement.

Erin M. Kennemer is a writer and artist living in Austin, Texas. Her education at Texas A&M taught her that not all roommates are created equally, which was part of the inspiration for *The Way She Grows*, which won an Honorable Mention in the L Ron Hubbard Writers of the Future Competition. Erin has published short stories in various imprints and online magazines, including the March 2015 issue of *Luna Quarterly*. Erin believes firmly that real life inspires good art, which is why she tries to say yes to everything. She lives with her daughter and husband, who have not personally observed this "saying yes to everything" business. Her current project is a science fiction novel exploring human society in the confines of space travel. Find her on twitter @emkennemer.

Steven D. Malone received a BA in History from the University of Houston. He has been a teacher of life skills and work skills to special needs students, adjudicated youth, and the visually impaired as well as teaching College English. He is a published author and blogger whose works have been featured in venues as diverse as *True West Magazine, SpeedX QSL* and *KOL Israel Radio*. Steven is the author of the historical fiction novel *Sideshow at Honey Creek* (2012, amazon.com).

Steven's novel, *Sideshow at Honey Creek*, is a historical fiction concerning a little known but ultimately tragic event, the Battle of Dove Creek, fought between Confederate troops aided by Texas militia and the Kickapoo nation in the last winter of the American Civil War. This epic family saga is based on genealogical research of Steven's ancestors, participants in the frontier defense of Texas during that war.

Steven's interests include ancient and Dark Age history, the Civil War and the American West, Taoist and Buddhist philosophy and classic movies. He is a certified teacher of Tajiquan. Presently, Steven lives in Texas with his wife, son and two cats.

Visit the author at his website and blog: www.stevenspen.com.

Rebecca Nolen writes, draws, paints and cares for people she loves at home in Houston, TX. Rebecca always wanted to be a writer and chose that as a career goal in High School. She has been a member of SCBWI, The Houston Writer's Guild, and Sisters in Crime for many years. She has won writing awards, including the top prize for Deadly Thyme at the Houston Writer's Guild writing contest. She has participated in many writing conferences, workshops, and advanced writing courses. Her books can be ordered at any bookstore. At the library ask for the book to be ordered, or if the author could send the library a copy. Contact her at: rlnolen@hotmail.com to request a copy and be sure and include the library name and address.

Patricia Flaherty Pagan grew up near Boston but has traveled extensively and lived abroad. After earning her MFA in Creative Writing, she founded Spider Road Press. In 2014, she coedited *Eve's Requiem: Tales of Women, Mystery and Horror,* which features her short story, *Bitter Sweets.* Her fiction has appeared in anthologies and journals such as *Spry, The Pitkin Review,* and *Robocup Compendium 2013.* She edited *Up, Do: Flash Fiction by Women Writers.* She enjoys hiking with her husband, rereading *The Lion, the Witch and the Wardrobe*, and co-parenting two feisty, Indonesian rescue cats. Visit her online at http://patriciaflahertypagan.com/.

John D. Payne writes fantasy, sci-fi, and literary fiction. His debut novel, *The Crown and the Dragon*, is also a major motion picture from Arrowstorm Entertainment and Flatiron Films. He lives near Houston with his lovely wife, charming son, and many shelves of beloved books.

Chantell Renee has written since the age of twelve. She fell in love with words. What made them so fascinating was the way words create worlds; how they can inspire physical and emotional experiences for those who read or hear them. While many writer's focus on the beauty of language, she tends to put emphasis on the way words can toy with readers, rattling their concepts of the normalcy in their everyday lives. Throughout this author's life, she has survived many things that have created a unique look at the world. Over the past five years she became influenced and educated through workshops and advice of fellow writers, many of which are published. This has given her tools to turn her distinctive point of view into engaging stories. Many of her ideas come from dreams, literally. Which is how *Effa On Fire* came into existence. Chantell is an Urban Fantasy writer that caters to New Adult. If you were to pick through her working projects, you would find: shape shifters, futuristic concepts of our world and a very tough, punk rock chick. The characters in these adventures are full of life and exciting adventures, unless they are meant to be eaten by Ghouls. Chantell is a native Texan, born and raised in Houston, where she currently resides. Her muses are Rugby the beagle and her two fussy cats, Ella and Ovo, who often try to add their own text while she's working. You can learn more about her at chantellrenee.com.

John "Fritz" Schwabenland, teaches math at an inner-city high school in Houston. When he's not planning trigonometry lessons or grading papers, he's hanging out with his wife and kids – or reading a wide mix of dystopian fiction, horror, and young adult. Summers and other breaks in the school calendar are devoted to traveling and writing.

He's a member of the Houston Writers' Guild, where he gets help from experienced and knowledgeable writers. Stimulation for his writing comes from his family.

"My family members motivate my writing through their courage. My wife and my mother are both cancer survivors and have each been featured in my published short stories. My son, who struggles with autism, is the inspiration for my nearly completed novel, *SPECTRUM*, while my teenage daughter lends me all the excellent YA books she reads and is becoming a fearless, passionate writer herself."

John has compiled a collection of short stories and hopes to soon publish at least one of the three novels he's working on.

Bethany Valles, a wife and mother of two children, lives in Houston. She is married to a math professor at a local university, and education is an issue near to her heart. A graduate of the University of Texas at Austin with a degree in English, her love for stories permeates her life. Bethany teaches language arts at the elementary school level and enjoys sharing her love for the written word with the next generation while coaxing them through the ever-present battle with subject-verb agreement. During the day she spends her time shuffling her son and daughter to band rehearsal, soccer practice, and Boy Scouts. After all the driving she unwinds by playing with her rescued mutt, Penny, and catering to her demanding fat cat, Rum Tum Tugger. When the sun goes down she spends her time writing contemporary thrillers with a paranormal twist, chugging copious amounts of coffee to keep her going. Her stories deal with issues ranging from werewolves to telekinesis to mostly-unhelpful psychic episodes. Bethany is a sixth-generation Texan, born and raised in small towns. She has lived in the dusty High Plains of west Texas and the shady Piney Woods of east Texas, weaving the colorful folklore, culture, and picturesque vistas of her home state into her writing, giving it a unique flavor. Strong women are at the heart of her stories, and no women on earth are stronger than Texan women. Follow her on Twitter @bethany_valles, or see her blog: texanamysterymama.blogspot.com.

Tides of Impossibility

Tides of Impossibility

www.ingramcontent.com/pod-product-compliance
Lightning Source LLC
Chambersburg PA
CBHW070623130626
46556CB00001B/449